Miss Match

A NO MATCH FOR LOVE NOVEL

OTHER BOOKS BY LINDZEE ARMSTRONG

No Match for Love Series
Strike a Match
Meet Your Match
Not Your Match
Mix 'N Match

Sunset Plains Romance Series
Cupcakes and Cowboys
Twisters and Textbooks

Other Works
First Love, Second Choice

Miss Match

A NO MATCH FOR LOVE NOVEL

#1 BEST-SELLING AUTHOR

LINDZEE ARMSTRONG

Snowflake
Press

Edited by Tristi Pinkston
Cover Design by Novak Illustrations
Interior Design by Snowflake Press

Tooele, UT
ISBN 978-0-9863632-2-1
Library of Congress Control Number 2015906687

To my mom, who sacrificed a lot of time to help me follow my dreams and never once complained. I love you!

Brooke's Rules for Staying in the Friend Zone

1. Absolutely no kissing on the lips.
2. Hugging is okay, but only for three seconds or less.
3. Cuddling is fine as long as we're doing something (like watching a movie) and not just cuddling for cuddling's sake.
4. We can call for emergency dates (for weddings, work events, that sort of thing) at any time, and the other person has to agree.
5. We can't call for dates just because we're bored.
6. Plans with each other can be broken for a "real" date.
7. Hanging out doesn't count as a date as long as we each pay for ourselves.
8. No extravagant or expensive gifts for each other.
9. If one of us needs help, the other will drop everything and come running—no questions asked.
10. We can each use the other as a fake boyfriend or girlfriend to dissuade unwanted attention from a persistent admirer.
11. Rule #4 and #10 are void if one of us is in a relationship.
12. We can stay overnight at each other's apartments, as long as we are in separate rooms.
13. No keeping personal items at each other's homes. That's what couples do.
14. Holding hands is okay, as long as neither of us is dating someone.

Chapter One

$\mathcal{L}$uke wrapped his fingers around the leather steering wheel of his Aston Martin One-77. He pressed the clutch and shifted gears, speeding through a yellow traffic light. His chest tightened as his heart constricted. *Just a few more minutes.* Then today would fade away as he lost himself in the bottom of a glass.

Five minutes later, Luke tossed his keys to the valet and walked into the exclusive Los Angeles club. The pulse of music made the black walls, draped in shimmery purple fabric, vibrate with every beat. His shoulders dropped and his breathing slowed as the music washed over him. Lights from the dance floor reflected off the chandeliers in tiny rainbows. The club smelled like expensive alcohol and perfume. Despite the holiday, or maybe because of it, the dance floor was crammed with people. He ignored them and headed straight for the bar. The women would come to him soon enough.

"Mr. Ryder," the bartender said. "I didn't expect to see you here today. The usual?"

Luke nodded and sank onto a barstool. The bartender made a Scotch on the rocks and handed it over. Luke downed it in two painful gulps. He noticed women turning his direction, whispering to their friends.

Here come the gold diggers. It's why he'd come to the bar instead of drinking at home, but he wasn't ready for them yet. It always took a few drinks to forget Brooke and enjoy the company of other women.

One broke away from her group and sauntered over. Luke knew her type immediately—microscopic party dress, bleached blonde hair, sun-tanned skin. Fake boobs and Daddy's credit card.

Wait. He didn't just recognize her type. He recognized *her*.

She sat down on the stool next to his, leaning forward so her cleavage was shown at its best advantage. "Luke Ryder, in the flesh."

"Candi. What are you doing back in California?"

"Buy me a drink and I'll tell you."

"For old time's sake," Luke agreed. He lifted his hand, signaling for the bartender. "I'll have another Scotch, and give this lady whatever she wants. A vodka martini still your drink of choice?"

"You remembered."

The waiter left to get their drinks. Candi played with the cuff on Luke's shirt. "What's a man like you doing here on Thanksgiving? Surely you have somewhere better to be."

He resisted the urge to shrug off her hand. It wasn't like Brooke was here to see. "I do." But the house had been too quiet without his dad whistling Christmas tunes off-key. The dinner table had been too empty with only him and his mom. The meal had been too bland, lacking his dad's jokes and famous deep-fried turkey. As soon as his mom had started to yawn, Luke had bolted.

Candi's lips turned down in a sympathetic pout. "This must be such a hard day for you. It's only been, what, a month since your father passed? I've been keeping tabs on you through the press."

Five weeks and two days. He'd felt every one of them.

The bartender returned with their drinks, and Luke took a sip from his.

Candi crossed one of her long, shapely legs over the other. "I'm sure you remember what a comforting person I am. I can make you feel better if you let me."

Luke didn't doubt that. Candi had been his college girlfriend, and another failed attempt to make Brooke

3

jealous. Luke and Candi's relationship had been rocky at best. She was a possessive and jealous girlfriend, prone to mind games. He'd been relieved when she got a job across the country and moved. But she *had* known how to make him feel better.

What would Brooke think? She'd never liked Candi much.

She'd think about Antonio, that's what. The ring on her finger made that much clear.

Still, he couldn't bring himself to encourage Candi. Not yet. "I'll stick to drinking, thanks." He took a sip to emphasize his point.

Candi's tongue flicked out and moistened her top lip. "You never used to drink much."

"My father used to be alive."

Candi leaned back, the flirtatious act dropped for the first time. "I understand. I lost my father almost two years ago. Lung cancer, same as yours. He couldn't give up smoking, even at the end."

"My father didn't smoke." But his grandfather had. Secondhand smoke, the doctors said. That's what caused the lung cancer. Eighteen years of living with a pack-a-day smoker. It always seemed cruel that his dad had to die for a choice he never made. "I'm sorry about your dad. I hadn't heard. Does it get easier with time?"

"No. But you get better at dealing with it."

Her honesty was unexpected and refreshing. Maybe she'd changed in the four years since he'd last seen her.

Brooke would hate that you're here with Candi, his mind whispered.

Brooke doesn't get an opinion. She has Antonio now.

Candi smiled at Luke. Her teeth were too white and too straight, her smile too wide. Obviously her career as a model had been successful enough to afford a few enhancements.

"I've thought a lot about you the last few years. Even thought about contacting you when I moved back a few months ago," Candi said.

"Why didn't you?"

"I figured if you wanted to find me, you would. But then I saw you here tonight and couldn't resist." Candi took another sip of her martini, then set it on the bar. She held her hand out to Luke. "Enough of this depressing talk. Let's dance."

Candi had been a lot of things. Crazy. Erratic. Possessive. But she'd also been fun, passionate, and great at making him forget his troubles. She was exactly what he needed tonight.

Luke let Candi lead him to the dance floor. Brooke was home, probably video chatting with Antonio and eating pie with her mom. Candi was here.

Candi grabbed his hips, moving them in rhythm with the music. Luke took a shot from a passing waiter and let the alcohol take over. For hours they danced. As his brain clouded, Candi grew more beautiful, the music became more exciting, and dancing more enjoyable than ever.

"My apartment's only a few blocks away," Candi told Luke after yet another dance. "Remember how much fun we used to have?"

Luke's muddled brain sharpened. *Brooke.*

She doesn't want me. Not like that.

Still, he wanted to at least try to be a gentleman. "Are you sure?"

Candi moved closer, pressing herself against him. Her skin glistened with moisture under the colored lights. "Yes. I'll help you forget all about today. I promise." And then her lips were on his. Her arms were like vises—soft, comforting vises that made him feel less dead inside.

And she'd always been a fantastic kisser.

He closed his eyes and imagined he was kissing Brooke. Imagined it was her arms wrapped around his neck, her fingers threading through his hair. Luke should've made his move on Brooke when he had the chance, despite the promise he'd made to his father. The lights of the dance hall flickered behind his closed eyelids as he let himself dream.

He was startled back to the present by a shout. "Luke!" The voice was relieved, with a hint of panic.

Luke tore himself from Candi. He struggled to make sense of that voice in this setting.

And then he saw her. She strode boldly through the crowd, looking out of place in her white peacoat, ripped jeans, and flip-flops. But he recognized the bag—a twelve-thousand-dollar pink Birkin bag he'd given her as a birthday present. She had no idea how much it cost, or that he'd been the one to buy it. He'd lied and told her it was a gift from a client, since that didn't technically violate Rule #8.

Brooke threw herself at Luke, wrapping him in a hug. Her chestnut curls, pulled back in a ponytail, tickled his nose. "You're okay." She moved back, glaring. "Do you have any idea how long I've been looking for you? I had to leave my mom's house early. Without any pie."

"What are *you* doing here?" Candi placed a hand on her hip and glared.

Brooke's eyes widened, apparently noticing Candi for the first time. "Look what the cat dragged in. I could ask you the same."

"Why are you here?" Luke asked Brooke. The words sounded slurred, even to his own ears. He winced. Brooke never touched alcohol, and hated it when he drank. Because of that, he'd never indulged much. Until the funeral.

She never mentions Antonio's drinking.

"Duh, I'm looking for you," Brooke said. "Your mom called and begged me to check in on you. And then Mitch called." She pulled out her phone and started texting. "Come on, we're going home."

"We were just leaving for my place," Candi said, grabbing Luke's arm possessively. "And three would be a crowd. You never did know when to butt out."

Brooke ignored her. "Let's go, Luke."

Candi stepped in front of Brooke. "He's coming with me. You're not his mom."

"But I am his best friend. That trumps ex-girlfriend any day."

Brooke stepped around Candi and tugged on Luke's arm. He stumbled, nearly knocking Brooke over. *Way to make an impression, Luke. Nothing makes a girl's heart flutter like a drunk.*

"You don't have to go," Candi called after them.

"I gotta," Luke mumbled.

"At least call me."

"Sorry," he said. He'd always picked Brooke over Candi, and he always would. He'd follow Brooke anywhere. Even when she was pissed.

"You really know how to pick 'em," Brooke said. "Were you seriously going to hook up with that psycho again? I was feeling sorry for you, but now I'm just mad. I left you like ten voice mails, but I guess I know why you weren't answering your phone."

"Couldn't hear it."

"Did you drive or take a cab?"

He had to think about that for a moment. "Drove."

Brooke's hands roughly patted his cheeks.

Had he fallen asleep?

"Luke. Luke! Where's the valet ticket?"

Valet ticket? He couldn't think clearly.

Brooke sighed, fumbling in one of his coat pockets, then the other. Luke's heart thudded in his chest, and he wanted to lean forward and hold her. That would definitely violate Rule #2. Probably Rule #3 as well. He pushed her hands away.

"Where's the claim number?" she repeated.

He reached into the inside breast pocket of his suit jacket and withdrew it. Soon Luke's car pulled up to the curb, the silver paint gleaming under the light of the protective awning. The valet opened the passenger door, and Brooke crammed Luke inside.

"Buckle up," she said.

When he didn't move, she leaned over and did it herself. Her breath tickled his cheek, and he inhaled the familiar scent of peppermint. He would happily spend the rest of the night filling his lungs with her fragrance if she'd let him.

9

She didn't. Instead, she climbed into the driver's side and drove toward his apartment. He admired the way she handled the clutch for about a block before falling asleep.

Luke woke when Brooke shook him. Both she and the valet for the apartment complex stared down at him. He squinted against the lights coming from the lampposts along the curb.

"I can't carry you inside," Brooke said. "Can you walk?"

Luke mumbled yes. He tried to support his weight as they walked into the lobby, but Brooke still bore the brunt of it. She grunted, her arm tightening around his waist.

"Do you need help, Miss Pierce?" the doorman asked.

"No," Brooke said. "Thanks."

Luke's foot slid on the white marble flooring, causing him to pitch forward. He pulled Brooke with him and she let out a gasp of surprise. The doorman rushed to their aid, but Luke caught himself before the stout man reached them.

"Maybe I should help get him upstairs," the doorman said.

"Once we're in the elevator we'll be fine," Brooke reassured him. "The elevator attendant can help if needed."

"Of course." The doorman hurried to the elevator doors, the chrome so shiny Luke could see a blurry reflection in them. The older man pushed the call button, and the doors opened almost immediately. Luke's stomach curled with humiliation as the doorman helped Brooke guide him into the elevator. The doorman stepped out, and the doors slid silently shut.

Luke slumped against the mirrored wall as they rode up twenty-nine floors to his penthouse apartment. He must've fallen asleep again. He heard the deep rumble of a male voice—the elevator attendant?—helping him into his apartment. Felt the soft silk of the duvet on his bed beneath his cheek. A tug as Brooke pulled off his shoes and socks.

He heard the clatter as Brooke dropped something—probably her cell phone—then a soft whisper as she spoke to someone on the other end of the line. "Hey, Zoey."

Ah yes, Brooke's roommate and trusty sidekick. He wondered if Zoey would be upset about being dragged into another episode of the drama that was his life. After eight years, it had to be wearing on her.

"Yeah, I found him, about to hook up with Candi. Yeah, that Candi. I don't know—he's totally wasted. Can you pick up my car? I'm going to stay the night to make sure he's okay."

That's when Luke fell asleep.

11

Chapter Two

Luke awoke to the banging of pots and pans in the kitchen. *Brooke*. His head felt as though it had been sliced in two with an ax. Now he remembered why he usually didn't drink. He squinted at his alarm clock. It was already ten in the morning. He rolled over and sat up, groaning. He was still dressed in his suit from the night before, minus shoes, socks, and jacket. His stomach churned. He wasn't sure if it was a result of the hangover or anxiety over facing Brooke. He'd made an idiot of himself. Again. And he knew she'd have a lot to say on the subject.

His feet hit the floor, sinking into the plush charcoal-colored carpet, and the bedroom lights flipped on. Heavy dark blue drapes—Brooke's choice—slid back from the large picture windows on one wall. "Good morning, Luke," said the cool voice of Talia, the computer running his home automation system. "Los Angeles is a chilly fifty-five degrees today. It's 10:09 a.m., and your schedule is blank for the entire day-day-

day." She repeated the last word three times, a glitch that happened a few times a day. Luke hadn't bothered to fix it. Talia was the last project he and his dad had worked on together. She functioned correctly most of the time.

The heated wood floors of the hallway warmed Luke's cold toes, and Josh Groban's voice drifted from the speakers in the kitchen—one of Brooke's presets. The unmistakable smell of frying bacon overwhelmed him. He sighed in relief. If Brooke was making breakfast, she couldn't be too mad.

"I miss you too." The voice was Brooke's, and Luke froze in the hallway. She must be on the phone with Antonio. He peeked around the corner. Brooke stood behind the six-foot long island, mixing some sort of batter—pancake, if the griddle was any indication. The diamond in her engagement ring caught the light, sending a rainbow across the white shaker cabinets and a knife through his heart. He still wasn't used to seeing it on her finger.

"I saw the pictures too. I'm sorry. But I couldn't let him go home with that floozy." A pause as she listened to something Antonio said in response. "I know I'm not being fair to you. I promise, you do come first. I'll set better boundaries in the future."

Luke closed his eyes and massaged his temples. He'd noticed Antonio and Brooke fighting more and more lately, and this confirmed his suspicion that he was a big part of that. He didn't like Antonio. He was always ordering Brooke around, and was a little too arrogant for his own good. But Brooke seemed genuinely in love, and Luke hated causing her trouble.

"I'll talk to Luke again. I'll take care of this, promise. I love you too. Bye."

Clearing his throat, Luke walked into the kitchen.

"Hey," Brooke said, glancing up from the batter. She looked adorable in her rumpled jeans and T-shirt from last night. Her face was devoid of makeup, her hair pulled back in a loose messy bun. "I was wondering when you'd wake up. I've been banging pots for twenty minutes. Aspirin's on the counter."

He grabbed the two white pills and swallowed them dry. "You could've borrowed a pair of my sweats instead of sleeping in jeans." Before Antonio, she would've done so without blinking. But since the engagement four weeks ago, things had been changing.

Luke dipped a finger into the pancake batter, and Brooke swatted at his hand. But it was playful, so maybe they were okay.

"I'm engaged now. I shouldn't be spending the night over here in any type of clothes. That's the last time I babysit your drunk butt."

He winced at the accusation in her tone. "At least it's a holiday, right?"

15

She grunted. "You made me miss out on Black Friday shopping."

"I'll buy you whatever you wanted."

Brooke rolled her eyes. "I'm not taking your money." She stirred the batter a few more times, then poured some on the griddle. "Breakfast will be ready soon."

"You didn't have to cook. And you didn't have to stay last night, either." If Antonio found out she'd slept over, he'd pout and throw a tantrum like a spoiled toddler. From the calm voices of the phone conversation, Luke was guessing she hadn't told him.

"The breakfast is to help make this conversation suck less." Brooke slid a tablet across the black granite counter top. "Mitch called. Google Alert directed him to this about an hour ago. Obviously he's thrilled."

"Mitch needs to relax." Luke woke the tablet with a swipe. A web page was already pulled up to a popular tabloid. One of the less reputable ones, if there was such a thing. And there, on the front page, was a photo of him and Candi, lips locked in a sloppy kiss. The picture was grainy, as though taken long-range with a cell phone. In big, black letters across the top, the headline proclaimed, "Billionaire Turkey Bags a Holiday Treat."

Luke clenched his hand into a fist. He never should've let Candi kiss him. He couldn't believe he'd almost gone home with her. He glanced at Brooke, hoping to gauge her reaction. She busily flipped bacon, but her lips were pursed into a line.

"Must've been a slow news day," he said.

"Read the story."

Oh no. He clicked on the article and opened it. There were two more grainy photos—one of Brooke helping him to the car, and another of Brooke and Candi talking. The photo made it look like they'd been in a cat fight. Luke didn't remember anything like that.

He read the caption. *Luke Ryder was seen leaving the club with Brooke Pierce, who still sports her engagement ring from artist Antonio Giordano. Pierce and Giordano met through a matchmaker at Toujour, where Pierce is an employee. Despite that, it has long been rumored that Pierce is carrying on a not-so-secret affair with Ryder.* Luke swallowed. The article couldn't be further from the truth.

"I'm sorry, Brooke. I didn't mean to drag you into this again." He sheepishly motioned to her phone on the counter. "I heard you talking to Antonio. He's pissed, isn't he?"

"Yes, and I can't blame him. I see red every time a girl so much as flirts with him. And you and I are constantly being linked together in the media. It's not easy for Antonio." She pointed her spatula at Luke. "I assured him I'd do whatever necessary to stay out of the papers and squash the rumors."

17

"I'm sorry," Luke repeated. He curled his fingers into his palm. She acted as if being linked romantically to him was the worst possible thing.

Brooke flipped the pancakes. "Out of all the girls in the club, you had to pick Candi. Have you forgotten how crazy she is?"

Maybe.

"You've been showing up in the media a lot lately."

"Not true," Luke said.

"Talia, how many times has Luke been mentioned online recently?"

"Fourteen times in the last month," Talia said, her voice surrounding them from all sides.

Luke's jaw clenched. "Of course I'm in the news a lot right now. Ryder Communications' founder just died."

Brooke grunted.

"There's nothing between me and Candi."

She removed the bacon and blotted it with a paper towel. "She didn't seem to know that. You two were quite the item in college." Was it Luke's imagination, or did she sound angry? Maybe even jealous?

Don't get your hopes up. Despite Antonio's many, many flaws, Brooke seemed committed. Why else would she have accepted the ring?

"I had a momentary lapse in judgment, nothing more," Luke said.

Brooke put a pancake on each plate, then took the saddle barstool next to his. "You're spiraling. I know you miss your dad. I do too."

"Of course I miss him. He's barely been gone a month."

"I know. And I won't pretend to understand what you're going through. But this . . ." She motioned to the tabloid. "She stole the door off your car when you broke up with her."

Luke savagely bit off a chunk of bacon. "I was drunk last night."

"You didn't used to drink very much or very often."

Life was easier to handle with alcohol. He didn't have to remember the death rattle he'd listened to for five hours or his mom's sobs after his dad breathed his last. He didn't have to recall how the company's stock still hadn't recovered and he was a woefully unprepared and inadequate CEO. He didn't have to think about how he'd lost Brooke. "So I showed up in the tabloids again. Their next big story is 'Stars Without Makeup!' I don't think I have much to worry about."

"Oh, I disagree. You know Darius and the rest of the board are going to hate this."

Luke grimaced. That much was true. Darius was old fashioned, and loudly disapproved of Luke's every action. As though being chairman of the board of directors gave him the right. "I can handle him. The most I'll get is another lecture on how I need to man up and act like I'm forty."

"Mitch is worried. He says stockholders are really nervous."

Luke snorted. "What does Mitch know? He's just my personal assistant."

"He's more dialed in to the company than you are. The anniversary gala is really important, and he wants to keep the focus on that and not you. Try to stay out of the papers for a week, okay?"

The anniversary gala next weekend. Just thinking about it made Luke want to take another drink, or maybe go lift some weights. His father had been so excited about the celebration—thirty years since he'd started the company out of his basement. He'd planned a lot of the event, and had been determined to be there. The memories stung. "I'm not going."

"You say that now, but you'll change your mind by next Friday."

"It's too hard, okay? I'll go to the press release for the lung cancer foundation next month, but not the gala." The company was nearly ready to announce their nonprofit, and Luke hoped it would help shareholders feel more positively about the dipping stock.

"You're strong. You can do this. You think the board is going to freak about the tabloid? Try not showing up to the most highly publicized company event of the decade. Besides, it'll destroy your mom if you don't attend. And it's disrespectful to your father's memory."

She was right—Brooke was always right. He'd have to go. "Are you coming with me?"

"Of course. Zoey and I will both be there. Antonio won't be back until the day after the party."

He knew she was bringing Zoey for Antonio's sake. Brooke hadn't been Luke's "plus one" to an event since she and Antonio started dating. Rule #11 effectively voided Rule #4. It was yet another reason to hate Antonio.

"Eat up," Brooke said. "You're braving the Black Friday sales with me. Maybe there's still some good deals left."

Luke rolled his eyes, but obediently shoveled another bite into his mouth. A day spent with Brooke was heaven, no matter where they went.

Chapter Three

Brooke poked her head into Zoey's bedroom, then rolled her eyes at the disaster she saw. Clothes were thrown haphazardly about, draped over the bed and littering the floor. Makeup spilled across the dresser, and a bottle of nail polish sat open. For just a moment, Brooke was taken back to the arguments the two of them had had as Freshman sharing a tiny dorm room. They'd both been much happier since moving into an apartment with two bedrooms.

"Zo?" Brooke asked. "We're going to be late."

Zoey poked her head out of her private bathroom. "Almost ready," she said. She disappeared again, and emerged less than a minute later. She stepped over the piles of clothes, carefully placing her stilettoed feet. She tossed aside a pair of jeans and a few shirts before locating her purse. She held it up, triumphant. "We can go now."

Brooke crossed her arms. Zoey looked glamorous and edgy as usual. Her dark ebony hair fell straight over her shoulders, highlights of bright pink throughout. Dramatic eye makeup made her brown eyes pop. She wore a pencil skirt and lacy blouse, sure to tempt all her clients to give up on Toujour and beg Zoey for a night on the town.

"If you would put your purse the same place every night, then you wouldn't make us late for work," Brooke said.

Zoey laughed. "We've never been late. You make sure of that." She shut and locked the apartment door, and they headed to Brooke's car.

"With an eleven o'clock start time, you'd think we wouldn't be rushing," Brooke pointed out. Not that she really minded. After eight years as friends, she'd gotten used to Zoey's penchant for tardiness.

Zoey stifled a yawn. "I didn't get home last night until almost three."

"Clubbing again?"

"On a date. He was kind of a jerk, but totally loaded. I ordered every dessert on the menu."

Zoey and Brooke chatted as they drove the short fifteen minutes to Toujour. Brooke parked her VW bug and they both got out of the car.

"Think you'll be able to keep busy all eight hours today?" Zoey asked.

Brooke grunted. "I hope so. I'm quickly running out of matches for a few of my clients."

Brooke swung open the front door to Toujour and was immediately hit with the spicy-sweet scent of Dragon's Blood incense. Even after five years, it still overwhelmed her every time she entered the lobby. Christmas music played softly through the hidden speakers, and a small Christmas tree decorated in hearts, cupids, and wedding ring ornaments sat in one corner of the reception area. Lianna, the receptionist, sat behind a tinsel-lined black desk.

"Good morning, Lianna," Zoey said.

Lianna glanced up from her computer. "Morning," she said. Her eyes were bleary behind her thick glasses frames, and her blonde hair was tousled as though she'd rushed getting ready. Brooke glanced at Lianna's computer. A game of Solitaire was pulled up. Lianna absently moved one of the cards.

"Phones are quiet this morning," Brooke muttered to Zoey. They walked down a short hallway that opened into the heart of the building. Cubicles filled the center of the large space, and small rooms called parlours lined the outside wall. Posters of happy couples were on the front of each door, no doubt meant to remind clients of the success they'd soon experience in love.

Zoey and Brooke's shared cubicle was near the center of the room. Zoey set her purse on the desk and they both sank into their chairs. Brooke fired up her computer, dread already curling in her stomach. She was

25

down to eleven clients, barely enough to keep her busy each day, and with each failed date the pool of potential matches shrunk even further.

"Have you decided if you're going to your dad's yet?" Zoey asked.

Brooke frowned. She clicked on the welcome icon and entered in her password. "I probably should. I haven't visited since the fourth of July."

"Wow, it's been that long?"

Brooke tapped her foot against the floor. "Yeah." Ever since her dad cheated on her mom, she hadn't been able to look at him the same. Their relationship had improved since the divorce, but she knew it would never be what it had once been.

Her dad had ditched Shandi, the woman he'd gotten pregnant while still married to Brooke's mom, not long after Jason was born. Now he was married to Miranda, a woman Brooke genuinely liked, and they had four-year-old twin girls together. She hoped this relationship would last.

"I should go," Brooke said. "To see my sisters, if nothing else."

"It won't be so bad," Zoey said. "You'll eat dinner, chat for an hour, and leave. I bet Miranda puts on a fantastic Thanksgiving spread, even if it is December now."

"That alone is reason enough to go," Brooke agreed. Miranda was a fantastic chef. Brooke pulled out her phone and quickly texted her dad. *A week from Saturday at one o'clock is great for a late Thanksgiving celebration. Can we bring anything?*

She hadn't expected him to text back right away. As a dentist, he didn't usually have a lot of down time during work hours. But he must've been between patients, because he quickly texted back, *Nope, I've got it covered. I'm so glad you and Antonio can come!*

"It's done," Brooke said, setting her phone on the desk. It would be good to spend time with her family again. She should make more of an effort with her father, so things wouldn't be awkward at the wedding. And she really did miss her brother and sisters.

"Good." Zoey unplugged her laptop and stood. "My client should be here soon. Cross your fingers the date went well, because if it didn't I have no idea who I'm going to match him up with next."

"Good luck," Brooke said. Zoey nodded and headed toward one of the parlours. Brooke pulled up her own list of clients, clicking on one of the profiles. She was a little concerned about finding a match for this woman. Kate had been on five first dates, and hadn't clicked with any of them. With barely one hundred clients left at Toujour, and less than half of those male, Brooke was running out of options fast.

She didn't understand why people weren't signing up for Toujour in droves. It was so much more than online dating. Toujour's professional matchmakers provided relationship advice, tips on dating, and spent hours finding the perfect match for their clients. And that was only the beginning. Brooke *knew* Toujour worked. It was how she'd met Antonio, after all.

Brooke reviewed the notes she'd taken the last time she met with Kate, making sure all the keywords were there for the computer. Then she clicked a button to run a search for matches. Anything above sixty percent compatibility was considered a good potential match, and anything less than fifty percent wasn't worth looking at.

While the computer ran Kate's profile against the men in the database, Brooke responded to a few emails. She clicked back over to Kate's profile. The computer had finished, and a flashing button said "five matches found."

Five. It wasn't much, but it was something. Brooke clicked on the button to display the matches. Two of them were below sixty percent, so she discarded those for the time being. Another one Brooke instantly knew wouldn't work. That particular guy was one of her clients, and she knew that the couple would never mesh. That left two matches. Two. What if neither of them worked out?

Brooke took a deep breath and started going over the profiles. One of them had to be the guy for Kate. She'd never had to turn a client away, and she didn't want to start now.

By the time Zoey returned, Brooke was looking into date options for Kate and Damon. "How'd it go?" Brooke asked.

Zoey let out a dramatic sigh. "Okay. He agreed to a second date, but I could tell he was reluctant." Zoey set her laptop on the desk. "If we don't get more clients soon, people are going to stop renewing their memberships for the sole reason that they've already dated everyone here."

"I know." Brooke chewed her lip, wondering what Charlotte, Toujour's owner and founder, would try to do next about the lack of business.

"Hey, are we still going to the anniversary gala on Saturday?" Zoey asked. "Someone asked me out, and I wanted to double check before telling him no."

"We're still going," Brooke said. "Don't ditch me now."

Zoey rolled her eyes. "I'm not ditching you. I just wanted to make sure nothing had changed." She flashed a grin. "I can probably meet way richer guys at the gala anyway. This guy was only a junior partner at a law firm."

Brooke laughed. "You're impossible."

"My grandma always said it's just as easy to fall in love with a rich man as a poor one. I'm taking her advice to heart."

Chapter Four

Brooke twisted her engagement ring around and around on her finger, anxiously watching the red carpet for signs of Luke's arrival. She'd spent all morning at his apartment, trying to convince him he needed to attend, and only left to get ready when Mitch arrived to take over babysitting duties.

Zoey's hand clamped over Brooke's. Zoey arched an eyebrow, her eyes looking larger than normal with the dark, smoky eye makeup. "Stop that, or the press will think you're breaking off the engagement. Mitch said they're on their way."

Brooke pulled the wrap tighter around her shoulders. "Sorry. I'm just nervous. There are so many ways tonight could go wrong." The gala needed to be flawless. Despite Luke's blasé attitude, Brooke was worried about his position with the company. She'd read the articles, and knew investors were antsy. She also knew that if she appeared in the papers, she'd be in hot water with Antonio. And her fiancé had put up with enough the last month. "We don't need a repeat of the tabloids last weekend."

"Well, let's hope Luke shows up on his best behavior. If worse comes to worst, I'll cause a distraction."

Brooke's hand stilled on her wrap. Zoey was impulsive enough to do just about anything. Brooke eyed the bright pink highlights in Zoey's hair. "Like what?"

Zoey shrugged. "I don't know. It'll depend on how drunk everyone is."

"Zoey . . ."

She sighed dramatically. "You're no fun."

"Please don't do anything that'll end up in the papers tomorrow. I can't keep an eye on Luke and you."

"He's here," someone shouted. Reporters rushed forward, converging on the black limousine that had pulled up to the curb. A door opened, but that was all Brooke could see with the reporters swarming. Not that it mattered. She knew it was Luke.

"Mr. Ryder! Mr. Ryder!"

"C'mon, let's wait for him inside," Brooke said.

Zoey followed. "You don't want to walk in with him?"

Brooke shook her head. "Too many cameras."

"Oh." Zoey's surprise evaporated into annoyance. "Antonio. Right."

Brooke nodded her thanks to the doorman, and they escaped inside the hotel. The doors swung shut, and the shouts of reporters were replaced with *O Holy Night* playing quietly through hidden speakers. A twelve-foot Christmas tree, covered in gold and red decorations, sparkled underneath the chandelier in the center of the hotel foyer.

Brooke and Zoey handed their wraps over at the coat check, then showed their invitations and were let into the opulent grand ballroom. Poinsettias sat in alcoves and on tables, and evergreen wreaths with gold and red Christmas balls hung from every window. A string quartet played holiday music on a raised platform, and tuxedoed waiters wandered through the crowd with trays of food. A banner proclaiming "Happy 30th Anniversary, Ryder Communications!" with the company's logo hung on the far wall. She hoped it wouldn't set Luke off.

A warm hand settled on her waist, and Brooke recognized the touch immediately. She shivered as lips brushed her cheek. "You look beautiful," Luke said, his voice husky. His breath smelled strongly of spearmint mouthwash—a sure sign he'd been drinking.

Brooke quickly moved away. He got extra flirty when drunk, something she'd discovered the past month. But when she turned around, her breath caught. He'd gelled his caramel hair into an organized mess, a look she adored, and the cerulean blue of his eyes popped underneath the chandelier light. He'd shaved away the three days of growth, showing off his strong jaw line. "You don't look so bad yourself."

Mitch was at Luke's side. Despite being almost thirty, at these events he always resembled a high school kid borrowing his dad's tux for prom. He was lanky, all limbs, and had a perpetually youthful face. Brooke doubted he could even grow facial hair. His dark chocolate skin was nearly the same shade as the black tux, and his lips were turned down in the slightest frown. Brooke watched Zoey grin flirtatiously. Mitch's eyes widened and he gulped.

What was that about? Did Zoey like Mitch?

Luke grinned, holding out his hand to Zoey. "Thank you both for coming."

Brooke frowned, her focus returning to Luke. "You're in a good mood."

He gestured grandly to the ballroom. "Well this party is just so *fabulous*. We have so much to celebrate."

Brooke's stomach clenched. "You're drunk."

"I had one Scotch before coming here. There's a difference."

"I know this is hard," Mitch said. "Just hold it together for a few hours, okay?"

Luke grunted. Brooke hoped that meant he planned on giving the speech without complaint. "Let's go say hi to Mom," he said.

"Of course." Brooke pointed. "She was over there a minute ago."

Karen saw them heading toward her and smiled. Brooke saw the relief in her expression. No doubt Karen had been as worried as Brooke that Luke wouldn't show. Her arms wrapped tightly around him, and Brooke saw the glisten of unshed tears in her eyes. "Thank you for coming," she said. "I know this is hard for you."

"Of course, Mom." Luke's voice was gruff as he hugged her back. "I'm here to support you."

Karen released Luke and hugged Brooke. "And thank *you*. I know you're probably the reason he's here."

Brooke opened her mouth to respond, but didn't know what to say. "The party's beautiful."

Karen nodded. "Rick would've loved it."

"Karen." An older woman with a beehive hairdo slipped an arm around Karen's shoulders. She was one of the board members, but Brooke couldn't remember her name. "How are you doing, honey? I've been thinking about you."

Luke took Brooke's hand and tugged her away. Karen gave a small wave of acknowledgment as they left.

"I can't be around board members right now," Luke muttered. Brooke knew things had been tense since he'd been appointed CEO days after Rick's death. "I'm not in the mood to listen to a lecture on how I'm failing the company."

"Things will get better," Brooke tried to soothe. *If you'll start showing up at the office.*

And that's when Brooke saw her. Candi. She walked into the ballroom in six-inch stilettos, her arm wrapped tightly around none other than Nathan Kendall, CEO of Kendall Home Systems. Her gold dress was slit nearly to her naval, and a full, sheer skirt left little to the imagination. She looked like part of the decorations.

And she was headed right toward them.

What is that vixen playing at?

Mitch had managed to engage Luke in a conversation about basketball. Brooke caught Zoey's eye and motioned discreetly toward Candi and Nathan. Zoey turned, then whipped back around to Brooke, eyes wide.

Luke raised an eyebrow. "You okay, Zoey?"

Brooke's heart thudded in her chest. She didn't know which would be worse for Luke—seeing Candi or seeing Nathan. Had Candi been playing Luke? There was no way it was a coincidence she was here with the competition. *There's no such thing as coincidence, especially where she's concerned.*

"I'm fine," Zoey said. "I . . . saw a former client. He and his fiancée called off the wedding and it's a little awkward."

Brooke stole a glance at Candi and Nathan. Candi had wrapped her arms so tightly around his bicep that she looked like an accessory to his tux. They were stopped a few feet away, chatting with an actress. What was Candi up to? Brooke could tell by looking at Candi and Nathan that the couple—if that's what they were— wouldn't last. The way they clung to each other spoke of lust, not love. If they were clients at Toujour, she'd be looking for new matches for both of them in a month.

Brooke took Luke by the arm, doing her best to make the action appear casual. "I love this song. Dance with me?" She pulled Luke toward the dance floor.

"Catch up with you later," Zoey called. Brooke looked back over her shoulder and saw Mitch already headed toward the pair, Zoey close on his heels. Zoey brushed her hand down Mitch's arm. Okay, something was definitely up with the two of them.

Luke's mouth twitched, completely oblivious to what was going on. "Is this supposed to be a Christmas song? I've never heard it. What's it called?"

Brooke blushed. Why couldn't the quartet have played *Deck the Halls* or *White Christmas* or something everyone knew? "Okay, I don't know the song. But I love the way the cello sounds." There was a cello in a string quartet, right?

Luke allowed Brooke to lead him onto the dance floor. "When did you become a music expert?" He pulled her into the classic dance pose—one hand at her waist, the other holding hers. As Luke turned her in a slow circle, Brooke caught a glimpse of Mitch and Zoey talking to Nathan and Candi in the far corner of the room. For the moment, the risk had passed.

"We're getting dangerously close to violating Rule #2," Brooke teased. "We've been like this for way more than three seconds."

Luke pulled her close. "I beg to differ. If both my arms were around your waist and both your arms were around my neck, then *maybe* we could consider this a hug. But this?" He held up their clasped hands. "We're just dancing. And I'm certain you haven't made a rule against that."

Brooke laughed. Once upon a time, back in high school, Luke had wanted more than friendship from her. But she'd turned him down. She'd seen how Luke was in relationships, and she wasn't willing to sacrifice their friendship for a fling. And that's all Luke ever had—flings. It reminded her too much of her father. Thankfully, his feelings seemed to have quickly faded to friendship, and he'd never pushed the issue.

A camera flashed, and Brooke flinched. "If that shows up in the papers tomorrow . . ."

The music blessedly ended then. Luke sighed and pulled back. "You and Antonio are still fighting about the tabloid." It wasn't a question.

"Can you blame him?"

Luke rubbed his eyes. "I need a drink."

"Your speech is coming up soon."

"I don't know if I can give my speech." Luke's jaw worked back and forth as he blinked.

"Do it for your dad."

"Check, check, check," a low voice echoed around the room. A hotel employee stood on the stage, handing a microphone over to Reginald Darius, chairman of the board of directors.

Brooke squeezed Luke's hand. "It's time."

He closed his eyes and nodded.

Chapter Five

Luke's stomach buzzed with nerves, and he clenched his fists to keep them from shaking. It would be okay. His father had helped him craft the perfect speech. All he had to do was read from the teleprompter.

"Welcome, friends," Darius said, his voice shaking with age. He was short and slight, with a full head of brilliantly white hair. "I am so pleased you could join us tonight to celebrate thirty years of a fantastic company, and to honor a dear friend of mine, Rick."

Luke clapped unenthusiastically. Brooke gave him a sympathetic smile.

"We had all hoped Rick could attend tonight. Unfortunately, he lost his battle with lung cancer a short month ago. But he's with us in spirit. Tonight, on our thirtieth anniversary, I'm pleased to announce the Richard L. Ryder Lung Cancer Foundation." A banner unfurled behind Darius with the foundation name emblazoned across it and a photo of Dad to the side.

Luke's mouth dropped open in horror. No. They were supposed to make the announcement at a press conference in a week or two. He had a different speech he'd been preparing for that event.

"Tonight we have the privilege of hearing our new CEO, Luke, speak on his father's behalf. Let's give Luke a big round of applause and welcome him to the stage."

"The bastard," Luke whispered.

The crowd turned toward them, polite smiles on their faces as they clapped and waited expectantly. His eyes met Brooke's. Her mouth formed a surprised "o" and her eyebrows arched above her beautiful blue eyes.

He wanted to run and hide. But instead he let go of her hand and walked toward the front of the room. He would kill Darius. Why hadn't he told him they were making the announcement tonight? Heat crept up the back of Luke's neck as he made his way to the stage, dodging women in high heels and waiters carrying trays. He tried to remember the speech he'd been working on for the press conference, but drew a blank.

The crowd's claps died down. The distance to the stage grew with every step. Luke felt hundreds of eyes burning holes into his soul. He passed a group of society matrons in glitzy dresses, gossiping loudly.

Just waiting for me to mess up. Crowds like this were always waiting for someone to make a fool of themselves.

A woman eyed him like a lion eyes its prey. Luke ground his teeth together. The speech his father had helped him so carefully craft was all about Ryder Communications' humble beginnings. It didn't seem to fit the announcement of the foundation.

Luke took the microphone from Darius with a tight smile. It felt cold and heavy in his hand. He blinked, trying not to squint at the stage lights. "I'd like to thank you all for coming here today," he said. *Great opening. Your father would be proud.* He cleared his throat. Glanced at the teleprompter.

He couldn't give that speech. Not now.

"Dad was a great businessman, and an even better father. My earliest memories are of watching him invent. When I was in high school, I jokingly suggested a home automation system. But Dad wouldn't let the idea go." Luke clenched the microphone, willing away the sting in his eyes. "And now, eight years after that idea, look at what he created." Luke thrust an arm toward the room at large. "He brought this company from a single-man operation to an international corporation. It wasn't right that he should die so young. He didn't deserve lung cancer. No one does. And Dad

43

wanted to make sure that even after he was gone, he could still help find a cure."

A spattering of polite claps filled the room, with a few enthusiastic "hear, hear's." Luke tried to remember what else he'd planned on saying, but his mind drew a blank. The teleprompter was stalled on the first line of his original speech.

Luke looked for Brooke's bright blue eyes and reassuring smile among the crowd. Instead, he found his mother, Karen. She stood in the front of the room, close enough he could see the tears sparkling in her eyes under the light of the chandeliers. She wore a conservative black dress—one he recognized from the last company event they'd attended. The one just before Dad's death. He was sure the papers would notice and comment on it.

Maybe the rest of the audience only cared about how their company stock was performing. But his mom cared about Dad. And so did Brooke.

Darius cleared his throat, and Luke blinked. He'd been quiet for too long. "Nothing can bring Dad back," Luke said. "But we can pay respect to his memory by finding a cure. Thank you all for coming." He shoved the microphone into Darius's hand. Darius fumbled and almost dropped it.

"Luke Ryder," Darius said, clapping. The audience followed his lead. The clapping sounded uncertain and strained. But what did Darius expect, springing this on Luke last minute? *Why* had he sprung it on him?

Luke wove his way through the crowd, eager to reunite with Brooke. "I heard they're having an affair," he heard one of the women whisper to a friend as he passed.

"But isn't she engaged?"

"So they say, but she doesn't act like an engaged woman."

"I heard she sometimes spends the night at his apartment."

Luke closed his eyes and willed the entire room to disappear.

It was his mother who found him first. She grabbed his arm and looped hers through it. "That was a very nice speech," she said. The chief director of the foundation spoke now on the stage, but Luke hadn't registered a word she said. When had they hired a director anyway?

"Did you know they were unveiling the charity tonight?" Luke demanded.

His mom blinked. "Darius mentioned it last night, and I agreed it was a good time to make the announcement. I thought you knew."

"I didn't," he said.

"I'm sure Reginald sent you an email." Her tone was reproving.

Luke ran a hand through his hair. He hated how his mother managed to make him feel ten years old again. "Dad hated these events. He wouldn't have wanted the charity announced like that."

"And how do you think it should've been done?"

"A press conference, like we'd discussed."

Someone patted Luke on the shoulder. "Excellent speech," the man said as he walked passed. Luke forced a smile.

"Your dad may have hated these events, but he knew they were necessary for the well-being of the company. Tonight was the perfect time to make the announcement. We have Los Angeles' richest in the room tonight, and they're all in a giving mood thanks to the holidays. Donations will pour in. Maybe it'll help us find a cure." Mom's voice was wistful, but hopeful too.

Luke wouldn't hold his breath. How long had scientists searched for a cure? Decades, at least. Even if they did find one, it wouldn't bring his dad back.

A woman smiled coyly at Luke. "Excellent gala, Mr. Ryder. Congratulations on thirty years."

Luke nodded, and the woman slunk away.

"I'd better go mingle," Mom said. "Looks like Brooke's headed over here anyway." She gave Luke a kiss on the cheek and left.

Brooke arrived seconds later. "You did great," she said, giving Luke a hug. "Especially for not knowing about the charity's unveiling." She pursed her lips as though tasting something sour. "Mitch is furious. Apparently they sent you an email but never mentioned anything to him. He's making phone calls now."

Luke's jaw clenched. "That's exactly the kind of crap that makes me avoid these events. Darius had no right."

"I agree." Her eyes focused on something behind his shoulder. She grabbed his arm. "Don't look now, but Darius is headed right for us. Let's go."

Luke swore, quickening his pace.

"Luke." Darius's voice was loud, drawing the attention of those around them.

Brooke stopped walking and looked up at Luke, her eyes apologetic. "If you don't talk to him, it'll make a scene."

"I have nothing to say to him," Luke hissed.

"Then make something up." Brooke's face melted into her best keep-the-client-happy smile. "Mr. Darius, we didn't see you. I spotted a waiter serving quiches and must've blocked everything else out." She laughed, a soft tinkling sound that sent shivers from Luke's head down to his toes. "What a fantastic turnout tonight. You must be so pleased."

Darius frowned, his laser vision focusing on Luke. "I was, until that speech."

Brooke's mouth fell open, but Luke wasn't surprised. "The speech I had prepared didn't seem appropriate in light of the charity being unveiled," Luke said. "If you ever spring something like that on me again, I'll have your spot on the board as payment."

Darius didn't flinch. "I sent you an email yesterday about the change and asked you to solicit donations from our guests."

"I didn't read the email."

"I gathered as much. As CEO you shouldn't let communication lapse. The board needs to be able to get in contact with you anytime, day or night."

Luke felt the anger spread like a rash. He clenched and unclenched his fists, and Brooke put a hand on his arm. "I'm grieving, Darius. And you're going behind my back, announcing my dad's charity?" His voice rose with every word. "You should've relayed the change over the phone, at the very least."

"Luke," Brooke said. "You're making a scene."

"I wasn't trying to go behind your back," Darius said. "Your father was one of my closest friends. Don't think you're the only one affected by his loss."

"Don't compare how you feel to how I feel. If you ever—"

Brooke stepped between the two men. "Okay, I think that's enough. In case you hadn't noticed, you're attracting attention."

Luke caught the eye of a tuxedoed man with a cell phone pointed in their direction. The man quickly slipped the phone into his pocket and walked away. A few other cameras flashed.

"Mr. Darius, I hope you can respect how hard this is for Luke," Brooke continued. "I know you meant no harm, but I think it's best if you discussed keeping the lines of communication open another time."

"Brooke, I hope you at least understand that I meant nothing by it." Darius took her hand in both of his. "I tried to keep him in the loop."

Brooke patted his hand. "I know, Mr. Darius. Oh, there's Mitch. He actually sent me to find Luke. We'd better see what he wants." She grabbed Luke's arm and whisked him away.

"Darius should be fired for that stunt."

"He made a mistake. Try to calm down, okay? You don't want the cameras capturing this."

Luke tugged at the collar of his tuxedo shirt. "I need a Scotch. Just one." *After what I've been through, the least she can do is give me one drink.* It wasn't like he could leave to go to the gym and release his stress.

"We'll get you a spiced cider. Or maybe some hot chocolate." She focused on something over his shoulder. "Oh crap."

And that's when Luke saw her, wrapped around Nathan Kendall like a piece of meat on a kabob.

Luke froze, his breath heavy. "What. Is. He. Doing. Here?"

"I have no idea."

"He's here with *her*?" Luke massaged his temples and tried to make sense of what was happening. With Candi, you never really knew.

"I know. Let's go get you that drink."

At the bar, Brooke ordered him a spiced cider. He leaned back against the counter, watching Candi cling to Nathan like plastic wrap. Any closer, and they'd be fused together.

"The gala's had a great turnout," Brooke said. He knew she was trying to distract him—trying to get him focused on anything but what he was seeing.

"Candi," Luke ground out. He felt no disappointment at seeing her with another guy. He knew last night would've only be a one-night fling. But to be here with Nathan, his competition? That seemed a little too convenient.

Candi leaned forward and pressed a lingering kiss to the corner of Nathan's mouth. And then she looked across the room, caught Luke's eye, and smirked.

"I can't believe it," Luke muttered.

Brooke glanced at Candi and Nathan, then grabbed Luke's arm and tugged him in the opposite direction. "I think I need some fresh air. And you definitely need to cool down."

"She smirked at me."

"Should we see if Zoey and Mitch want to go with us?"

"She kissed him then smirked."

"Is that the girl from the tabloid?" an unfamiliar voice asked.

Luke whipped his head around, and saw two old biddies whispering together.

"What a hussy." The second woman, who sported a sequined dress, actually harrumphed. "Young people these days. His girlfriend is engaged to another man, and he's seeing a scarlet woman on the side."

"Oh, I heard the engagement's being called off."

Sequined Dress raised an eyebrow. "Really?"

"Well, that's what the magazines are saying. I also heard Brooke and Luke haven't ever dated, but are just friends."

"They can't really think people believe that. Best friends don't act like those two."

Luke clenched his jaw. "What a disaster."

Brooke put a hand on his arm. "It's fine."

He shook his head. "No. I keep bringing you into the papers, and people think . . ." He couldn't even say it.

"It doesn't matter. You and I and Antonio know the truth."

The two biddies moved away, giving him a clear view of Candi, who threw back her head and laughed. She pressed herself suggestively against Nathan and slipped one hand beneath his tuxedo coat, her lips turned up in a smirk the entire time.

Is she a corporate spy? If so, she wasn't a very good one. He hadn't spilled any company secrets, and now that he knew she was with Kendall, there was zero chance she'd get anything out of him. Besides, even Kendall wouldn't try something that dumb.

"Brooke, darling." Mrs. Darius threw her arms around Brooke, nearly toppling her. Luke reached out a hand to steady her. Brooke's expression was one of surprise and horror. "I'm so glad you're here. I've been looking for you all night."

"Mrs. Darius," Brooke said. Luke heard the caution in her voice, but doubted anyone else would. "It's nice to see you again."

"You must meet my grandson." Mrs. Darius tugged Brooke away from the bar. "I think I've told you about him before. Andrew's visiting from Oregon for the holidays. He's so ready for a wife, but doesn't have time to find a suitable woman to date."

"Toujour sounds perfect for him then." Brooke's eyes flicked to Luke's. He knew the matchmaking firm she worked for was struggling, and he saw the desire for a new client battling with her obligation to stay with him. "Luke and I were just enjoying a spiced cider together."

Here it was, his chance to get a Scotch. "Don't worry about me. Who knows when Andrew will be in town again?"

Mrs. Darius beamed. "He's really unsure about the whole matchmaker thing, but I think if you explained it to him . . ."

Brooke grabbed Luke's arm. "Don't. Just don't," she whispered.

He waved her off. "I'll be fine. Give Andrew my best."

"Oh, we will, dear," Mrs. Darius said, and she and Brooke disappeared into the crowd.

Luke whipped around to the bartender. "Give me a Scotch on the rocks, and keep 'em coming until that woman returns."

The bartender grinned and quickly poured Luke a glass. "I've seen her in the papers with you before. They say she's your girlfriend."

I wish. "Best friend. And she doesn't like it when I drink." Luke downed the Scotch in one painful gulp. The bartender's eyes widened, and he quickly poured another. Luke devoured that one too. The speech. Brooke. The gala. Candi. Nathan. It was all too much.

The room was starting to spin when he felt a tap on his shoulder. He turned around to see none other than Nathan and Candi, still fused together.

"Luke," Nathan said, holding out a hand. Luke shook it warily. "I had to stop by and congratulate you on the foundation's creation. We'll find that cure eventually."

Luke grunted. "I'm surprised to see you here, Kendall." He heard the slur in his words, but couldn't bring himself to care.

Nathan pulled his face into a look of faux offense. He wasn't much older than Luke, maybe thirty or thirty-one, but he still managed to treat Luke as though he were a child playing make believe. "I know we're competitors, but I'm here tonight as a guest celebrating your company's success." He motioned to Candi. "You already know my girlfriend."

"Girlfriend, huh? She seemed pretty available last night," Luke said. "She's a great kisser, man. And even better in bed."

Nathan's jaw clenched. "I'm here to offer my congratulations. Let's not make things ugly."

"You're the one who's crashing my party."

"Luke," Candi said, her lips turning down in a pout. "Please. I know it was wrong of me not to tell you I was seeing someone, but I was so mad at Nathan last night. We had a horrible fight." She laughed, and it sounded like breaking glass. "Turns out it was all a silly misunderstanding."

Ah, I was the means to piss off Nathan. Luke decided to push the envelope, just to see what would happen. "Are you sure it wasn't a pathetic attempt to get company secrets?"

Nathan laughed. "We don't need your secrets. Talia's a joke and your product's floundering. I'm launching a new system in January that's going to make yours look like something out of the Dark Ages."

"Talia is *not* a joke."

"She's got more glitches than a government website. And you refuse to even consider replacing—"

Luke's fist flew and landed in the middle of Nathan's face. Luke felt the crunch of cartilage as hand met nose. Felt the skin on his knuckles split. Blood exploded, splattering all over Nathan's face and onto Luke's white tuxedo shirt. Candi let out a dramatic scream. The bartender yelped. Nathan fell to his knees, his hands covering his bleeding nose.

Nathan let out an expletive. "What was that for?" His voice had a distinct nasal sound now.

And that's when Luke saw Brooke.

Chapter Six

Brooke stood frozen in horror as she watched blood ooze from between Nathan's fingers. It'd taken a while to extricate herself from Mrs. Darius and her grandson, but not *that* long. His careful language and easy blush had spoken of a girlfriend he obviously hadn't told his grandparents about—a bummer since she really could use another client.

Someone in a glittering green dress pulled a cell phone from her bra and snapped a picture. Brooke took a step forward, then paused. Antonio would freak if she ended up in the papers so soon after their conversation. A picture of her talking to the mayor at the gala was explainable, but not this.

Another camera flashed. Brooke lurched toward Luke.

"You're crazy," Nathan yelled at Luke. Candi helped him to his feet. A waitress hurried forward and handed him a stack of cocktail napkins for his nose.

"What were you thinking?" Brooke hissed at Luke. "What happened?" A few more people took out their phones. The reporters, clearly differentiated by the press passes on lanyards around their necks, were converging on the scene. The flashes of their cameras were nearly blinding.

"Mr. Ryder, was this a provoked attack?" one asked.

An old woman pointed an accusing finger at Luke. "I saw him punch Mr. Kendall in the nose."

This is a nightmare. Brooke grabbed Luke's arm, pulling him away from the crowd. His breath was heavy, and he shook his hand as though it stung. They had to get out of there.

"I'll sue you to bankruptcy for this," Nathan yelled at their retreating figures.

Mitch pushed his way through the crowd. "What's going on?" he asked Brooke.

"He insulted Talia," Luke said through clenched teeth. "I had to hit him."

"Was the confrontation over the voice recognition feature in your home automation system?" a reporter asked, shoving a small voice recorder toward Luke. "Or was it because Kendall is dating your ex-girlfriend?"

"Don't say anything," Mitch said. He was already pulling up the contacts list on his cell. "Not until we talk to the lawyers."

Paramedics pushed their way through the crowd, a gurney helping to cut a path. "Stand back," one of them said. "Give Mr. Kendall some space."

Nathan let a paramedic help him onto the gurney. "I think he broke my nose."

"Wimp," Luke said, and not quietly either.

"Shut up," Brooke hissed.

"Does this have anything to do with the fact that you're having an affair with Mr. Kendall's girlfriend?" a reporter asked.

"Get him out of here," Mitch said to Brooke.

Brooke quickly reviewed the contingency plan Mitch always had in place for these situations. Escape through the service entrance into the kitchen. Go to the back of the hotel. A car would be waiting. She grabbed Luke's arm and tugged.

Two burly men in uniforms pushed their way through the crowd. "Security. Let us through. Security!"

Brooke's heart sank. "Let's go," she said.

A hand fell on her shoulder. "Not so fast. Mr. Ryder, the police will need a statement."

"Then they'll have to make an appointment," Brooke snapped. "Mr. Ryder isn't feeling well and needs to leave."

"I'm afraid that leaving isn't an option, miss," the security officer said.

"At least let us go outside to talk." Brooke motioned to the cameras.

"Mr. Ryder, how much have you had to drink?" a reporter called.

The security officer looked around, then nodded and escorted them from the room. The door to the ballroom swung shut behind them. But not before a few last camera flashes captured the moment.

Antonio is going to be thrilled. Brooke groaned at the thought. She was supposed to pick him up at the airport in less than twenty-four hours—plenty of time for this to go viral.

"Thank you," Brooke told the security officer. He nodded and helped them escape into the relative anonymity of the hotel's parking garage. A police officer arrived moments later.

"What happened?" the police officer asked.

"Nathan was mouthing off," Luke said, his words running together. "Insulting Talia. Insulting my father. And now he's trying to steal our clients."

The officer looked at Brooke.

"I didn't hear the confrontation," she said.

Mitch arrived then, nearly blending into the darkness with his ebony skin and black tuxedo. "Nathan grudgingly declined pressing charges," Mitch said. Brooke let out a sigh of relief. "I think he wants to look noble in front of the press."

"Let him try to sue me," Luke said. He stuck out his chin belligerently. "I'd love to take him on in court."

Brooke felt like slapping Luke. Didn't he care about how this was affecting everyone else involved?

Mitch swore. "You think you're in hot water with the board now? They'd have boiled you alive if Nathan had decided to press charges. And it's my job on the line too. I'm supposed to stop this sort of crap from happening."

The police officer held up a hand. "Let's all calm down." His radio beeped to life, and he spoke quickly into it, then listened. "Looks like Mr. Kendall is indeed feeling generous. Since he isn't pressing charges, I don't need to take your statements. You can go." He nodded his head toward Luke. "Make sure he doesn't drive himself home."

"Thank you, Officer," Brooke said as the police officer and security guards left.

"I'll get him home," Mitch said, motioning to Luke.

Brooke nodded. She needed some space right now. And she needed to figure out how to spin this to Antonio. Maybe she should call and explain, before it started circulating around the web. No, better to delay.

"He provoked me, Brooke," Luke said as she helped him into the waiting limo.

Brooke closed her eyes and took a deep breath. "I doubt the media will care." She slammed the door shut and turned to face Mitch. "How bad is it going to be?"

Mitch sighed. "Hopefully Nathan doesn't change his mind about pressing charges. The press heard him decline so I doubt he'll flip. I've already got people on damage control. All we can do is wait and see."

Brooke leaned against the car. "When is he going to come back?" she asked. "I miss Luke."

Mitch awkwardly patted Brooke on the shoulder. "He'll bounce back soon."

"If I don't kill him first. My fiancé is going to lose it when he finds out about this." Brooke took a deep breath and blew it out. "I'm going home."

Chapter Seven

Brooke tossed and turned all night before finally giving up and going for a run. The trees in the park reached toward the sky like skeletons, and the cool air hurt her lungs. She ran a few laps around the paved trail, enjoying the stillness of the park. The sky was beginning to light, and she heard a few birds chirping nearby.

Her phone buzzed in her armband, knocking her out of her thoughts. Who would call this early?

Brooke slowed to a jog and slid a finger across the screen of her cell. *I'm sorry.* It was a text from Luke.

Brooke angrily shoved her phone back in her armband and picked up her pace. He should be sorry. His behavior last night had been out of line.

And now she'd get to explain the whole debacle to Antonio.

Brooke ducked her head and increased her pace even more, her feet pounding against the asphalt. She and Antonio were a perfect match, or practically perfect at least. When Brooke had approached Charlotte two years ago about signing as a client with Toujour, she'd expected Charlotte to insist a matchmaker couldn't also be matched. But Charlotte had been excited to help Brooke find true love, and agreed to let her join. It took only two okay dates before she was matched with Antonio. His Italian family was ultra-traditional, and his parents had met on their wedding day through a matchmaker. They wanted their son to find happiness the same way. Brooke and Antonio had a seventy-one percent compatibility rating, which was excellent.

It only took three dates for them to decide to be exclusive. They'd been together ever since.

Her phone buzzed again. Brooke ignored it and kept running. The sky was now a dusty pink, and the trail was starting to fill with other runners. One more lap, then she'd get ready to pick up Antonio.

She was unlocking her apartment door when she received another text. Brooke sighed and pulled her phone out. Both texts were from Luke.

I'll explain what happened to Antonio if it'll help.
Please don't be mad at me. I'm sorry.

Brooke closed her phone without replying. She'd decide how to respond after gauging how upset Antonio was.

Brooke took her time getting ready. She curled her hair into loose beach waves, the way Antonio preferred, and put on a little more makeup than usual. Then she paired her favorite jeans with stylish boots and left for the airport.

Traffic was a nightmare, but she still arrived at the airport early. She parked in the short-term lot and headed inside. *Maybe the story hasn't hit the newsstands yet.* And maybe Antonio hadn't been online.

Curse Luke Ryder. She'd looked forward to Antonio's return since he left ten days ago, and now because of Luke she dreaded it.

Three car rental counters advertised various savings, but thankfully didn't have any newspapers with Luke's face on display. Maybe not enough time had passed for the story to be in print. Brooke found baggage claim and four more newsstands, but none of them had a front page photo of Luke either.

Brooke closed her eyes and wished she could rewind last night. What could she have done differently? Maybe she should've told Mrs. Darius to bring her grandson to the bar. Maybe she should've made Luke go with her. Maybe she should've refused to leave his side. Maybe she should create a rule to avoid ever being in this situation again.

Maybe Luke should grow up and stop acting like a child.

Last year at the company party, Luke had joked and charmed everyone in the room. Brooke's only concern had been making sure things didn't get too awkward between him and Antonio. Now Brooke felt more like a babysitter than best friend.

A small gift shop stood in one corner of the baggage claim area. Brooke looked at her watch. She still had at least thirty minutes to kill. She wandered into the shop. *Santa Baby* played on the overhead, and Christmas ornaments were prominently displayed on the front counter.

"Hi," the store clerk said. "How can I help you?"

"Do you sell newspapers or magazines?" Brooke asked.

The woman popped her gum. "Sure do. They're on the back wall."

"Thanks." Brooke headed to the back of the store. None of the newspapers or magazines showed a picture of Luke on the cover. She let out a sigh of relief.

"Next up, Luke Ryder in a jealous rage."

Brooke's head jerked up. She zeroed in on the television in the corner, showing *E! News*. A picture flashed of Nathan Kendall, blood spurting out of his nose.

"Last night, Luke Ryder punched Nathan Kendall in the face," the reporter said. He motioned to the picture behind him.

"You've gotta feel bad for the guy," the female reporter said. "His dad just died, and now he's CEO of a billion-dollar corporation that isn't doing so hot. And the competition is moving in on his old girlfriend."

"He's already having an affair with an engaged woman," the male reporter said. "Does he need to add another one to his list?"

"Kendall didn't press charges, so he's coming out of this looking like a hero," the female reporter said. "Looks like Luke won't get either woman to break up with her significant other anytime soon."

Brooke looked away in disgust. They hadn't even mentioned the purpose of the gala, or the announcement of the lung cancer foundation. The two positives had been overshadowed by the one negative.

"Delta Flight 435 from Atlanta, Georgia has now landed," the airport announcer said over the intercom system. Antonio's connecting flight.

Brooke checked the time on her cell phone. The flight was nearly thirty minutes early. Her stomach clenched. She turned away from the television and wandered over to wait by the security exit. Soon she and Antonio would be reunited after ten long days apart. The tabloids—and Luke—better not ruin this.

She had missed Antonio so much. Had longed for him to come home. All she wanted was to finish planning their wedding, say "I do," move into an apartment together, and start their married lives. *I'm so mad at you, Luke.* He always seemed to be the wedge in her relationship with Antonio. She'd created the rules in high school to avoid this exact situation. She wanted Luke and Antonio to be friends, not enemies.

Brooke heard a tap and glanced to her side. An elderly woman with a cane stood beside her. The woman caught Brooke's gaze, and Brooke gave a tentative smile.

"Waiting for someone important?" the woman asked.

"My fiancé. He's been visiting family in Italy for almost two weeks."

The woman's eyes widened. "Oh my. That's a long time to be apart."

Brooke had wanted to go to Italy with Antonio, and had even talked to Charlotte about taking time off. It wasn't like Toujour was busy at the moment. But when she'd mentioned it to Antonio, he'd said it made more sense for her to stay home and save up her vacation time for their honeymoon. "I've missed him very much."

The woman smiled kindly. "You must be excited to see him."

Brooke faked a smile. *I was. Thanks again, Luke.* She would find every bottle of Scotch in his penthouse and pour it down the kitchen sink. If she ever decided to speak to him again.

"I am excited," Brooke said. As long as the drive home didn't revolve around Luke.

"When's the wedding?" the woman asked.

"September fifth." This time Brooke smiled for real.

"Young people have such long engagements these days." The woman leaned forward conspiratorially. "My husband and I were engaged on Thanksgiving and married on New Year's Day. We thought it was very romantic. A new beginning and all that."

"That's so sweet. Is that who you're waiting for—your husband?"

"No, my dear Harold passed on three years ago, may he rest in peace." The woman quickly crossed herself. "We were never apart for more than a day in all our fifty-one years together."

Tears pricked Brooke's eyes. "I'm so sorry."

"I know I'll see him again. Today I'm waiting for my grandchildren." The woman's voice brimmed with joy. "My daughter and her family are moving home after fifteen years away. The last three years have been lonely, and I'm glad to have family close again. Oh, here come some people now." Weary travelers wandered into baggage claim. "I wish you and your fiancé a lifetime of happiness, dear."

"Thank you. And I'm glad your family is moving home."

The woman nodded, her attention focused on the crowd. Brooke scanned the passengers for Antonio.

"Grandma!" A girl with bouncing brown curls broke away from the crowd and ran into the woman's arms. A few moments later, she was swarmed by two more children and two adults. They laughed and hugged each other.

Brooke smiled. She was glad she'd talked to her. She and Antonio could be like that woman and her husband with a little work. Brooke and Antonio had their fair share of problems, but they loved each other, and she was committed to their relationship.

Even if it means giving up Luke? a tiny voice whispered in the back of her mind. She shook it aside. Antonio wasn't a fan of Luke's, true. But he knew how much their friendship meant to her, and would never ask her to give that up completely.

She searched the crowd, looking for Antonio's shaggy locks and flirtatious smile. He was only five foot ten, and easily hidden in a crowd by all the taller men. Businessmen in black suits with stern expressions entered baggage claim. A mother alone with three young children. A group of what looked like high school students with a few tired looking chaperones.

And then she saw him. He had his trademark five o'clock shadow, a dark gray winter scarf nearly obscuring it. His curls were even more unruly than usual, and he reached up with one of his strong hands to brush them out of his eyes. She could just make out flecks of paint on the back of his hand.

Her heartbeat quickened, and she couldn't help the grin that spread across her face. "Antonio!" She raised on tiptoes and waved.

He looked up and saw her. His mouth turned up, and he hitched his carry-on bag higher on his shoulder and jogged over to her, a portfolio case in his other hand. "*Mia dolcezza,*" he exclaimed, dropping the portfolio case and bag and catching her in his arms. His lips quickly found hers, and she let her hands weave into his hair as he kissed her breathless. Several long moments later, he pulled back, their foreheads still touching. "I've missed you," he whispered.

Brooke kissed him again. "I'm glad you're home. I love you."

"I love you too." He released her, reaching down to pick up his bag and portfolio. "Let me grab my bag from the carousel."

"Here, let me." Brooke took his portfolio and carry-on, and waited while he picked up his bag.

"Let's go home," Antonio said. "I'm exhausted."

Brooke made a sympathetic noise in the back of her throat. "Long flight, or long trip?"

"Both."

Brooke breathed easier now. He hadn't brought up the gala. *All I have to do is keep him away from any form of media for the next week or so, and we'll be golden.* She mentally kicked herself. *Yeah, right.*

"How did the last few art deals go?" Brooke asked as they loaded his luggage into the back of her little VW Bug.

"I ended up selling all but three pieces at the show last night, and was commissioned for twelve more. And I signed an exclusive contract with a gallery for my landscapes."

"Antonio, that's fantastic."

"I know. And the money is amazing. Enough that I could buy you this." He reached into his pocket and pulled out a box. He opened it and handed it to Brooke.

She gasped. "Oh, it's beautiful." A white gold chain held a gemstone-encrusted pendant—a painter's palette and brush. He took the necklace from the box, and she lifted her hair so he could clasp it around her neck.

"Now we'll never be parted again," he whispered into her ear, then leaned down to kiss her neck.

She shivered, and turned around to kiss him on the lips. "Thank you. I love it."

"I knew you would. Now let's go home."

Brooke nodded, getting in the passenger side of her car. Antonio always drove when they were together. "Tell me more about your trip. How's your family?"

Antonio started the car and pulled out of the parking space. "Doing well. They miss me, and are anxious to meet you in September." He paid the attendant at the booth, then pulled out of the parking garage. "What I really want to talk about, *mia dolcezza*, is how, just days after our conversation, you managed to end up plastered across the Internet."

Brooke's mouth fell open. *Shoot.* And she thought she was doing so well. "How did you find out?"

"Twitter. 'Nathan Kendall is Thankful for Health Insurance After Luke Ryder Punches Him at a Charity Gala.' Nice headline. I especially loved the photos of you in the article."

"I'm sorry," Brooke said. Maybe if she downplayed the situation, he wouldn't get too mad. "Everything was going so well, and then . . ." She sighed.

"I'm not interested in what went wrong. What I'm interested in is why you were in the middle of it. Again. I understand supporting your best friend, but this is getting ridiculous."

"I wasn't in the middle of it. I was trying to keep Luke from getting arrested. He punched Nathan while I was off talking to some guy who didn't want to hire me as a matchmaker."

Antonio glanced over. "I'm not even going to ask about that. What I am going to ask is why my fiancée can't respect even the simplest of my wishes."

Brooke clenched her teeth together. He was right. She knew her relationship with Luke was unusual, and Antonio was more understanding than most men would be. He had asked one thing of her—one simple request—and she had failed. "I'm sorry. I was trying to help out a friend. Rule #9 and all that. You know Luke's going through a hard time."

"And it seems like our relationship is always what suffers." Antonio shook his head, causing curls to wave around his face. "It's like Luke is your fiancé, and I'm your best friend."

"You know that's not true." Brooke's voice shook. "It's *you* I'm in love with. It's you I plan on spending the rest of my life with."

"Yes. With Luke always in the wings."

"He's only affecting our relationship because you make such a big deal over our friendship. Luke kept me sane during my parents' divorce. He's been there for me every time I needed him the past eight years. I'm trying to return the favor."

"*I* need you now, Brooklyn. I need you to put me before him." His words were sharp, angry.

Brooke drew back, stunned. "I do."

"Then why do you keep doing exactly what I ask you not to?"

Brooke put a weary hand to her forehead. He hadn't even been home an hour, and already they were fighting. It was the same conversation they'd had a thousand times before, and she was sick of it. Luke never attacked her over her relationship with Antonio. Sure, he wasn't a fan of the engagement. But he didn't make demands of her like this.

Just put Antonio first, a voice in her head insisted. *Then this will all go away.*

I do put Antonio first. But Luke needs me right now. I'm all he has.

He has his mother.

That's not the same.

"I'm sorry." Brooke put a hand on Antonio's arm. "I'll do better. Please, let's not fight anymore. You just got home and I've missed you."

Antonio kissed the top of her head. "I've missed you too. I love you, Brooke. I don't want something as trivial as a friend to come between us."

But he's not trivial. He's my best friend. Brooke squeezed Antonio's arm and didn't say a word.

Chapter Eight

Brooke didn't sleep well. She rarely did at Antonio's, with his hard-as-a-rock mattress and the ceiling that made her feel claustrophobic. Antonio's apartment was a studio, with the bedroom as a loft. When sleeping, the ceiling was only four feet above her head. She spent a lot of the night staring at Antonio, wishing there was an easy solution to Luke constantly driving a wedge between them. Eventually she gave up on sleep and got ready for the day before climbing back up the ladder to the loft. Antonio still lay sprawled across the bed in his boxers, the sheets only half covering him. She lifted his arm and slipped underneath it, cuddling against him.

Antonio stirred. "*Mia dolcezza,*" he said, smiling sleepily.

"I'm sorry about yesterday," Brooke said. "You're right, I need to set better boundaries with Luke. I don't want to fight anymore."

"Me either." Antonio caressed her lips with his own, and Brooke wrapped her arms tightly around his neck.

"Let's go to the beach," Brooke said. "We can eat brunch at that café we like and do some shopping. Maybe catch a movie."

"Sounds wonderful," Antonio said. "Give me twenty minutes."

Brooke made the bed and tidied Antonio's apartment while he got ready to leave. Her phone buzzed. Luke. She rejected the call.

Antonio walked out of the tiny bathroom, a towel wrapped around his waist. "I'll be ready to leave as soon as I get dressed," he said.

Brooke wrapped her arms around his neck, kissing him deeply. "I love you."

"I love you too." He took her hand and played with her engagement ring. "Let's not talk about anything stressful today, okay? We'll talk about the big stuff tomorrow. I just want to enjoy spending time with you after so long apart."

"Deal," she said. Her phone buzzed with a call. Brooke rejected it again. Today was about her and Antonio.

They had a fabulous time reconnecting. It was too chilly for playing in the water, but they walked along the beach and browsed the shops nearby. They enjoyed a leisurely brunch at the café, and ended up forgoing the movie when they discovered an art festival downtown.

"I'm glad you're home," Brooke said as they sat on his balcony that night, watching the stars. Antonio sipped a glass of red wine while Brooke drank coffee.

"Me too. Let's never again be apart for so long."

"Next time you go to Italy, you're taking me with you."

"Deal."

On Monday morning, Brooke picked up Zoey and they headed to work early. Charlotte had called a staff meeting for ten o'clock.

"What do you think the meeting is about?" Zoey asked.

Brooke signaled left, her car brakes screeching at the turn. "How slow business has been." It wouldn't be the first staff meeting they'd had to discuss the lack of clients. They'd tried everything—marketing campaigns, sales, special promotions, training for the employees.

Brooke pulled into Toujour's parking lot and killed the engine.

"If she'd add an online dating branch to the company, we'd be doing fine." Zoey unclicked her seatbelt and they got out of the car.

"Don't you dare suggest it." Brooke locked the door and they walked toward the building. "Have you forgotten Janet?"

"'Course not." Zoey scowled. Janet had been fired on the spot for suggesting online dating. "I'm just saying Charlotte's being an idiot."

The open sign in Toujour's front window wasn't lit, but the front door swung open when Brooke gave it a try. The space felt empty without Lianna at the desk. The silence where Christmas music usually played made the whole thing feel even more foreboding.

They wandered past reception and through the cubicles. People were visible through the clear glass of the boardroom.

"The *Jaws* theme song is playing on repeat in my head," Zoey said.

"I'm sure Charlotte has some new idea she wants us to try on how to drum up business."

"Ugh. Please tell me she isn't bringing more people over from the French office."

Brooke grimaced. A few months ago, Charlotte had brought her top matchmakers over from France for an intensive two week training session with all the matchmakers. To say there'd been some culture clash would be putting it mildly. "Let's get in there so we can figure it out."

The boardroom was already mostly full with employees. Toujour wasn't a large company—a staff of around twenty, most of them matchmakers. All the chairs around the large oval table were taken, so Brooke and Zoey took seats at the back of the room.

"My hands are sweating," Zoey said.

"Join the club. Where's Charlotte?"

Just then Charlotte walked into the room, the last of the employees trailing after her. They quickly took their seats and settled down. Lianna stood at the front of the room, counting heads. "Everyone's here," she told Charlotte.

"Good," Charlotte said in a thick French accent. "Then let us begin."

Everyone looked at Charlotte expectantly. She took a deep breath, placing her hands on the board table in front of her. Her French manicure stood out starkly against the chocolate of her skin. "I'm sure you're all aware of how slow business has been the last few months. The last ten years, if we're being honest. Things never got off the ground like I hoped they would when I opened Toujour, and it's been—what's the American expression?—'uphill' ever since."

"I think you mean 'downhill,'" Lianna said.

Charlotte scowled. "Downhill is easy, not hard. None of your American expressions make sense." She sighed. "That's not the point. What I mean to say is that Americans don't appreciate matchmaking the way the Europeans do. Our numbers haven't increased since my French staff came three months ago. Toujour is still losing money and I've made a difficult decision. Unless we can turn things around in the next three months, I'm closing the business."

The room went from silent to thunderous before Brooke could blink. Her heart thudded. Her pulse throbbed in her neck.

"You can't just close," Lianna said loudly at the front of the room.

"What'll we do?" one of the matchmakers asked.

We have to fix this.

"She gave us a time frame," Brooke said to Zoey. "We're not giving up just like that." Brooke stood, raising her voice to be heard over the chatter. "You said three months. That means we have three months to change your mind, right?" *Please, let it be so.* She couldn't lose Toujour. Not her dream job. She'd begged and harassed Charlotte as a college freshman until being hired as an intern, then worked her way into being Charlotte's protégé, the top ranked matchmaker at the firm. All that hard work couldn't be for nothing.

The room quieted down. People looked back and forth between Charlotte and Brooke.

"So we still have a chance?" someone asked.

Charlotte caught Brooke's eyes. Her black corkscrew curls spiraled all over her head, and she wore a cheery yellow dress that set off her dark skin—and contrasted sharply with the room's general mood. But Brooke couldn't miss the circles underneath Charlotte's eyes. The woman was exhausted. "I've tried everything I can think of to save the company and I'm out of ideas. So I'm bringing it to you."

"What will you do if we close?" Zoey asked.

"I had planned to return to France soon regardless of what happens here. If I close the office, that'll just speed up the process. I have five matchmaking firms thriving in Europe." Her nose wrinkled in disgust. "Americans only want their online dating and temporary relationships. No one here is interested in real commitment."

That's not true! We just need to try harder. Brooke had matched up dozens of couples interested in real commitment. That's why she'd become a matchmaker. And she and Antonio had been matched. They were proof that Toujour worked.

"I want everyone to take a few days to think how we can make this work," Charlotte said. "Submit your ideas to me, and on Friday I will announce which idea I have chosen. We have until Valentine's Day to implement the idea and start turning a profit."

If Toujour closed, where would Brooke go? There wasn't another matchmaking firm in the state. Would Antonio agree to move if she found a position elsewhere? They couldn't survive on only his income.

No. She couldn't think like that. She would save Toujour.

Maybe if we start a Valentine's Day campaign. Single people always get desperate around the holidays.

"You're dismissed," Charlotte said. "You've got thirty minutes until we open for the day. Start brainstorming ideas."

The room broke apart and filled with a distressed buzz as people started talking. *That's it—find a solution or you're fired?* Desperation washed over Brooke in waves. There had to be something they hadn't tried. Something that could save the company. She stood, pushing through the crowd of upset co-workers toward Charlotte's retreating figure.

"Brooke," Zoey called.

"I'll be back," Brooke muttered. Charlotte had five other firms to go home to, but Brooke's career would disappear if Toujour closed.

It's not like I'm surprised. I barely have enough clients to spend a full eight hours at work each day. Brooke shrugged the thought aside. It didn't matter. There had to be another way.

What if we do a special promotion—buy a three month package at a discounted price. We could use social media to spread the word.

The door to Charlotte's office stood closed. Brooke knocked, then entered without waiting for a response. Charlotte looked up, her mouth opened and face scrunched in a scowl. She relaxed. "Oh, it's just you. Come in, and close the door behind you."

Brooke did as she was told, taking a seat in front of Charlotte's desk. "I can't believe you didn't tell me," Brooke said. Her voice sounded wounded, even to her own ears.

Charlotte looked up from the papers she leafed through. "I'm sorry about that, Brooke. But I didn't tell anyone until that meeting. I didn't want word to get out and cause a panic." She turned back to her papers.

"So that's it?" *I can't believe this is happening.* "Turn a profit in three months or we're done?"

Charlotte slammed the papers down on the desk. Brooke jumped in her chair.

"Do you think I want to close Toujour? This was supposed to be my big break in the United States. But the company has been losing money for nine months. The fact is, Americans aren't interested in traditional matchmaking."

85

"I'm proof that's not true."

"Most Americans don't care, then. They don't care that we can get them discounted tickets to sold out events, or reservations at the best restaurants. They don't care that my matchmakers help them overcome their flaws and past relationship baggage. All they want is online dating, with its instant gratification and cheap monthly fee."

"You talk like saving Toujour is impossible." Brooke choked on the words.

"Toujour is thriving in Europe. Come with me, Brooke. Any office, your pick. Maybe Italy. Antonio would like to move home, wouldn't he? You're too talented not to continue on as a matchmaker."

"Antonio and I want to stay here for at least five years. We have a plan."

Charlotte sighed. "I'm sorry to hear that. I'll write you an excellent recommendation, of course. You should have no trouble finding another position here. Maybe not as a matchmaker, but something. And when you do move to Europe, you'll have a job with me."

Luke. He can help. Give Charlotte a no-interest loan or something.

"I'm not moving to Europe." Brooke placed her hands flat on the desk, splaying her fingers wide. "I'm friends with Luke Ryder. I'm sure he would be a financial backer for the company, if it's money you need." Brooke silently apologized for involving him without his knowledge. But she had to save Toujour. Matchmaking was the only thing she was truly good at.

And if matchmaking didn't work, what did that say for her future with Antonio?

"All the money in the world isn't going to help this place. It's clients we need. Lots of them. And I don't know how to make that happen."

Brooke massaged her temples. *Think!* "There has to be something. Maybe if we start a refer-a-friend program with existing clients. Or what if we implement a free trial? Or maybe get a celebrity client to attract notice?"

Charlotte froze, her eyes locked on Brooke's. "What did you say?"

"A celebrity client . . ." Brooke's eyes widened. "Someone like Luke Ryder." Brooke stared across the table at her boss. Had she really just suggested signing Luke as a client? Would he even consider it?

Charlotte leaned forward, her dark eyes sparkling. Brooke could almost see the circles underneath them disappearing. "If Luke Ryder were to sign up for Toujour's services, women would flock to join."

"They'd all want a chance at dating Luke," Brooke said eagerly. "And then men would sign up, hoping for a chance to date all those beautiful women."

"After a while, they'd all start to find real happiness. Things would—how do you say it?—'iceball.'" Charlotte's eyes darkened. "But Luke would have to really want to find a soul mate. If news got out that he was a marketing plant, my reputation would be destroyed."

Brooke grimaced. Luke wasn't really relationship material, and the situation with Candi wouldn't help things. "Everyone's looking for a lasting relationship, right? Some just don't know it yet."

"I've taught you well, Brooke." Charlotte leaned back in her chair. "It's all a spout dream. If I thought I could just ask a celebrity to sign, I would've done it months ago."

"You aren't friends with any celebrities. I am."

"Do you really think Luke would do it?"

"He'll sign if I asked him to." *I'm sorry, Luke.*

"Are you submitting this as your official proposal?"

Brooke nodded. "The best part is, we won't even have to spend a lot of money on marketing—the media will give us all the free advertising we want if Luke's involved."

Slowly, Charlotte nodded. "Hopefully the media attention will be more positive in the future, and not like what happened at the gala. But I'm willing to take the risk. Unless someone comes up with a better idea, we'll try it."

"And if we turn a profit in three months, you'll keep Toujour open."

Charlotte smiled. "I'll do you one better, Brooke. If this works, I'll leave you as head of this office when I go back to France. I think you're ready."

Brooke's eyes widened. "Are you serious?"

"Yes. I wouldn't leave until I had trained you adequately, but you're ready. I'm warning you though—it will take a miracle to turn this business around."

"I'm counting on it."

Chapter Nine

Luke sat straight up in bed, gasping as icy water numbed his face. He spluttered, wiping it away with cold fingers. He blinked it out of his eyes, bringing Mitch into focus.

Luke swore, then swore again. "What was that for?"

Mitch smiled grimly. "The board has called an emergency meeting, and your presence is requested. I figured you hadn't checked your email again and didn't know. Since you apparently had a few nightcaps after I left last night, I couldn't wake you up by conventional means. Get dressed. We don't want to be late."

Luke sank back against his sheets, then sat bolt upright as the water seeped into his shirt. "My bed's all wet now."

"Talia, make sure the housekeeper knows to change Luke's sheets when she stops by today," Mitch said.

"Sure, Snitch. I'll tell her. Do you want me to start the shower for you, Luke?"

"Yes," Mitch said.

"I was talking to Luke, Snitch."

Mitch rolled his eyes. "When are you going to get that glitch fixed?"

"Start the shower, Talia." Luke stood, pressing his feet into the heated carpet in a vain attempt to get warm. "I'm freezing."

"I'm dead serious about this one, Luke. You want to be at this meeting."

Luke scowled, then wandered into his master bath and shut the door with a click. Steam from the hot water already filled the room. Luke quickly undressed and stepped under the spray. He doused his head, relishing the warmth returning to his body.

This had to be about the gala. Had Nathan decided to press charges after all? That was the only disaster that could necessitate an emergency meeting. The company stock was still not great, but it hadn't dropped significantly since the initial dip. They weren't struggling with the release of any new products. Luke seriously doubted this was about a product recall.

It had to be the gala. It was the only explanation that made sense.

Luke frowned, vigorously shampooing his hair. He shouldn't have to explain his personal business to a stodgy board of directors. What had happened between him and Nathan had nothing to do with Ryder Communications. *Bunch of old geezers.*

Mitch pounded on the bathroom door. "Time to get out, Luke."

"Can it," Luke said.

"I'll tell Talia to shut it off if you don't hurry."

Luke sighed. He could turn the water back on, of course, but he didn't want to engage. "Off, Talia," he said. The spray instantly disappeared. He toweled dry, then slipped into a clean pair of boxers.

Luke wandered back into his bedroom. A suit lay across his bed, with a matching shirt, tie, and shoes. A crisply folded pocket square even waited to be placed in the front breast pocket of the jacket.

"You picked out my clothes?"

"You need to look like a professional today, not a frat boy with a hangover. Besides, we're in a hurry. We're leaving in five." Mitch stalked out of the room and slammed the door.

A pit of worry congealed in Luke's stomach, and he quickly dressed. He opened the bedroom door four minutes later to see Mitch leaning against the hallway wall, still scowling. "Let's go," Mitch said.

Luke followed Mitch the penthouse's foyer, where the private elevator waited for them. "You want to tell me what this is about?"

The elevator door pinged opened, and the attendant greeted them with a smile. They rode to the lobby in complete silence. Luke nodded to the doorman, and they exited the building and climbed into a waiting car.

"I really wish you would've held it together at the gala, man," Mitch said.

"I've already explained myself."

"I know." Mitch rubbed his head. "There are some things I need to tell you before we get to the meeting."

"Out with it, Mitch."

"There's been a lot of talk the last few months, especially since Rick . . . They're talking about replacing you as CEO."

Luke's eyes widened, and he swore. "How could you keep this from me?"

"It was just talk, and you were going through stuff." Mitch sighed, rubbing a hand over his face. "It was mostly the newer guys blowing off steam because they're pissed about picking up the slack. 'Can Luke hack it as CEO?' That sort of thing. They all think you're too young and inexperienced, but the board only brought up generalities. You were in such a bad place, so I didn't mention it to you. Your chi's already out of whack."

Luke clenched his hand into a fist, resting it on his knee. "This is *my* company." *And Dad's.* "Who do they think they are?"

"The freakin' board of directors! They control fifty-five percent of the company. I've already been placed on a verbal warning for not keeping you in line. They *can* replace you, if they feel it's justified. They already took on a lot when Rick refused to appoint an interim CEO and worked through his illness. Now that Rick is gone, they want a CEO who is focused on the job. And after Saturday . . ." Mitch let out a long breath. "If you go, I'm out, too."

"So you're telling me this meeting is to fire us?"

"I don't think they'll outright fire us. Not today. But I've got a bad feeling about this."

Luke sank back against the upholstered seat of the limo. "Well thanks to you, so do I."

"Just don't do anything stupid, okay? Act penitent. Contrite. Promise to do better. *Something.* It's not just your butt on the line anymore."

"If you'd told me about this earlier, it never would've gotten to this point."

"I shouldn't have to tell you to do your job."

The limo pulled up to Ryder Communications' corporate office—a fifteen story monstrosity in downtown Los Angeles. *Put on your game face, Luke.* Maybe this meeting had nothing to do with the gala.

Maybe hell would freeze over, too.

I can fix this. I will do anything to fix this.

Luke straightened his tie, then stepped out of the limo and followed Mitch. He squinted as sunlight glared off the reflective surface of the building. They passed tall palm trees and a modern art sculpture that Luke had never understood. A fountain gurgled softly right outside the entrance, but it did nothing to soothe Luke's nerves.

"Mr. Ryder," the receptionist said, her eyebrows raised in surprise. Luke scowled. It wasn't like he never showed up at the office. He'd spent fourteen hour days at this place until a few weeks before his father's death. Taken on a lot of CEO responsibilities while his dad grew sicker and sicker. Every long weekend and school break during college had been spent here. He'd been one of the first to arrive and last to leave the office every day until his father's cancer progressed to the final stages.

"We're heading up to the conference room on the fifteenth floor," Mitch told the receptionist.

"I'll let them know you're on your way." She picked up the phone and dialed.

Luke followed Mitch to the elevator. The sensors detected their presence as soon as they were in range and the doors opened automatically. When they arrived on the fifteenth floor, the secretary there was hanging up the phone. "The last of the board members just arrived," she said.

"Thanks," Mitch replied. The conference room doors swung open as they approached, and Mitch waited for Luke to enter first. *Trying to keep me from running away?* With the board threatening to oust him, there wasn't a force in the world that would keep Luke from this meeting. *Whatever it takes.* Saving his father's legacy was worth whatever promises, half-truths, and outright lies he had to tell.

They weren't taking Ryder Communications from him. He wouldn't let them.

Fifteen of Los Angeles' stodgiest men and women sat around the mahogany conference table, chatting amiably with each other. Floor to ceiling windows flooded the room with light and a view of the Los Angeles skyline. None of the board members seemed to notice Luke and Mitch's arrival. *That's because they're all half blind and mostly deaf.*

"My daughter just announced she's expecting a baby," Walter said to Harold.

"Congratulations." Harold pushed his glasses up his nose. "How many does this make?"

"Five grandchildren." Walter chuckled. "The missus is tickled pink."

Luke rolled his eyes, but kept his mouth shut. He took a seat next to Mitch at the end of the table—closest to the door.

"Luke, nice of you to join us," Walter said.

Luke almost grunted, then remember his resolve. "Feels good to be here, Walter."

"Can I get you some coffee, Mr. Ryder? Or maybe some tea?" A girl in a smart business suit gave Luke a timid smile. An intern, maybe? She couldn't be more than eighteen. He used to know everyone in this place by sight, if not by name. Had so much really changed in two months?

"Coffee is fine. Black."

The girl nodded and turned to Mitch for his order.

"It's good to see you." Emma, in the chair next to Luke's, patted his arm. "We've missed you around the office."

"Nice to see you, too," Luke lied.

A large hand fell on his shoulder. Luke looked up into the solemn eyes of Darius.

"Lucas," Darius said. "So glad you could join us. I wasn't sure if you'd come."

"Why wouldn't I be here?" Luke asked.

"I thought maybe you were neglecting your email again. Since everyone is here, we'll start."

Luke glowered. Darius may be the chairman of the board, but Luke was CEO. *He* should call the meeting to order. He should call the meeting, period.

"Your coffee, Mr. Ryder."

Luke took the cup from the intern with a mumbled, "Thanks."

Darius sat at the head of the table. "I think we're ready to start," he said. Fifteen pairs of eyes shot toward Luke. "Where's Andrea? Someone needs to take minutes."

"Here," said a small voice. A woman scurried over to sit at the back of the room, behind Darius.

"Good," Darius said. He sank into his chair, then placed his arms on top of the mahogany table and steepled his fingers. "Luke, we're here to discuss the future of Ryder Communications. I'll come right out and say it—we're not sure you're the CEO for the job. We were uncertain from the moment your father suggested the idea, and your behavior since his death has confirmed our worst fears. We think it might be time to reevaluate your position with the company."

Luke's heart thudded. He hadn't disbelieved Mitch, but he hadn't expected Darius to be so blunt, either. "I didn't realize things were this bad." He knew he'd been acting mainly as a figurehead the last two months, and the board had been the ones running things. But he was still working through his grief.

Harold snorted. "You're in the tabloids constantly. You're drunk more than you're sober. You've got a new woman every night. The investors are concerned about the stability of the company. We need a capable, strong CEO to reassure stockholders that even though our founder is gone, the company is still thriving."

"You could at least have the decency to fake a stable relationship for appearance's sake," Silvia piped in. "The gala was a disaster. I don't care who Nathan Kendall is sleeping with, that was over the line." She let out a harrumph. "It made it look like our CEO cared more about his latest booty call than keeping the company afloat. I've received half a dozen calls this morning from concerned shareholders, and four times that many emails, not to mention all the calls I got over the weekend."

"This isn't you," Emma said. "We need the Luke who had an MBA by twenty-two and practically lived at the office. And frankly, we haven't seen any evidence he still exists the last two months."

A general murmur of agreement circulated around the room.

Luke took a deep, calming breath. *You can rage in the privacy of your own house later. For now, be the CEO.* He struggled to slip into the persona that used to come so naturally. "I'll admit the gala wasn't my finest moment.

But that wasn't about Candi—it was about Talia. Kendall said their new product will destroy us."

"It very well might," Darius said. "Talia is a disaster. You have to stop being stubborn on that matter. She needs a complete overhaul or another company will steal our spot in the automation world."

Luke opened his mouth to protest, but Harold spoke up. "It's not just Talia. Stock is down, and people are getting nervous."

Luke was losing his cool. He couldn't keep this up much longer. "We knew stock would dip after Dad's death. You can't possibly blame that on me."

"You're the CEO," Harold said.

Darius held up a hand, and the room quieted. "We know this has been tough on you. We all miss Rick, but it's time to move past his death and focus on his legacy—*Ryder* Communications. We understand you need time to grieve, but we won't allow it to affect the company any longer. We don't want to replace you. But something has to change."

The boardroom started spinning. Luke gripped the arms of his chair. *This can't be happening. They can't take the company from me. They can't!*

"We had our misgivings about you taking over at such a young age," Darius said. "In fact, I suggested to Rick that we appoint an interim CEO while you learned a bit more. But Rick assured me you were up for the task."

"I am," Luke said. "I was doing half Dad's job before his death."

"Which is why we agreed to appoint you," Darius said. "But your behavior the last two months has made us question whether or not you can do this without your father's guidance."

"We're all worried about you," Emma said. "We've watched you grow from a gangly teenager into a man. We want to see you succeed."

"But we aren't willing to continue to put the company at risk," Darius said.

"Or to continue working weekends to pick up your slack," Walter added.

Luke wanted to scream. He wanted to fight back and curse and storm out of the room after flipping them the bird.

But he wanted to remain CEO more. They could fire him, and Mitch. They would, if things didn't change.

"Just don't do anything stupid, okay? Act penitent. Contrite. Promise to do better. Something." Had it really been less than an hour ago that Mitch told Luke that? Luke glanced over at Mitch, who slowly nodded his head as if to say, *Give them what they want.*

"I didn't realize my personal life was causing the company so much distress," Luke said. The words caught in his throat, but he forced them out anyway. "It wasn't my intention to endanger the company. I'm as interested in seeing Ryder Communications continue to succeed as the rest of you, obviously."

Darius smiled. "I'm glad to hear it."

Luke swallowed hard. "I've allowed my grief to overcome my good sense the last few months, but I see that it's time for me to put that all behind me. What can I do to regain your trust?"

The next two hours were grueling. The board's demands were numerous, but nothing he hadn't been doing daily until two months ago. Show up to work every day. Show up sober. Show up before nine. Stay out of the tabloids. Get back on track with the corporate version of the home automation system, and launch it by summer. Either fix Talia's bugs, or start over with a new voice automation system.

"We want shareholders to feel like the company's making progress," Darius told Luke as they finished up. "It's been a while since our successes with the security features and integration systems of early models. We need to restore confidence in you as CEO, and Ryder Communications as a company. Let's see if we can't launch some new products and get stock up, okay?"

And if I don't? But Luke didn't ask that question. He already knew the answer.

"I'll handpick a team today for the corporate automation system and revamping Talia," Luke said. "And I'll personally oversee both." He hadn't brought anything with him to the meeting, but the intern had graciously brought his work laptop from his office. "I'll get to work immediately."

"Excellent," Darius said. "We're pleased you're willing to work with us. I feel like we've made good progress today. We're hopeful things can turn around. Let's reconvene in a month and see where we are. Meeting adjourned."

The room broke up into individual conversations. Members of the board left the conference room, rushing to whatever it was they did with the rest of their time. Luke closed the lid on his laptop and stood.

From behind, Darius clapped Luke on the shoulder. "I hope we weren't too harsh with you. Your father was a dear friend of mine. I don't want to see his company destroyed because you're mourning."

Luke clenched his jaw. "It's my company too, Reginald."

Darius frowned. "I hope you can handle the job. To be CEO at twenty-five . . . I'm sorry such a burden has been placed on you."

Me too. But Luke wasn't about to let Darius know that. "My father was twenty-five when he started Ryder Communications. If he could do it, so can I."

"Yes, but back then he was the company's sole employee, and mostly doing contract work. Plus he had your dear mother to help him."

Luke stood and grabbed his laptop off the table. *Don't say a word.*

"Karen supported and helped him through the hard times. Family is really all we have, when you think about it. I doubt Ryder Communications would've ever gotten off the ground without your mom's help." Darius smiled. "I'll check in with you regularly, and if you need any help, don't hesitate to call. I'm on your side."

Luke gave Darius a tight nod and left the room. Mitch trailed his footsteps. The two men were silent as they walked down the hallway to Luke's office. Luke's personal secretary looked up in surprise, jumping to her feet as they approached.

"Mr. Ryder," Krista said. "I thought you'd head home right after the meeting."

Luke raised a hand to his eyes and rubbed. His tie felt like it was suffocating him. Had he really been so unreliable lately? "No, I'm back to my regular schedule. Mitch and I have business to attend to. Hold my calls, and don't let anyone bother me for the rest of the day."

"Of course, Mr. Ryder."

"I need a list of all project manager stats and current projects as soon as possible," Luke continued.

"I'll bring it right in."

Luke nodded. He opened the door to his office, and shut it behind Mitch. His vision was tunneling, and he blinked rapidly.

"You handled that well," Mitch said. "I think if we keep our heads down for the next few months, this'll blow over. If they see you're trying, they won't even consider—"

"I can't believe this is happening." Luke grabbed his hair and pulled, his breath coming in gasps.

"Luke?" Mitch put a hand on his shoulder.

Luke shrugged it off. He fell to his knees, his heart racing. His hands tingled and he shook them violently, trying to get rid of the sensation. "They're going to fire me. And I'm going to lose the company." *It's all I have left of Dad.*

"Calm down." Mitch crouched next to him. "Breathe. Look at me, Luke. Look at me!" He shook Luke roughly, and Luke stared into Mitch's concerned face. "I'm not going to let you lose this company—it's why I gave you a heads up about the meeting. Do you hear me? You're not going to lose it."

Luke's heartbeat started to slow as he followed Mitch's lead and took deliberate, even breaths. "It's overwhelming," he whispered, feeling like an idiot.

"I know. But we'll make a plan and make lists and get everything done. I'm on your side. I'm here to help."

Luke nodded, rising from the floor and brushing off the knees of his suit. "What do we need to do first?" he asked Mitch, even though he already knew the answer.

Whatever it takes.

Chapter Ten

"What was that about?" Zoey asked when Brooke arrived back at their shared cubicle.

Brooke sank into a chair. "I'm going to sign Luke."

Zoey's eyes widened. "You're joking."

"I'm not." Brooke quickly explained the discussion she'd had with Charlotte. "It makes sense. It's risky, but it's the only thing I can think of to save the company."

"But Luke?" Zoey folded her arms and shook her head. "He's your best friend. He's been in love with you for eight years."

Brooke rolled her eyes. She booted up her computer and swiveled back to face Zoey. "That was ages ago."

"If you gave him any encouragement, he'd be all in."

"You're being ridiculous." Brooke clicked on the icon to log into her computer. "What I'm worried about is whether or not he can handle it right now. He's not great with relationships."

"I can't believe you're going to be Luke's matchmaker. That's messed up."

"I'm not—Charlotte thinks it's best if someone else is his matchmaker. And you won't be complaining when we can still make rent next month."

"That's even more messed up. What will Luke say? What will Antonio say?"

"Luke will do it for me. Antonio will get used to the idea." He would hate that Luke was doing her a favor, but love that he was dating others. "I'm taking off early for our cake tasting this afternoon. I'll tell Antonio then."

It was a fairly slow day, which was becoming more and more typical. Brooke spent a few hours scanning the database for client matches, and then had two client appointments before logging off for the day at five.

"Leaving for the cake tasting?" Zoey asked.

"Yes." Brooke tossed Zoey the car keys. "I'll have Antonio drop me back at home."

Zoey grinned. "I love chocolate, if the maid of honor's opinion holds any weight. Just sayin'."

"I'll keep that in mind."

Zoey nodded, waving a hand absently as she returned her focus to her computer screen. Toujour's database was open, but it didn't look like Zoey was having much luck finding her client a match. *That'll all change as soon as Luke signs.* With more clients in the database, it wouldn't be as hard to find matches.

The chatter of employees conversing was overtaken by music as Brooke made her way to the front lobby. Antonio was already there, waiting for her. He leaned against Lianna's desk, his head tilted toward hers as she laughed at something he'd said. "Oh, Antonio." Lianna swatted at his arm playfully.

Antonio chuckled. "Careful, Lianna. You've displaced the poinsettia." He straightened the potted plant on one corner of her desk.

Brooke swallowed back the jealousy that threatened to choke her. Antonio was only being friendly. Women always flirted with him. It didn't mean anything.

"Hey," Brooke said.

Lianna turned to Brooke, her cheeks flaming pink. "Brooke. I didn't hear you come in."

I'll bet you didn't. Brooke tried to smile, but she worried it came off more as a glare.

Antonio strode over to Brooke and leaned down to kiss her on the lips. "*Ciao, mia dolcezza.* You look absolutely ravishing today."

That at least made her feel better. Antonio didn't look the least bit flustered at her arrival. *He was just flirting.* They were going to look at wedding cakes, for heaven's sake. They were committed. Seventy-one percent compatible. *He isn't my dad.* She needed to pull herself together. "Ready to go?" Brooke asked.

Antonio nodded. "If I stay here much longer, this incense is going to give me a headache."

"Bye, Antonio," Lianna called as they left.

Brooke inhaled sharply, sticking her hands deep into her pockets and curling her fingers. It didn't escape her notice that Lianna hadn't said goodbye to her. She turned right and walked rapidly down the sidewalk. The bakery was only a few blocks away, and she needed to burn off steam. They could come back for Antonio's motorcycle later. *Lianna has some nerve.*

Antonio followed, completely oblivious to Brooke's jealousy as usual. His shoulder brushed hers, and he pulled her hand from her pocket and held it. "Slow down, *bella*. It's such a beautiful day, and I want to enjoy it with you."

Brooke's heart melted, and the last of her anger disappeared. Antonio hadn't meant to flirt, and neither had Lianna. Probably. Either way, Brooke wasn't that insecure in their relationship. *Let it go.* She needed to tell Antonio about her deal with Charlotte—before she told Luke tomorrow—and she didn't want to have that conversation while fighting. It would be dicey enough without the added tension.

"How has your day been?" Antonio asked.

She wouldn't find a better opening than that. "Stressful. Today Charlotte gave us an ultimatum—start turning a profit in the next three months, or she's closing Toujour."

Antonio stopped, turning to face Brooke. "Are you serious?"

Brooke tugged his hand until they were walking again. "Unfortunately, yes."

"You knew Toujour wasn't doing well." Antonio rubbed his thumb over her knuckles. "Oh, *mia dolcezza*, I am so sorry for you."

Brooke blew out a breath. "If it weren't for Toujour, we'd have never met. This is my dream job, Antonio. I worked so hard to get where I am with the company. I can't give up."

The bakery shop windows were cheerily decorated with fake snow and an appealing display of holiday-themed baked goods. Antonio opened the door and held it for Brooke. A bell tinkled as the door shut behind them.

"It's not giving up," Antonio said. "It's unfortunate it's come to this, but three months won't make a difference."

The words cut Brooke. She glared, lowering her voice to a harsh whisper so the employee at the counter wouldn't overhear. "Are we even having the same conversation? I told you I'm losing my job. Let's forget the fact that I love where I work, just for a minute. Let's forget about how an entire business is closing, putting twenty employees out of work. All that aside, we need my income if we're ever going to move out of your studio apartment into something larger. We can't survive on just your commissions."

Antonio grinned. "But that is what I wanted to tell you today. Your news makes the timing even better. The art gallery I signed with in Rome wants me to move there this spring. Isn't that fantastic?"

Brooke's breath caught in her throat, stolen by the announcement.

"Welcome to Sweet Dreams," the woman behind the counter said, smiling broadly. "How can I help you?"

Antonio stepped up to the counter. "We have an appointment with Sara. For a cake tasting."

The girl smiled. "Oh, you must be the five-fifteen. Let me take you back to our tasting room."

Italy!

Antonio took Brooke's hand again, and she let him lead her to the tasting room. She barely registered the music playing overhead, or the sample cake displays along the back wall, as she and Antonio took their seats.

"Sara will be with you shortly," the girl said, then left and shut the door.

Brooke whirled on Antonio. "When were you going to tell me about this?"

"About what?"

"Rome!"

Antonio shrugged. "I didn't want to ruin our happy reunion yesterday. I thought today would be a better time to bring it up."

"I thought we agreed to stay in the States for at least five years." Brooke had counted on those years. They had a plan—work for five years, have a baby, *then* move to Italy.

Antonio leaned forward, grasping both Brooke's hands in his. "This is an amazing opportunity for us. The gallery wants me to paint for them full time. I'd make enough money that you wouldn't have to work."

Brooke pulled away. "And what exactly would I do all day in a foreign country where I don't speak the language?"

"Your *Italiano* is coming along well. And you'd take care of the *bambini*, of course."

Brooke shot out of her chair. She pressed a shaking hand to her stomach and swallowed down the bile in her throat. "I thought we decided to not have children for at least a few years."

Antonio shrugged. "Yes, but that was before. Now that I'll be earning enough to support us both, there's no need to wait. Italians always have big families. My mom can't stop talking about grandchildren."

"That's not what we talked about."

"Toujour is closing." Antonio stood as well. "It makes the decision easy. What's keeping us here?"

Brooke folded her arms. "Oh, I don't know. My family. My friends. My job. Toujour isn't closing—not yet, at least. Charlotte gave us three months, and I made a deal with her. She said if I could turn a profit by then, she'd make me head of the U.S. office when she goes back to France. This is what I've been working for."

Antonio snorted. "And how exactly are you going to turn a profit in three months?"

Brooke had planned to break it to him gently, but he was being absolutely infuriating. She wanted to make him as mad as he'd made her. "Luke. I'm going to ask him to sign with Toujour and we'll run a marketing campaign around that. It's going to work."

Antonio's mouth fell open. "You've got to be joking."

The door opened then, and a middle-aged woman entered. She wore a white baker's coat, and had glasses perched on her nose. She froze when she saw them standing. "Am I interrupting something?"

Brooke sank back into her chair, and Antonio followed suit. "Not at all," Brooke said, making her words purposefully light. "Antonio and I were just discussing work."

"Okay." The woman smiled uncertainly, sitting on the third chair around the small table. She set a binder on the counter, and held out her hand for both of them to shake. "I'm Sara. I wanted to start off by getting a feel for your wedding, and what kind of a cake you envision." She opened the binder, withdrawing a form and writing their names at the top. She looked up at them, her pen poised above the paper. "When is the wedding?"

"September fifth," Brooke said.

Sara wrote the date down. "The weather is perfect that time of year. What are the wedding colors?"

He wants to move to Italy. Brooke couldn't believe it. She'd always known it was a possibility—no, inevitable. But she thought she had years to prepare for this. At least five, like they'd agreed.

"Brooke's decided on coral, gray, and turquoise," Antonio said. "But the swatches she's chosen hold a lot more warmth than those tones typically have."

Sara smiled and wrote it down. "I'm impressed. The groom usually has no idea about these things."

"I'm a painter. I always pay attention to color."

Sara laughed. "Well, aren't you adorable. Where's the venue?"

"A vineyard just outside the city," Brooke said.

Antonio grinned. "I'm Italian. It seemed fitting."

Sara nodded. "Oh yeah. This wedding sounds fabulous."

Italy. By spring. That was before the wedding. If they moved to Italy, would they still get married in California? And he expected children immediately now, too?

No. This was *not* what she'd agreed to.

Now is not the time. After the appointment, she and Antonio clearly needed to have a serious conversation. But for now, she was going to savor this experience. She'd been planning her wedding her whole life, and she wanted to enjoy every minute of choosing her wedding cake.

Even if she ended up having to choose a new one in Italy.

Two hours and eight tastings later, the cake was chosen—a three-tiered white raspberry fondant cake with gray and turquoise accents and coral-colored sugar roses. Brooke and Antonio thanked Sara, and left Sweet Dreams hand in hand.

As soon as they were outside, Antonio pulled his hand away from Brooke's. "That's your plan to save Toujour—involve Luke?" He threw his hands up in the air. "Why do I feel like that man is destroying our future every time I turn around?"

"It's a good idea. It's going to work."

"Oh yes. Luke is the picture of stability."

Brooke folded her arms, walking briskly ahead of Antonio. She heard his footfalls as he hurried to catch up. "You're being pretty selfish about this. It's not only my job we're talking about. Twenty people will be unemployed if this doesn't work."

"And they'll find new jobs."

"I thought you'd be more sentimental. Without Toujour, there'd be no us. Don't you want to give other couples that chance?"

"I'm grateful for Toujour because it brought me you, but it's not the only way to find love. You know I'd never have signed if my parents hadn't pressured me."

Brooke whirled. "You just want to move to Italy."

"And why shouldn't I? It's my home. *Mia famiglia* is there." He took her hands in his. "This is a great opportunity for us. This gallery sells millions in art every year. We'd have more euros than we'd know what to do with."

Brooke brushed tears away with the back of her hand, angry at herself for letting them fall. "This isn't what we agreed to," she repeated stubbornly. "I can't believe you didn't consult me on this sooner. If I'd known you were going to Italy to find a job so we could move—"

"I wasn't. But after signing the contract with the gallery, they mentioned how much more they'd be able to do for me if I was in the city. You'll love Rome. We'll eat gelato at the Trevi Fountain every Friday, just like we've always talked about." He touched the tip of her nose with his finger. "I know the timing is unexpected, but we've discussed this."

"And what about the wedding? Would we even still get married in California?"

"Of course, if that's what you want. It'd be more challenging to plan the wedding from Italy, but people do destination weddings all the time. This would be no different."

Brooke wiped away her tears. "California isn't my idea of a destination wedding." She sniffed. "I have to save Toujour. I have to at least give it a try."

Antonio frowned. "So you won't even consider what I'm saying. You don't want to move because of *him*."

"No, I don't want to move because Charlotte will make me head of the office here. That's a big career move for me."

"And this is a big career move for me. You know Charlotte will let you work in her Rome office, and you'll be director there soon enough. Neither of us has to sacrifice our career goals. Come with me, Brooke. Let's just go."

She wasn't about to tell him Charlotte had already offered her a job in Rome. "It's not that simple."

"It's not that difficult, either."

She put a hand to her head. "Give me a second. I need to process."

Antonio's voice softened. "How about a compromise? I won't complain if Luke joins your matchmaking service, as long as you agree to consider Italy. If you really think about it, you'll know this is the best choice for us. But that doesn't mean you can't save everyone else's jobs. And maybe you'll find Luke a wife."

Think, Brooke. Luke's involvement at Toujour in exchange for thinking about Italy. Was it worth it? They'd always planned on moving to Italy eventually. And she had fantasized about living there quite a bit. It wasn't like she was promising to move by taking the deal. Yet.

"If I agree to this, you won't so much as complain about Luke," Brooke said.

Antonio swallowed. "I don't like it, but yes. If he agrees, I won't say a word. *If* you think about Italy. I mean really think about it. You know what this means for my career."

That's what made this whole thing so crappy—she did know. This was huge for Antonio. Brooke could even keep matchmaking, regardless of the Los Angeles office's fate. And Italy appealed to Brooke too. The vineyards and ancient Roman ruins and romance. But talking about someday was very different from dealing with reality.

She couldn't give up on matchmaking here. Giving up meant admitting it didn't work. That maybe the little conflicts she and Antonio had experienced lately were a sign of a deeper compatibility issue, whatever their seventy-one percent said.

"Okay," she said reluctantly. "I'll think about Italy, if you let me save Toujour. And if you promise we'll still get married in California, no matter what."

"Deal." Antonio wrapped a strong hand around the back of her neck. He pulled her toward him, and she sank into his kiss, letting herself think of nothing but how his lips felt against hers.

Several pleasant moments later, Antonio pulled away. "Are you sure you don't want to ditch Zoey and move in with me now?"

Brooke kissed him playfully. "I'm sure."

Maybe it's better if we move. Antonio has to be my first priority now, and Luke needs to find a wife. Maybe we need some distance.

Luke clearly wasn't in a place for a real relationship. Maybe she could help match him up with someone who would change his mind.

She smiled at something Antonio said. Right now, she needed to focus on saving Toujour. She could worry about everything else later.

Chapter Eleven

Luke stared at the list of names and brought the can of Dr. Pepper to his lips. He pushed the intercom button next to his computer. "I want the stats from the last six months for these six people," he told his secretary, and immediately rattled off some names.

"You're doing good, Luke," Mitch encouraged. He sat in a chair on the opposite side of the desk, his tablet in hand. "The tech department confirmed they'll have Talia 2.0 available for pre-order on our website by the end of the week at the latest. And marketing scheduled a meeting for this afternoon to bounce around ideas for advertising the business automation system." Mitch busily tapped buttons on his tablet. "When will you have a decision on project managers for both those projects?"

"Hopefully by lunch," Luke said. "Once Krista gets me their stats, the decision should be easy." Luckily he'd only been out of touch for two months and still more or less knew which project managers were capable of what. He rolled his shoulders and glanced at the clock in the corner of his computer screen. Nine-sixteen. He shook his head. He hadn't seen nine a.m. since the funeral.

Luke's cell phone buzzed, sliding across the smooth mahogany desk with the movement. Brooke's ring tone. His heart jumped. She hadn't answered a single one of his calls since the gala. He was used to her ignoring him for a few days after Antonio got back from a trip, but she usually at least sent a text. He knew she was pissed, and he didn't know how to fix it. He was desperate to see her. To talk through what had happened at the board meeting.

"Hey, Brooke."

"Where are you?"

He frowned, looking around his office. "Work."

"Seriously? Why?"

Luke rolled his eyes. *Ouch.* "Um, because it's my job. Where are you?"

"At your apartment. I'll be at your office in ten." The phone clicked before Luke could reply.

"What was that about?" Mitch asked.

"I'm gonna guess that Brooke's finally ready to yell at me about the gala." Luke downed the rest of his Dr. Pepper and sent his computer to screen saver mode. "I won't be able to focus until after she gets here."

Mitch nodded and closed the cover on his tablet. "I'll go make some calls in my office then. Let me know when you're done."

Luke nodded and Mitch left.

It was a long fifteen minutes until his secretary announced Brooke's arrival. Luke tugged at his tie, making sure it was straight. The doors opened and Brooke entered.

"Hey," Luke said, giving her a hug. She stood stiff, but then slid her arms around his back for a quick squeeze. *Victory.* Luke let her pull away. Heaven forbid they violate Rule #2. "Did you come to yell at me about the gala?" he teased, hoping Brooke would smile.

She didn't. "No."

Luke sighed. "You're mad at me."

Brooke folded her arms across her stomach. "Of course I am. Did you see what the latest papers are saying?"

"Yeah, but I was hoping you hadn't."

"That's not what I'm here to talk about."

"Are you saying you forgive me?"

Brooke sighed. "You know I can't stay mad at you. I'm just tired. I miss the old you. The you that was so passionate about his job I'd have to force him to go home and sleep. It's really good to see you here." She set her purse on his desk, the one she had no idea had cost him twelve-thousand-dollars, and kicked off her heels. She looked amazing in a gray skirt that hugged her legs and a blouse that was tailored in all the right places, her dark hair tumbling around her shoulders. "What brought you to the office?"

Luke motioned for her to sit on the couch and sank down beside her. "You were right—the board is pissed. We had a meeting yesterday, and they're threatening to oust me."

Brooke's jaw dropped. "They can't do that."

"They can."

"I know they have the power to, but it's not right. Darius wouldn't really fire you, would he? He was so close to your father."

Luke rolled his shoulders. He could feel the tension gathering there, making his neck ache. "Maybe that's why he'd do it. They were nice enough to point out that I've been destroying Dad's legacy the last two months." *How could I have been so negligent?* He never would've forgiven himself if the board hadn't stepped in and he'd ran the company into the ground.

Was that what he was doing with Brooke—refusing to step in and letting Antonio take his place? It had been eight years since she'd turned him down. After that initial dismissal, the timing had never been right. He'd give up on Brooke and start dating someone, and by the time he broke up with the girl, Brooke would have a boyfriend. But in eight years his feelings had only grown stronger. Certainly there was still a chemistry between them. He had been getting up the courage to suggest they start dating, hoping the timing was finally right, when she signed with Toujour and Antonio entered the picture.

She doesn't see me that way, he reminded himself.

"Hey." Brooke took his face in her hands, forcing him to look at her. Her palms were soft against his cheeks, and he barely held back a shiver. "You lost your father. Anyone would struggle after something like that." She dropped her hands, and he wanted nothing more than to put them back on his face. To pull her onto his lap and hold her close until their lips were touching and—

"Well I'm not willing to lose the company over grief," Luke said. "Two months was enough time to wallow. It's time I start acting like the CEO."

Brooke smiled, and there was so much pride in her gaze. He wanted to deserve her faith in his abilities. She wrapped her arms around him in a quick hug. "You're going to be a fantastic CEO. I'm glad to see you at work again."

"Aren't you supposed to be at work?" Luke asked.

"That's actually why I'm here." She frowned. "Now I don't know if I should ask."

Luke's heart warmed. "You can ask me anything."

"It's big, Luke."

"Ask away."

Brooke tucked her feet underneath her and her eyes clouded with misery. "Charlotte's closing Toujour if we can't turn a profit in the next three months."

Luke's heart lurched. And after she had worked so hard. He'd watched her tenaciously badger Charlotte into an internship, then claw her way to becoming top matchmaker at the firm. She had so much faith in Toujour she'd placed her hopes for a relationship in the hands of another matchmaker. He scooted closer and wrapped an arm around her shoulder. She sat rigid for a moment, then relaxed and leaned her head against him. She didn't cry, but he could feel the disappointment and sorrow radiating from her in waves.

"I'm sorry. When did she tell you that?"

"Yesterday," Brooke admitted.

He scrubbed his face. "And after I acted like a complete jerk at the gala. Not a good weekend for you."

She chuckled. "Definitely not one of my better ones."

"Is it about money? I'm more than willing to—"

Brooke shook her head, pulling back. "Money is *a* problem. We've been in the red for months. But the real issue is we don't have enough clients."

That should be an easy enough fix. "Maybe if she tried a new marketing campaign. I can recommend someone and foot the bill."

She blew out a breath, causing a strand of hair to puff outward. He ached to reach out and tuck it behind her ear. Brooke hadn't made a rule specifically against that, but he knew it would piss her off. "You're sweet to offer," Brooke said. "But we need your help in a different way. I sort of volunteered you for something without asking you first." She paused, as though waiting for him to respond.

"Go on."

"Charlotte and I came up with a plan. If we sign a celebrity client, people will trip all over themselves to sign up for the chance at a date. And the media will give us all the free publicity we want." She raised an eyebrow, as though this should mean something to him.

Did she want him to call in favors and get his high profile friends to sign up? His brow furrowed. He doubted anyone in his contact list would be willing. Maybe—

I'm an idiot. It was so obvious.

"Me," Luke said.

Brooke nodded. "Who better to attract new clients than America's favorite bachelor? I know I should've discussed it with you first, but I felt backed into a corner."

Why didn't I see this coming? Luke had watched Brooke in action since eleventh grade—even been the recipient of her matchmaking efforts a time or two. But never anything like this.

"You want me to sign with Toujour?" Luke clarified.

"Yes." Her eyes lowered. "Charlotte said if it works, she'll make me head of the U.S. division when she goes back to France. But now I don't feel like I can ask that of you. You need to focus on your job."

"This will save Toujour?"

"And get me a promotion. Kind of selfish, huh? To put you on the spot like this because I don't want to find work somewhere else. Especially now." Her foot tapped against the floor, a sure sign she was agitated. "I mean, the gala . . . well, you sort of exploded. Obviously you've got a lot on your plate."

"The gala was an accident. I was an idiot. It won't happen again." Luke frowned. "Antonio's upset about this, isn't he?"

Brooke's foot tapped at double time. "No."

"You're doing this against his wishes. I know he hates me."

"Antonio doesn't hate you." She swallowed. "In fact, we have an agreement. He won't complain about you signing with Toujour if I'll think about moving to Italy."

Luke's eyes bulged. "*What?*"

"Yeah, I know. He just told me yesterday. He signed with a gallery in Rome and they're really excited about his work, but fear the distance will limit their profits. They want to hire him exclusively instead of on a contract work basis. And they have an amazingly wealthy clientele. It's the break Antonio's been hoping for. Charlotte's already offered me a job at any of her European offices, so I wouldn't even have to give up my career."

Italy. Brooke—his beautiful, funny, adorable best friend—was going to leave him. Maybe. Luke's mind churned. Perhaps it was time for Ryder Communications to open an international office, headquartered in Rome. Of course, as CEO and with a forty-five percent investment in the company, Luke would need to go to Rome and oversee things himself.

Stop it. Following Brooke to Italy would be too obvious, and too much like stalking. No, he had to convince her to stay in Los Angeles. Moving would be his Plan B.

This is really happening. While he'd had his head in the clouds—or been in a drunken stupor—Brooke had been moving on with life. Without him. If something didn't change, he'd really lose her.

I can't lose Brooke too. I can't. Luke couldn't swallow past the lump in his throat. Losing his dad had crushed

133

him. Losing Brooke would destroy him. "Do you want to move to Italy?"

"I don't know." Brooke rolled her eyes. "I should. It's every girl's dream, right? I knew we'd move there eventually. Right now, I'm going to focus on Toujour. If I can't save it, then there's really no reason not to move and the decision will be easy."

"I'll do it. I'll sign with Toujour and save everyone's jobs."

"If you say yes, you're agreeing to try to find true love. Are you sure you're ready for that? You already have a lot going on right now."

"I'm not looking for love, so I'm not going to find it." The whole idea was absurd. He'd already found love. He just needed to convince Brooke to stay. And the first step to convincing her was keeping her in California. "I'm going to fake a relationship to help you with publicity. No big deal."

She folded her arms, and her eyes had that hint of steel he loved and hated all at once. "I won't sign you if it's not for real. I can't do that to my clients, even if it will save the company."

He held up a hand. "Okay, okay. I'll try to be open to a real relationship." Not.

"This is for real. Our clients are genuinely looking for forever. I've been in their position. I know how hard it is to put yourself out there, and I'm not going to subject them to someone who isn't committed."

He couldn't resist—he reached out and tucked a strand of hair behind her ear, ignoring the way she flinched. "I don't need another girl in my life. I've got you."

"You need a girlfriend. And I won't let you sign if you aren't genuine."

Luke frowned. Her lips were pursed, brow furrowed—a sure sign she was digging her heels in. "Okay. I'll really try to find a relationship."

"Promise?"

"I promise." Anything for Brooke.

Her shoulders relaxed. Brooke looked down, fidgeting with a button on her coat. "You deserve to find love, Luke."

I found you. His hand rested on hers. "And I'll find it someday. Maybe with Toujour."

"I think you will. I did." She threw her arms around his neck, squeezing tight. *One. Two. Three. Four. Five!*

She released him, but Luke's heart fluttered. She'd broken her own self-imposed rule. That never happened.

"You're sure you can handle this? It won't throw you over the edge or anything? Get you in trouble with the board?"

"It'll be fine."

Brooke grinned. "Luke, you're a lifesaver. I could kiss you!"

I wish you would.

"Charlotte will be thrilled. I'll make sure she assigns you an awesome matchmaker."

Another matchmaker? Luke caught her hand. "Brooke, I'm only doing this if you're my matchmaker. I thought that was obvious."

Brooke toyed with her coat button. "Charlotte is worried about how it will look after the gala and the speculations the media is making."

"I'm not negotiating on this. She'll give me what I want."

Brooke sighed. "Yeah, she will. We're desperate."

"It's settled then."

"I'm a fantastic matchmaker, Luke. You *will* fall in love if I'm matching you up."

"Maybe." He pulled her forward, kissing the top of her head. "What do I need to do?"

"Come down to the office and sign up. You can finally do that much online at least, but Charlotte will want to talk to you. Once you sign, you meet with your matchmaker—me, I guess—and fill out a questionnaire. I can't start finding matches until I have that info."

"Sounds boring." He nudged her shoulder. "You could answer the questions for me."

She laughed. "Not a chance. Only a client can fill it out." She kissed his cheek, her warm lips sending fire through his veins. "Thanks, Luke. You're the best."

Chapter Twelve

Am I really doing this? Luke grabbed his tie, loosening it a bit. He held the door open for Brooke and followed her inside Toujour. Luke had been there a thousand times before, but today the whole place looked different. He'd never noticed the photos of happy couples in the front lobby, or the cork board covered in wedding announcements behind the reception desk. He was sure Brooke's invitation would be added to the board once she had them printed. An English copy of Charlotte's international bestseller, *Finding Love*, sat on a small table in the waiting room. Maybe he should read the book. Find out what he was getting himself into.

Luke shook his head. Were his hands seriously sweating? *It's not like you're really here to find love. Whatever you told Brooke.* He'd already found love—with the girl who was about to become his matchmaker.

Lianna waved as they passed the reception desk, but she was on the phone so they didn't stop to chat.

The decorated front lobby gave way to gray cubicles and small conference rooms barely big enough for four people.

Brooke stopped outside Charlotte's door. "You're going to do this for real, right?"

"Absolutely." *Not on your life.*

Brooke swallowed. "Okay then. Let's go tell Charlotte." She raised her hand and rapped on the door.

"Come in," said a voice with a French accent that had to belong to Charlotte. Luke had seen her a few times, but they'd never had what he would call a conversation.

"Here goes nothing," Brooke whispered, and let them both inside. The room matched the tone of the rest of Toujour. Sleek black bookcases lined one wall, and a quote about love in swirly lettering was on the wall directly behind the uncluttered desk. Charlotte rose from her chair immediately. She was what most would call "breathtaking," with her rich chocolate-colored skin and black curly hair, along with a slender, tall frame and exotic brown eyes. But all Luke could think about was this was the woman who would want him to fall in love with anyone but Brooke.

"Charlotte, this is Luke," Brooke said.

Charlotte leaned over the desk and extended her hand toward him. Her handshake was firm and professional. Luke liked her immediately. "I know who you are, Mr. Ryder. Please, sit down."

"Thank you," Luke said, and they all took their seats. The high-backed chair forced him to sit uncomfortably straight.

"I spoke to Luke about our plan," Brooke said. "He's agreed to help."

Charlotte clasped her hands together. "Oh, I'm so pleased you've decided to become a client, Mr. Ryder. Let me assure you, you're making the right decision."

Luke shifted in his seat, trying to find a position that didn't make his back ache. "I really want to help Toujour."

Charlotte crossed one leg over the other, looking pleased. "I'm confident you will. You've given us all hope. We will find you the most meaningful relationship of your life. You'll like Raine. She's a superb matchmaker. You're in good hands."

Luke set his jaw. "I want Brooke as my matchmaker."

Charlotte frowned. "Surely Brooke explained to you why that might not be the wisest choice. How will it look to the media?"

"Like a friend is setting a friend up on blind dates." Luke leaned forward, his arms on the table. "Brooke is your best matchmaker here, right?"

Charlotte inclined her head. "She does have the highest success rate."

"Once the media finds out I've signed, they'll scrutinize every inch of Toujour. How's it going to look to them when they find out you assigned me anyone but the best?"

Charlotte sighed, pulling out a paper and making a notation. "I can see you're determined, and perhaps you're right. Let's hope the press focuses on Brooke's numbers and not your personal relationship."

"I can pad a few pockets if necessary. I'm friendly with a few reporters," Luke said.

"No. I don't want anything that can harm my reputation."

Like a client who's in love with his matchmaker? He cleared his throat. "Then it's only fair I tell you I'm not great at relationships."

"That's all about to change. Brooke will coach you through your dating pitfalls and help prepare you for long-term happiness with the partner of your choosing. Everyone is looking for a meaningful relationship. Some just don't know it."

"I'm willing to give it a shot," Luke said, even though he wasn't. If only Charlotte could put him in her database and match him up with Brooke. Maybe then Brooke would realize they were meant to be together.

"But don't be disappointed when I leave here alone. I don't want it to hurt the company."

Charlotte laughed. "I can assure you, you won't leave alone. Here at Toujour, we're very good at our jobs. I've spent years researching love. What attracts a couple to each other, what keeps them together. Traps to avoid. Eighty-nine percent of our couples are still together after five years. This is the beginning of the rest of your life."

Luke swallowed.

Charlotte spun around in her chair and opened a file cabinet. She placed a small stack of papers in front of Luke. "This is our basic agreement. All our clients undergo background checks, of course. Our fee is paid monthly, and you're at liberty to terminate our contract at any time. We can only terminate the contract if you violate our regulations, which are listed here." She pointed. "Mostly things like if you're in a relationship and don't tell us, if you run into legal trouble, that sort of thing."

Luke took the contract, glancing apologetically at Brooke. "I need my legal team to look over this. I hope you understand. I can have it signed and back to you no later than tomorrow." *No need to make legal more furious than they already are.*

"Of course, of course. I would expect nothing less from a businessman such as yourself."

"So how exactly does this work?" Luke asked.

Charlotte pulled a pamphlet out of a desk drawer and handed it to him. "Finding your soul mate isn't something we take lightly. I have developed a sophisticated database to help find matches with a high chance of success. You'll fill out an extensive questionnaire with your matchmaker, in this case Brooke. Likes, dislikes, goals, hobbies, what you want out of the relationship, that sort of thing."

"Just like online dating," Luke said.

Charlotte's eyes turned fiery. "It's nothing like online dating. Our matchmakers are love experts, not computers. They coach our clients on how to be their best selves, offer relationship help and advice, work with them on personality characteristics or mannerisms that might be interfering with their ability to find love. Once the computer finds matches, Brooke—not a computer—will comb through each one, looking for the best match. She will talk with the woman's matchmaker to find out more about her. Only when she is convinced a relationship is possible will she set you up on a date."

"Wow." Luke blinked. "I didn't realize it was so involved."

Charlotte sniffed. "Most don't. They think they can sign up with some online dating company and get the same result. But nothing can compare to our personalized service."

Luke glanced at Brooke, who smiled apologetically. "So once I have a match, then what?" Luke asked.

"Brooke arranges the first date, and afterward each client meets with their matchmaker to discuss how things went. If both parties are interested, you proceed to a second date, and so on. Once the couple deems themselves exclusive, their files go on hold until the relationship proves viable or dissolves."

She spoke of love so scientifically, like matching up the right formulas. Already Luke dreaded the process. He knew how to deal with barfly types. He picked them up at clubs for one-night stands all the time, providing he was drunk enough. But serious women looking for a serious relationship? That he wasn't familiar with. And to be honest, he wasn't sure how to handle it. Or how to avoid getting *too* serious. What exactly was "too serious?" Now that he thought about it, he wasn't sure.

"Brooke will be there to guide you through every step of the process," Charlotte said. "And as you yourself pointed out, she's the best."

Brooke's cheeks stained red, but she didn't refute Charlotte's claim.

"I can't wait to get started," Luke lied. "I'll get this over to legal immediately."

"Thank you," Charlotte said. "I'll follow your case closely. You are my first priority right now."

Luke barely avoided shivering. He didn't know if he should feel like a valued customer or stalked celebrity. How did Brooke work matchmaking day in and day out?

You'll find out soon enough. He'd probably be on his first date by the weekend.

"Snitch is arriving." Talia's voice was all the warning Luke had before Mitch burst into the apartment.

"You're signing with a matchmaker?" Mitch held a folder in the air as evidence. "And not with just any matchmaker, but with *Brooke Pierce*? Your best friend and the girl you're head over heels for?"

Luke scrubbed a hand over his face, leaning back against the couch. "How'd you find out? I only decided to sign like three hours ago."

"Legal called me, of course. They thought it was a joke."

"It is. Sort of."

Mitch ran a hand through his hair. "You are seriously screwing with my Zen, man. I've been diffusing oils all day and it's not even putting a dent in my stress level."

Luke rolled his eyes. He rose, going to the kitchen and pulling out two beers. Clearly Mitch needed a drink. "This'll help more than any essential oil."

Mitch grabbed the beer from Luke. "It's barely four o'clock, and neither of us are drinking. Now tell me about Toujour."

Luke shrugged. "It's all for show. Not that I can let Brooke know that." He quickly explained his conversation with Brooke, and his meeting at Toujour. "I'll take out lots of women, maybe go on a third or fourth date with one. Then I'll tell her things aren't working out and break it off. Toujour gets their publicity, and I get to help Brooke while dating hot women. It's a win-win situation."

"Or the media will guess you're faking it and leak the story. Then Toujour's integrity will be called into question, and you'll be American's most hated bachelor instead of most loved. And Brooke will be furious. You're right—nothing could possibly go wrong."

Luke grinned. "That's the spirit."

Mitch leaned across the counter. "You're on tenuous footing with the board right now. This isn't going to help."

"Are you kidding me? Darius will love that I'm 'settling down.'" Luke made air quotes with his fingers.

"Besides, it's my life. The board doesn't get an opinion."

Mitch snorted. "I dunno, man. They have opinions about everything you do right now. Are you sure you aren't trying to play the hero to Brooke's damsel in distress?"

"Of course I am. What did legal say about the contract?"

"They sent it back with a few minor revisions, which Charlotte accepted. Everything's on the up and up." Mitch glared as though it were Luke's fault the contract had been approved.

"Great." Luke snatched the papers out of Mitch's hand and rummaged in a kitchen drawer for a pen.

"That doesn't mean you should sign. This has trouble written all over it."

"Thanks for the unsolicited advice. I need you to help me write a press release. Something about the holiday season making me reconsider my future, wanting a fresh start, blah blah blah. Whatever sounds good and casts everyone in a favorable light."

"You've got to be joking."

"How else do you expect the media to find out? It shouldn't take us more than an hour, and then we can watch the game."

Mitch blew out a breath. "I'm going on the record right now, stating this is a terrible idea and I've been against it from the start."

"You aren't going to try to stop me?"

"Stopping you is like trying to stop a hurricane. Not gonna happen. I'm saving my energy for damage control."

Chapter Thirteen

Brooke knew the moment Luke issued a press release, because the phones at Toujour started ringing off their hooks. Brooke watched in amazement as the normally calm and quiet office exploded in activity. Instead of silently working in their cubicles, matchmakers were fielding calls and tapping away on their keyboards. Chatter floated from the lobby—a rare occurrence, indeed.

"It's working," Zoey said as she scanned her email. "I already have two new client appointments today. Lianna just sent me an email."

"Twitter's going crazy," Brooke said. "There are about nine hashtags to follow."

"Positive response?" Zoey asked.

Brooke shrugged. "Mixed, but slanted toward the positive I think." She opened her desk drawer and pulled out her purse. "I hate to leave now, but it's too late to reschedule with the wedding planner."

"Aren't you doing the intake appointment with Luke this afternoon?"

"Yeah, I'll be back by then."

Brooke had to squeeze her way through the crush of waiting women in the front lobby, something she was positive she'd never had to do before. She hoped that men would start signing up soon.

Antonio waited for Brooke in the parking lot, his motorcycle parked next to her car. "Hi, sweetie," Brooke said. She leaned in and gave him a firm kiss. "Sorry I'm late. Things are nuts today."

Antonio took the keys from Brooke, unlocked the car doors, and they got inside. "I can tell—the parking lot's never this full. While painting this morning, I heard them mention on the radio a few different times that Luke had signed. That's good, right?"

"Absolutely. I know this is going to work. No way Toujour will close now."

Antonio pulled onto the freeway and rapidly increased their speed to eighty. "I hope you really can find a woman for Luke. I think it would make things easier with us."

Brooke reached over and squeezed Antonio's hand. If that's what it took to make Antonio and Luke get along, she would try her best. But only if the girl was right for Luke, of course.

"Have you thought any more about Italy?" Antonio asked.

"Maybe."

"Ah." Antonio raised an eyebrow. "*Italia* is calling to you. We wouldn't have to stop there either. With what they'd pay me, we could travel all over Europe. Madrid. Athens. Paris. You name it, and we could go there. We'd take pictures and I'd paint from them."

"It does sound nice," Brooke said. More and more she was struggling to come up with reasons why they shouldn't move to Italy. There was only one, really. She'd miss Luke terribly. But there was texting and video chats and vacations for that.

"We could visit California often," Antonio prodded.

"We could live here and visit Italy."

He laughed. "My funny, stubborn girl."

The meeting with the wedding planner went well, but took longer than it should have. Traffic was a nightmare on the way back. Two blocks from Toujour, the car came to a complete stop. Brooke pulled out her cell phone and glanced at the time. Two minutes late.

"I'm late," Brooke said.

Antonio shrugged. "This traffic isn't moving."

"I'm going to walk."

"Are you sure? It's just Luke. He won't mind if you're late."

"He's a client now, and it's unprofessional to keep him waiting."

Antonio looked like he wanted to protest, but nodded instead. "I'll see you tomorrow."

Brooke gave Antonio a quick kiss and jumped out of the car. She jogged to the sidewalk and started speed walking. She glanced at her cell phone. Eight minutes late. She uttered a curse and picked up her pace as she rounded the corner to Toujour.

A camera bulb flashed. "Miss Pierce," a reporter called. "How will being Mr. Ryder's matchmaker affect your personal relationship?"

"How does your fiancé feel about this?" another asked.

Brooke blinked, trying to school her face into a blank expression and hide her surprise. Well, the media had arrived. She ignored the reporters and opened the doors to Toujour, eager to get away from the chaos.

It wasn't much better inside. Brooke looked around in amazement. There were eleven women and two men in the waiting room, and she didn't recognize any of them. That meant they were new clients. Lianna talked on the phone, and Brooke could see from the blinking lights that three other lines were on hold. Several of the waiting clients held clipboards and were filling out their initial information. And Brooke thought they'd been busy when she left two hours ago. The transformation from yesterday was astonishing.

Brooke shook her head and made her way toward her cubicle. Phones rang throughout the office, and the chatter of voices filled the room. Brooke saw several matchmakers in parlours with new clients, probably doing initial profiles.

Luke's dark hair was visible above her cubicle wall, and his and Zoey's laughter floated toward her. "Sorry I'm late," Brooke said.

Zoey smiled. "Luke was entertaining me with guesses of what kinds of women you'll set him up with."

"Ouch," Brooke said, but she knew they were only teasing her. "I set you up with some good ones in high school."

Luke rolled his eyes. "All girls I was totally uninterested in."

"You're difficult to please."

"How'd the appointment with the wedding planner go?" Zoey asked.

"Fine," Brooke said. If it was just Zoey, she'd talk about the gorgeous monogram that would be projected onto the dance floor and the way the fabric on the chair backers really complimented the table centerpieces. But she knew Luke hated hearing about the wedding. If she was marrying someone else, would he be so opposed? Was it the wedding he hated, or Antonio? "It took longer than I anticipated." Brooke leaned around Luke, unplugging her laptop. "I'm ready."

"We're not doing it here?" Luke asked.

Brooke shook her head. "I scheduled Parlour Two. That's the French spelling, of course." She looked around the room. "Good thing I did. Already you're bringing in business."

"I'm glad." Luke followed Brooke. "So everything's good with the wedding, huh?"

Brooke glanced back at him. *Why is he asking?* "Yep." Brooke had approved the final save the date, in fact, and the planner had assured her they'd arrive at her apartment in no more than a week so she'd have time to address and mail them. She wanted to give the Italian guests plenty of time to make travel arrangements. "Here we are." She stood back and let Luke enter the parlour. It had two overstuffed arm chairs and a sleek, modern-looking coffee table. Quotes about love and relationships were stenciled on the walls.

"Love is friendship set to music. Joseph Campbell." Luke raised an eyebrow. "Do you believe that?"

Brooke shrugged. Her spine tingled, and she felt inexplicably uncomfortable. "A solid friendship is usually the basis for a good relationship. Most of the couples I match develop a friendship before they develop a romance. Of course, there has to be a mutual physical attraction as well."

"And do those couples last?" Luke sank into a chair, and Brooke followed suit.

"I have a pretty good retention rate. But I've only been in the business a few years." Brooke opened her laptop and pulled up the questionnaire under Luke's profile.

"You sound like you expect the couples to break up."

Brooke glanced up. "That's not what I meant. Yeah, a lot of people do break up. But it's a choice, just like staying together is. The problem with couples today is they give up too easily. When things get tough, they bail."

"I couldn't agree more." Luke's eyes drilled into hers. "But I know you, Brooke. You're not a quitter. You don't give up when something is hard."

Brooke shifted in her seat uncomfortably. "Are we talking about my relationship history, or are we talking about relationships in general?"

Luke leaned back in his chair. "Generalities, obviously. I meant you don't give up on your clients."

"Oh. Well, everyone has that perfect match out there. It just takes some searching. After a first date, it's usually obvious if a couple will be compatible or not. Most of my couples who make it past the third date end up together long term."

Luke raised an eyebrow. "Huh. I didn't know that. What do you think makes some people work and others not?"

"It's intangible. That something you can't put your finger on. When things don't work out, it's not necessarily anyone's fault. It just means it wasn't meant to be."

"And who do you think I'm meant to be with?"

Suddenly it was hard to swallow. "I guess we'll find out." Brooke focused on her laptop screen. "I already filled in all the basics for you—name, age, occupation, that sort of thing. Hope you don't mind."

He put a hand to his chest in mock horror. "I thought only a client could fill out this questionnaire. Isn't that what you told me last night?"

She rolled her eyes. "I can delete it all and we can start over."

"No, no." He sniffed dramatically. "I can tell you're trying to get rid of me as quickly as possible."

And there he was—a glimpse of the old Luke. Brooke grinned. Maybe this matchmaking thing would be good for him after all. "Okay, first question. What qualities are you looking for in a partner?"

"Oh, that's easy. Someone hot."

Brooke burst out laughing. "And what exactly is your definition of 'hot?'"

"I'm looking at it."

Brooke's laughter died. Her cheeks heated, and she looked away. "Be serious."

"I am."

"Luke, you can't tell me I'm hot."

"Why not? It's true."

"Well, because . . ." *Because Antonio would hate it. Because I'm glad you find me attractive.* "Because I'm engaged."

Luke raised an eyebrow. "Being engaged doesn't diminish your hotness. It's not like there's a *rule* against complimenting you."

"Maybe there should be." Her heart pounded.

"We don't want to mess up our lucky number fourteen by adding another rule."

"Fourteen isn't a lucky number."

"Relax, Brooke." Luke motioned to her laptop. "Honestly, I want someone compassionate. Someone loyal. I want a girl who cares more about others than she cares about herself. Someone who likes me for me and not for my money."

"That's a pretty generic answer."

He shrugged. "I could make up something better."

Brooke quickly typed out the answer and moved on to the next question. "How long do you feel a couple should be in a relationship before entering into an engagement?"

"Is that seriously a question?"

"Yeah, I know. Kind of a weird one. But you'd be surprised how often that becomes an issue—one person wants to move quickly and the other one wants to take things slow. So what is it?"

"Eight years. That's how long we've known each other, right?"

Brooke's fingers curled against the keyboard. What was with him today? "Stop it."

"Stop what?"

"Stop flirting."

"Why?" He leaned forward. "I like flirting with you. We always flirt."

"Not like this we don't. And we especially shouldn't now. I'm getting married."

He sat back in his chair, jaw clenched. "I couldn't possibly forget that—you remind me every five seconds."

Brooke closed her eyes and took a deep breath. "You're out of line, Luke."

"Admit it—you like me this way."

"That's it, I'm making a new rule. Rule #15—no flirting when one of us is in a serious relationship."

"Define 'serious.'"

The man was impossible. "I think an engagement would qualify."

Luke rubbed his jaw. "You can't make up a new rule whenever you feel like it."

"I just did." She couldn't make her toe stop tapping against the floor. Her laptop bounced on her lap with each tap. "I think we should get back to the questionnaire. Now answer the question—how long should a couple be in a relationship before they get engaged?"

Luke glowered. "Fine. But know I'm not accepting Rule #15 as a real rule."

"Yes. You. Are."

He ignored her. "Here's my real answer—I think it depends on the situation. When it's right, it's right, and we'll both know it. Maybe that'll take a few months. Maybe it'll take years." He held up his hands. "I don't know. Don't you think that depends a lot on the couple?"

"Fair enough," Brooke said, breathing easier. What had that been all about? Had she overreacted with instituting a new rule? Luke always flirted, and it had never bothered her before today.

Forget about it and focus on the job at hand.

"How many children do you want?" Brooke asked. Then she laughed. "Three, of course."

"Same as you."

Brooke nodded. "Same as me." Antonio on the other hand wanted at least five. Somehow she knew that if they moved to Italy, he'd end up winning that battle. "Okay, this question is kind of random but actually says a lot about someone." Brooke held back a grin. "If you won a million dollars today, what would you do with it?"

But Luke didn't laugh. "Nothing. I would stay right here in Los Angeles, with my best friend and Ryder Communications. All my millions mean nothing without those two things."

Brooke's hands stilled. "If you keep bringing me up, these girls are going to run for the hills. They'll think we're an item. It's bad enough the press is constantly speculating about our relationship."

Luke shrugged. "If a girl can't deal with the fact that you're a permanent part of my life, she isn't the one for me."

"I feel the same way. About guys, I mean. But a first date isn't the right time to bring it up."

Luke raised an eyebrow. "Could've fooled me."

Was that what this was all about? "Luke, I do feel that way. You're my best friend, and that's never going to change. Once we're married, Antonio will feel more secure in our relationship, and the press will hopefully back off and stop spreading wild rumors about you and me."

"Or they'll spread even more. Only this time I'll be cheating with a married woman in their gossip columns."

Brooke rolled her eyes. "They'll get bored of the story eventually."

"Maybe." He motioned to her laptop. "So what happens after we finish this questionnaire?"

"I'll run your profile through the database and the computer will populate matches. Then I go over each profile in detail and pick the girl I think you have the highest chance of success with. I'll talk to her matchmaker, and if everything looks good, we'll set up your first date. That could take a day or two—we've had twenty women sign up this morning already."

"So I could be on my first date in a couple days."

A twinge of discomfort rocketed through Brooke's middle. "Yeah, I guess so."

For another hour, Brooke asked questions and Luke answered. Most of the answers came as no surprise to Brooke, things like hobbies, favorite color, and the like. But other answers did surprise her. She'd always assumed Luke couldn't care less about relationships, but his answers showed he had thought about it before. Maybe he was finally growing up and considering settling down.

"Last question," Brooke said. "But it's one of the more important ones. What are you looking for in a relationship?"

"I've never really thought about it." Luke pursed his lips as though concentrating. Was he mocking her, or taking this seriously? His eyes locked onto hers. "I guess what I'm looking for is a best friend. Someone I can tell everything to. Someone who knows me better than I know myself. But I want chemistry, too. That unidentifiable something that draws two people together, no matter how hard they fight it. Basically, I want a girl just like you."

Chapter Fourteen

Brooke clenched her hands together in her lap, glancing over at Antonio as he drove. *Did Luke seriously say what I think he said?* It had been two days, and she hadn't been able to stop obsessing about it. She looked out the window at the tree-lined streets as they wove toward the gated community where her father lived.

Why was Luke choosing now to be all flirty?

"Is Jason going to be here today?" Antonio asked.

"No, I think it's his weekend to be with Shandi," Brooke said. She could barely keep the distaste for her half-brother's mother out of her voice. She'd never liked Shandi, the woman her father left their family for. Brooke had cried no tears when their marriage had ended almost as quickly as it began. But she did love her eight-year-old brother, Jason. "It'll just be Dad, Miranda, and the twins."

"I bet they're getting big," Antonio said.

"I bet they are." Brooke pushed away the guilt at not making an effort to see them more often.

Antonio exited the freeway and began the climb to the affluent communities in the hills. Palm trees lined the roads and BMW's sat in the driveways. Her dad had nowhere near as much money as Luke, but was still a successful dentist with his fair share of assets. The homes were all white stucco with arched windows and terracotta shingles.

Her dad's house didn't stand out from any other on the street. It had the same decorative rock in the front yard, and a basketball hoop on the side of the driveway for when Jason was around. Brooke noticed the twins' toys were missing from the front porch though. She didn't have to step over any bikes or Barbies on her way to the front door. *Miranda must've made them pick things up.*

Brooke rang the doorbell. She stared at the front door, realizing what looked different about the house.

"They painted the door," Brooke said. "It used to be white, not turquoise."

Antonio made a face. "I love the color. But the tone doesn't match the stucco at all. The door has too much blue in it, and it doesn't work with the warm yellows."

Brooke thought the turquoise paint looked fine, if a little bright. But she frowned, scrutinizing the door. "This doesn't look like Miranda's style."

The door swung open, and her dad stood there with a grin on his face. He was tall and fit, with graying hair and a trimmed beard. Brooke knew women found her dad attractive. She hated that about him.

"Sugar Bee." He enveloped her in a hug. "I've missed you. How've you been?"

"Great, Dad." Brooke stepped inside, and Antonio followed behind her.

"Good to see you, Daniel," Antonio said.

"You too, son. How was Italy?"

"Wonderful." Antonio's eyes flicked to Brooke's. "I signed a contract with a gallery that wants me to relocate to Rome."

Brooke glared at Antonio. She hadn't expressly asked him to keep that information quiet, but it had clearly been implied.

Dad rubbed his beard and shut the door. "That's quite an opportunity. Can't say I relish the thought of Brooke being so far away."

"We haven't decided if we're moving yet." Brooke gave Antonio a warning glare.

"Well, come in," Dad said.

Brooke's stomach clenched as she followed her dad and Antonio to the sun room. The grandfather clock that had been in Miranda's family for centuries was gone from the entryway. In the hallway, the photos of the family had been switched out for art. It was tastefully done, but not something Miranda would choose. One wall of the sun room had been painted the same vibrant turquoise as the front door.

"Sit down." Dad sank into a chair and motioned to the couch across from him. "Food should be delivered soon. I ordered from that Italian restaurant you love."

"Miranda isn't cooking?" Brooke asked. But she already knew the answer. Miranda had moved out. The whole house reeked of another woman. Even the air smelled different, like lavender and roses instead of baking bread and vanilla.

Dad sighed, shifting in his chair. "Miranda isn't here."

Brooke folded her arms tightly across her stomach. Antonio gave her a helpless look of concern. "What's her name?" Brooke asked.

"Miranda and I have been having problems for a while," Dad said. "It wasn't going to work. We've been fighting a lot, and we thought it would be healthier for the girls if they moved out."

Brooke knew what that meant—Miranda had caught him cheating with the new mistress. "Oh, please. You got bored with 'normal life' and found someone new and exciting. Is she a dental hygienist at your office again? A chef at a restaurant? A pole dancer at a strip club?"

"Her name is Lexi, and she's a paralegal."

Brooke angrily tapped a foot against the floor, memories flooding over her. *Poor Sabrina and Lucy.* Her heart ached for her sisters, too young to understand what was going on. First he'd left Brooke. Then Jason. And now the twins.

"She'll be here soon. I want you to be civil, Brooke. She's really excited to meet you. I know this is unexpected, but you'll like Lexi."

"Unexpected?" Brooke barked out a laugh. "You've done this three times now. It's becoming your mode of operation."

"That isn't fair. It's not like I go into relationships expecting them not to work out."

"Are you sure about that?" Brooke let out another laugh, running a hand through her hair. "Is she at least older than me?"

"Love can't be restricted by things like age."

Brooke snorted. Antonio gave her another uncertain look, like he didn't know what to do. She suddenly wished that Luke was here. Luke, who'd helped her through her dad's previous two divorces. Eight years ago he'd held her while she cried, after finding out her parents' divorce was final. Six years ago he'd stayed up with her all night while she talked through her complicated emotions over Shandi and her dad's divorce. Antonio hadn't been there and hadn't seen the depth of her pain.

You have to let him in, Brooke reminded herself. She took Antonio's hand in hers, trying to draw comfort from his grip. She closed her eyes. Why couldn't her dad stay committed to one woman?

The doorbell rang, and Dad rose. "That's either Lexi or the food. I'll be right back."

As soon as he disappeared down the hallway, Antonio wrapped his arm around Brooke in a side-hug. He kissed her temple. "You okay?"

"Why does he have to do this again?" Brooke whispered.

"I don't know," Antonio said. Because in Antonio's family, no one ever got divorced. His sister, his parents, his grandparents . . . they were all the picture of stability. Brooke accredited some of that to the fact that most of them had been introduced by professional matchmakers.

Dad walked back into the room. A woman clung to his arm, her red nails standing out even from across the room. She wore tailored jeans and a lacy blouse, and her hair was pulled halfway up. Her makeup was subtle instead of gaudy, but it couldn't disguise her obvious youth. She had to be close to Brooke's own age.

The woman let go of Dad and strode across the room, wrapping Brooke in a hug. Brooke let out a surprised yelp as her arms were crushed to her sides. "I am so happy to meet you," Lexi said. "Daniel constantly talks about how proud he is of you. He said you're a matchmaker. I bet that career is fascinating."

Brooke opened her mouth to respond, but Lexi was already hugging Antonio. "And you must be the fiancé. I hear the wedding is going to be at a vineyard. I can't wait."

Brooke stared. Who said this woman was invited to the wedding? Who said she'd even be around come September? "This is Antonio," Brooke said. *You home-wrecker.*

The doorbell rang again, and Brooke prayed it was the food. She couldn't wait to get out of here.

Lexi giggled and flirted with Dad all through dinner. Brooke shoved one bite in her mouth after another, not even able to enjoy her favorite pasta dish. Lexi was disgusting. She was . . .

She was Luke's type. Brooke closed her eyes as the realization washed over her. Lexi reminded her of a career-girl version of Candi. Brooke would change all that, though. She would match Luke up with amazing women and teach him how to have a real relationship.

Brooke quickly ate her last bite of food. "Well, it was great meeting you," she said, standing. "But we really need to go."

Dad glanced at his watch, frowning. "So soon? It's barely two-thirty."

Yeah, Brooke was aware. The last ninety minutes had been excruciating. "Antonio's got work to do."

Antonio raised an eyebrow, then quickly nodded. "Uh, yes. A landscape to finish."

"I'm such a fan of your work," Lexi said as they all walked to the front door. "Daniel and I would love to attend one of your shows."

"I'll let you know when the next one is," Antonio said.

Brooke ground her teeth. She didn't want to spend any more time with Lexi than necessary. "It was nice to meet you," Brooke lied, nodding to her. She gave her dad a quick hug. "Thanks for dinner, Dad."

"It was good to see you, Sugar Bee. Come back soon, okay? The kids miss you. I'll have all three of them next weekend."

"Maybe," Brooke hedged. She did miss her brother and sisters. But her skin crawled just being in the same room as her father right now.

Brooke quickly got in the car and impatiently waited for Antonio to start it up. Dad and Lexi stood on the front porch, his arm around her waist. They both were smiling like lunch had gone fabulously.

Brooke forced a smile and waved. She let her hand drop the second they rounded the corner.

"Are you going to be okay?" Antonio asked.

Brooke brushed away the tear that trickled down her cheek. "Why does he do this?"

"I guess he has 'the grass is greener' syndrome."

"I can't believe he's doing this again." Brooke tapped her foot against the floorboard. "I'm so mad at him."

"I know." Antonio gave her a sympathetic smile. "Chocolate shakes?"

"Absolutely."

Chapter Fifteen

Luke stole the basketball from Mitch and dribbled down the court. He threw, aiming for the hoop. The shot went wild, bouncing out of bounds.

He couldn't believe he'd gone there. Two days later and he was still obsessing over their conversation at Toujour. Brooke had stared at him, eyes suspiciously wet, and said, *"Find someone just like me. Got it."*

What had he been thinking?

Mitch ran and grabbed the ball, then jogged back to Luke. "You okay, man?"

"Yeah."

Mitch blew out a breath. "Is this matchmaking thing going to send you into another spiral?"

"I was never in a spiral."

Mitch snorted. "That's not what your aura said."

"Okay, okay. But I'm fine." Luke threw the basketball at the wall, frustrated. He caught it when it bounced back and threw it again. He had to work out some of this energy.

"You're not fine—you're doing too much at once. You've got work and Brooke's wedding and now dating. And *Brooke* is the one setting you up." He shook his head. "I don't see how this can possibly end well. Seriously, tell me what happened with her. You've been on edge ever since your appointment at Toujour."

Luke raised the basketball and tapped the back of his head with it. "I ended up confessing my feelings and crap like that."

Mitch grunted in surprise. "You what?"

"Yeah, I know. But she's getting married in September. And I can't let her do it. Not without telling her."

Mitch grabbed the basketball from Luke and made a shot. "This is big."

"I know."

"What if she still marries Antonio? That could ruin your friendship."

Luke closed his eyes. "I *know*."

"So what did you say?"

"Basically that I wanted a girl just like her."

"Oh." Mitch dribbled the ball with a little more purpose than he had before. "That's not so bad. Are you sure she understood what you were trying to say?"

"Not really."

Luke's phone rang, and he jogged to the side of the court. He picked the cell phone up off the floor and saw Brooke's number flash across the screen. He swallowed hard. Was she calling to discuss the weirdness that had happened, or to tell him he had a date? "Hey, pretty lady."

"Rule #15, Lucas." Her voice was cool, and use of his full name was never a good sign. "I found a match."

Luke rubbed a hand over his face. So she was determined to ignore what had happened. "That's great."

"Her name is Tamera. She's twenty-four and a real estate agent. She loves sports, just like you. Can I set up a date for you two sometime next week? She, of course, is more than agreeable to the arrangement."

"Sure," Luke said slowly. Was he supposed to be distant and cool, like Brooke was being? "So how does this work? Do I arrange the date?"

"You can offer suggestions, of course, but I typically do that." Brooke's words were less stiff now, her tone more friendly. Luke sighed in relief. "There's a playoff game at UCLA. I thought that would be perfect, since you both love football. You'll have plenty of time to talk, and you can get hot dogs or whatever at the stadium. How does that sound?"

"Whatever you think is best."

"Great." Now she was cheerful, trying hard to act like there wasn't anything weird between them. But he heard the strain. "I'll arrange everything and use the card on file to pay. I'll let you know the details tomorrow. Bye."

"Bye," Luke said. But Brooke had already hung up.

"Brooke?" Mitch asked, nodding at the phone.

Luke nodded. "My first date is next week. A football game."

"Even if the chick is a total bore, at least you'll see the game, right?"

"Right." Luke set his phone back on the ground and grabbed the basketball. "I've got thirty minutes before I need to leave." And he took off down the court.

Today was the day. Luke took a deep breath and looked himself over in the mirror, hoping he'd struck the right balance with his outfit. He'd gotten stuck late in a meeting with the Talia team and had rushed home to change. He should've picked out his clothes yesterday. He wanted to look nice, but casual—it was a football game, after all. He'd chosen his favorite pair of jeans and a Ryder Communications hoodie and baseball cap. But did he look too much like a frat boy instead of a CEO?

The press would be there, and he didn't want to reflect badly on Brooke or Toujour. Should he go with a button-up shirt, but no tie, and a blazer? Or would that be too dressy?

He sighed. Brooke had coached him yesterday on everything from topics of conversation to appropriate physical contact on a first date. But she hadn't covered dress. Or maybe she had and he hadn't been listening. It'd been so bizarre to have her coach him on dating.

Just call her.

He hit the speed-dial before he could talk himself out of it. If he pretended things weren't weird, maybe they wouldn't be.

She picked up after only two rings.

"I have no idea what to wear on this date," he said.

"Hello to you too." Brooke sounded like her old self. Maybe she'd also decided to put aside the weirdness. One could hope. "We went over this yesterday. Were you even listening?"

He frowned at his reflection in the mirror. "I was distracted by how weird the whole thing was. Can you please help me? Is a hoodie a bad choice? Or a baseball cap?"

"I suggested a tee and leather jacket, but a hoodie could work. I think Tamera will probably find it very endearing. You're showing you're a person and not just a billionaire CEO."

Luke groaned. "This is ridiculous. I doubt I'll go on a second date with this woman, so it shouldn't matter."

"You promised to really try. Give Tamera a chance. I think you'll like her. I can't wait to hear how it goes."

Luke hung up, his chest tightening in anxiety.

At the stadium, Luke had the driver drop him off at the appropriate gate. He scanned the crowd as he made his way toward the entrance, looking for Tamera. Brooke had shown him a photo, so he knew more or less who he was looking for. Food vendors sold ice cream and pretzels from little carts, and a few people loitered outside the gates trying to sell tickets.

"I think you're meeting me."

Luke turned around. His smile came without forcing it. Tamera was beautiful—dark brown hair cut in a bob, hazel eyes, a petite figure. The photograph hadn't done her justice. She wore an NFL football jersey over a long sleeved white T-shirt. He was glad he'd gone with the hoodie. "Tamera." Luke held out a hand, and she gave it a firm shake. "It's so nice to meet you. I'm Luke."

She laughed, and he heard the nerves behind it. "Well of course I know who you are." She blushed. "I mean, I've read about you in the papers."

Great. She's one of the tabloid followers. Her hotness factor dropped a solid point. That's one thing he'd always liked about Brooke—she didn't follow celebrity gossip. It surprised him Tamera did. Brooke had described her as very down-to-earth.

Tamera and Luke stood there awkwardly for a moment, both smiling at each other.

Click. "Mr. Ryder, is this your date?"

The paparazzi were here and ready to work.

"What's your name, honey?" a woman photographer asked.

Tamera's face glowed bright red, but she grinned from ear to ear. "Tamera Hadley."

"How's the date going?" another photographer said.

"Well we just introduced ourselves—" Tamera began.

Luke held up a hand, forcing a smile. "Thanks, but that's all the time we have right now." He lowered his voice so only Tamera could hear. "Let's go in."

"That sounds great."

Luke shoved his hands in his pockets to avoid any awkward hand holding and walked beside Tamera to the entrance. Then he wondered how the press would interpret that. What would Brooke want him to do? She'd said hand holding was okay, but she probably hadn't meant from the get-go.

Too late. They were already at the front gate. The college student checking tickets stared at Luke with wide-eyed wonder. "Are you really Luke Ryder?"

"I am. This is my date, Tamera."

The boy's eyes grew to the size of silver dollars. "My girlfriend isn't going to believe this. Can I take a picture with you?"

"Sure," Luke said. He glanced over at Tamera. She grinned so wide he worried her face would split.

The boy handed his cell phone to her. Luke blinked. He'd assumed she'd be in the picture. The kid quickly moved to Luke's side.

"Say cheese," Tamera said.

"Cheese," the boy said. Luke remained silent, forcing a smile. He saw several of the paparazzi snap photos as well.

The boy took his phone back, and Luke handed him their tickets. "You're at the fifty yard line, first row," he said. "Awesome seats. Enjoy the game."

"Thanks," Luke said.

"I can't believe there are photographers here," Tamera said as they walked inside. *Snap snap snap.* "Am I going to be in the papers tomorrow?"

Luke shrugged. "Probably. Sorry about that."

"Are you kidding? This is awesome. The paparazzi are photographing our date!" She blushed. "I'm sorry, I'm being such a ditz. But I can't believe I'm on a date with Luke Ryder."

I can't believe I'm on this date either. Why hadn't Brooke told him Tamera was the star-struck type?

They'd discussed Tamera's likes and interests at length so he'd know what to talk about if the conversation stalled. Celebrity gossip hadn't been mentioned.

They wandered through the people waiting near the restrooms and standing in line at the concession stands. Luke led the way through the small tunnel underneath the seats. It opened up, and Luke took in a deep breath. He loved the smell of freshly mowed grass and humidity. A vendor wandered up the stairs, selling foam fingers. Luke walked in the opposite direction, down the stairs and toward their seats.

"Mr. Ryder, can we get a statement?" a photographer asked. Luke ignored him, but it didn't stop the camera flashes from following them. He found the right row and stepped aside so Tamera could sit down first.

"Wow, they are really in your face," she said. "How did they get in the stadium?"

Keeping this date normal would be harder than he'd expected. "They must've bought tickets. Are you a fan of either team playing tonight?"

Tamera shrugged. "I don't follow college football too closely."

"Oh." Hadn't Brooke said their mutual love of sports was one of the reasons she'd matched them up? And she was wearing a jersey.

"Oh, I love football. But I follow the NFL mostly." She motioned to her shirt. "Go 49ers. Are you a fan of college football?"

Click click click. Luke tried to ignore the photographers, leaning against the railing only a few feet away. "Yeah. I feels nice to be back at UCLA's stadium. Brooke attended here. We spent a lot of time together on campus. Went to lots of games too." Whoops. Brooke had stressed more than once that under no circumstances should he talk about her.

Tamera's smile drooped. "Right, you and Brooke are best friends." Her voice was purposefully casual. So she knew about his and Brooke's relationship. Probably read about it in the papers every time there was a story. "I don't know her that well since she isn't my matchmaker. I'm sure she's a lovely person."

Whenever Brooke entered the conversation, his dates had a tendency of spiraling downhill fast. Time to avoid the topic like Brooke had coached him to. This date had to go well. For Brooke's sake. "What led you to Toujour?"

Tamera brushed her hair behind her ear. "Oh, you know. I was in a miserable relationship for three years, and when we broke up I didn't know how to reenter the game. After six months of awful dates, I signed with Toujour."

And now she was bringing up old relationships. Luke swallowed. Brooke had mentioned that Tamera was still working through some hang-ups, but said she'd made lots of progress the last few months. He really hoped the reporters couldn't overhear their conversation. The chatter of the crowd was loud enough he didn't think they could. "I'm sorry to hear that. About the relationship, I mean."

Tamera shrugged. "It happens. Caleb was such a jerk. Did you know that he left me for my sister? And last night she called to announce they're engaged. She wants me to be maid of honor. What am I supposed to say to that?"

"I don't know." Luke tapped his fingers against his leg. *Where are you when I need you, Brooke?* This was so far out of his wheelhouse. She'd told him to avoid discussing old relationships, but hadn't told him what to do if Tamera was the one who brought them up.

"Yeah, me either. I faked a bad connection and hung up. I've ignored thirteen calls since."

"That sounds bad."

"Yeah." She laughed. "I can't believe I'm telling Luke Ryder about my family drama. This is unreal. Anyway, real estate keeps me pretty busy so I don't have a lot of time for the whole bar scene. That's another reason Toujour's so helpful—they do all the leg work for me. They can get you into any game, any play, any restaurant. VIP treatment the whole date. And they do background checks, although I guess a few bad eggs could still slip through." She slapped him playfully on the shoulder. "You're not a bad egg, are you, Luke Ryder?"

Sort of. Luke laughed uncomfortably. What would Tamera say if she knew he had no interest in a long-term relationship? At least not with anyone but Brooke.

"So what brought you to Toujour?" Tamera asked.

Brooke had told him that was a common topic of conversation on first dates, but he still hadn't come up with an answer that sounded believable without being an outright lie. "Same as you—I'm ready for something more serious, but with work I don't have time for the searching." He cleared his throat.

"Cold beer," a vendor called as he made his way down the stairs. "Ice cold beer, seven dollars."

Luke stood, signaling the guy over. "Want one?" he asked Tamera. There was no way he could get through this date without alcohol.

"Sure," Tamera said. Luke bought two pints from the vendor and handed her one.

The pre-game mercifully started then, and Luke didn't have to talk much. Tamera quickly finished her beer. "Want another?" Luke asked. She nodded. He didn't buy one for himself, though. Brooke would kill him if he got drunk on this date. She'd stressed that yesterday during their coaching, too.

The game eventually started, and Luke sat back, ready to enjoy it. Tamera hadn't been lying about her love of football. Before the end of the first quarter, she was on her feet, screaming at the refs for bad calls. He wondered if that was normal behavior for her, or if the two pints of beer helped. Brooke had said she had a strong personality, but he hadn't pictured this. Her face turned 49ers red, perfectly matching her jersey, and her voice grew hoarse from yelling.

"Can you believe that?" Tamera turned to him as the cheer squad ran onto the field for their halftime routine while the crowd cheered. "That call was ridiculous. Are the refs blind? That was clearly a fumble."

Luke glanced at the score board. "We're ahead twelve points."

Tamera shrugged. "Every point counts."

Her hotness level dropped yet again. There definitely wouldn't be a second date. "Want something to eat?" Luke asked. "I'm starving." And maybe if she had food in her mouth, she wouldn't be able to scream. Maybe it would help counteract the two pints of alcohol she'd consumed.

"Sure."

Luke rose. "What do you want?"

"I'll come with you." Tamera tried to stand and tripped, nearly falling into the lap of a middle-aged man. Her laughter was lost in the clapping of the crowd.

"No, I've got it. You sit down and enjoy the halftime show." *Please.*

Tamera giggled and complied. "Such a gentleman. I'll have nachos, I guess."

He nodded. "Be right back."

The cheers of the crowd faded as he walked toward the packed concession stands. He'd barely gotten into line when a reporter sidled up next to him. "Can I get a statement?" the reporter asked.

This is for Brooke, he reminded himself. Luke moved forward with the line, then turned to the reporter. "Tamera's a great girl, and I'm grateful that Toujour has given me the opportunity to meet her."

The reporter nodded, holding his voice recorder closer to Luke. "She appears drunk. Given your recent love affair with alcohol, are you pleased or upset that she might drink you under the table?"

Luke smiled stiffly. "Looks like it's my turn to order." He turned away from the reporter, and the man left with a grumble. Luke bought two nachos, two hot dogs, two hot chocolates, a giant bag of popcorn, and four candy bars. He hoped it was enough food to last the last half of the game, and he hoped Tamera didn't start hurling until the date was over. He asked one of the stadium employees to help him bring everything back to their seats.

"You missed it," Tamera said. "The halftime show was phenomenal." She flung her arms out, nearly toppling the bag of popcorn Luke held. "They shot cheerleaders out of a cannon."

"Wow." Luke thanked the stadium employee, taking the food from him and giving a big tip in exchange.

Tamera's eyes widened. "You got all this for us? Oh my gosh, I love candy bars."

Luke passed over her food and took his seat. "I was hungry, and figured you probably were as well. Nachos alone are hardly a meal."

"Oh." Tamera's eyes narrowed. "Thanks."

Brooke had mentioned dinner as a possibility after the game, but said if the date didn't go well he wasn't obligated. He hoped Tamera wasn't expecting dinner, or she'd be sadly disappointed.

The quarterback called out the first play for the quarter. Luke turned his attention back to the game. He hoped he could be done with this whole matchmaking thing soon. This was painful.

The quarterback threw the ball, and the receiver struggled to hold on to it as he went down. He landed hard on one shoulder and the ball slipped loose. A player from the opposing team jumped on it.

The ref threw a flag. "Down by contact," he exclaimed. The crowd roared.

Tamera jumped to her feet. Luke reached forward and steadied her cup of hot chocolate before it could spill all over her shoes. "What is wrong with you?" she screamed at the refs. "That was clearly an incomplete pass."

Luke sank a little lower in his chair. He wished the press wasn't here. He could see at least four photographers clicking away. Tamera was . . . well, she clearly took sports very seriously. So did he. Or he thought he had, before seeing her in action. If he acted anything like this, no wonder Brooke hated it when he drank.

The third quarter dragged. Luke tried to block out Tamera's insults and focus on the game, but it was impossible. The girl was totally sloshed, and for a moment Luke wished he could join her. Maybe if he was drunk, he'd find this date enjoyable.

But he would keep it to the one beer he'd already had. He hoped Brooke appreciated the sacrifice.

The fourth quarter began. Luke prayed it would go quickly. Tamera was getting more and more unruly as the game continued, and had progressed to yelling obscenities at the referees and players.

"Pass it," Tamera screamed. "He's wide open. Pass it!"

The player threw the ball and it was intercepted by the other team, who started running it down the field. The frat boys sitting behind them jumped to their feet with a roar, cheering on the opposing team. The player successfully avoided three attempts to tackle him, sprinting down the field and into the end zone.

"Touchdown!" the row behind Luke and Tamera yelled.

Luke turned around. The four guys were all on their feet, pumping their fists in glee. Their faces were painted the other team's colors, and one of them even had a foam finger. Luke grinned. His team was still up by sixteen points. He could afford to be generous.

"Idiots," Tamera yelled. She turned to the frat boys. "Don't get so cocky. You got lucky."

One of the guys held up his hand. "Hey there, lady. We're just enjoying the game."

"Well don't."

One of the other guys scowled, folding his arms across his chest. "You need to pipe down."

Luke closed his eyes. *This cannot be happening.*

"Don't tell me to pipe down," Tamera said.

The third guy leered at her. "Then at least sit down. It's hard to watch the game when all we can see is your butt in our face. We drove five hundred miles for this game."

Oh boy. Luke had never fully appreciated Brooke's commitment not to drink until this moment.

"Are you freaking kidding me?" Tamera said.

Luke stood. Time to take matters into his own hands. "Sorry to bother you," he told the frat guys. "How about I buy you another round?"

Tamera whirled on Luke. "They insulted me, and you're buying them drinks."

"Maybe you should stop buying drinks for people," Frat Boy #1 said. "Looks like your girlfriend's had more than enough."

The photographers were going nuts with their cameras. Luke lowered his voice, speaking to Tamera. "Please. I don't want to cause a scene."

Tamera pointed an accusing finger. "They're the ones causing a scene."

The frat boy stood, and the half full cup of beer sloshed in his hand. "Now listen here, lady. We went to a lot of trouble to make it to this game."

"Luke!"

How did I end up here? Luke took a deep breath. There hadn't been anything like this mentioned in Tamera's profile. *How would Dad approach this situation?* "I'm sure we can resolve this somehow."

The crowd jumped to their feet with a roar. Tamera whipped around. "What did I miss?"

One of the men swore. "Another touchdown, you stupid woman."

Tamera's face was 49ers red again. "Take it back."

"No."

She launched herself at the man. Luke threw himself between them. He wasn't sure who needed protecting more—Tamera or the frat guy. Or him.

And that's when the cup of beer went flying. All over his hoodie.

Chapter Sixteen

"So tonight's Luke's first date, huh?"

Brooke sank onto the couch beside Zoey. "Yeah."

"Who'd you set him up with?"

"One of Kendra's clients. I wanted to give him something easy for this first date, and the girl loves sports."

Zoey frowned. "Sounds like a match made in heaven."

"Let's hope so."

Zoey tucked her feet up under her. "I'm shocked, actually. I thought you might try to sabotage his relationships and set him up with girls that were all wrong for him."

Brooke's mouth dropped open. "What on earth would make you say that?"

Zoey shrugged. "What if this actually works? You're a phenomenal matchmaker. If you find him the perfect woman, then it really is all over for you." Zoey leaned forward, her eyes intent. "I know the system said you and Antonio are highly compatible. But what if the computer's wrong?"

"You're a matchmaker, Zoey. You know the computer isn't wrong."

Zoey sighed. "I don't know. You and Antonio feel off."

"There's nothing off about us. You're just so used to it being me and Luke that it's hard to adjust your thinking."

"What happens when you get offered the promotion and Antonio still wants to move to Italy? You have to know his career will always come first."

Brooke clenched her jaw. She knew Zoey was right, and it didn't sit well. "In Italy, we both get our dream careers. I might have to wait longer to get promoted, but it will still happen. It might be a struggle the first year as we adjust. But we'll get through it. Love means making sacrifices." And she was willing to make those sacrifices. Antonio was worth it. He loved her, despite their culture clash, and he always made her feel loved. Like the way he'd left a single red rose on her car windshield for her to find after work today. Or how he sometimes surprised her with breakfast in bed on Sundays.

"Okay, I get that love means making sacrifices. But what about Luke? You'll break his heart if you move."

Brooke's heart twisted at the thought. She knew Zoey was right, but she also knew she couldn't make her decision based on that alone. "This can't be about me and Luke. There isn't a 'me and Luke' and never has been. Not like that. We'll miss each other, sure. But I'm going to find him a girlfriend, so he'll be fine."

"That man only has eyes for you, and you know it."

Brooke folded her arms across her stomach. *Don't cry, don't cry.* She willed her voice to be steady when she spoke. "If he has eyes only for me, then why does he keep hooking up with Los Angeles' finest skanks?"

"Give him a chance. You two are so perfect together."

Brooke held up a trembling hand. "Stop. I can't keep having this conversation with you."

A knock at the door silenced them both. "Are you expecting someone?" Zoey asked.

Brooke shook her head. "You?"

Zoey headed to the door. "Nope." She looked through the peephole, then turned the deadbolt. "It's Luke."

Brooke scrambled to Zoey's side. "What?"

Zoey flung the door open, a smile on her face. "Hey. We weren't expecting you."

Luke entered the room, his face grim. He wore his Ryder Communications hoodie like he'd told her he would, but a stain covered one sleeve and most of the front.

"I need to talk to you," he said, shutting the door behind him.

Zoey sat down on the couch, grinning. "Oh, this is going to be good."

Brooke glared at Zoey, then turned back to Luke. He stood so close she could smell the stale beer. How many had he had? "Nice hoodie. If I'd known it was stained, I would've told you to go with the white tee and leather jacket."

"Oh, the stain wasn't there when I left the house. No, that happened when I got between Tamera and the frat boys she started a fight with."

Brooke's eyes widened. "Okay, that needs an explanation."

"Turns out Tamera is quite competitive. And a loud and obnoxious drunk."

Panic bubbled up in Brooke, and she covered her mouth to hold in a horrified laugh.

"Tamera spent the entire game yelling at the refs. When the frat boys behind us celebrated a touchdown by the opposing team, she turned crazy," Luke said.

"That doesn't sound like Tamera," Brooke said. How would this impact her plan to save Toujour? Surely he was exaggerating. "None of her other dates

198

have given that kind of feedback." She'd been so careful in her selection. Tamera and Luke were sixty-two percent compatible, and she'd spoken with Kendra extensively before they'd decided to set up a date between the two.

"Maybe the paparazzi stressed her out or something, I don't know. All I know is the date ended with me being doused in beer."

Zoey howled with laughter. "Good pick, Brooke."

He's not drunk. Relief swept through Brooke at that knowledge. The beer was on his shirt, not his breath. She hoped. But the relief was quickly replaced with embarrassment. "I'm sorry, Luke. I had no idea. Nothing in her psychological profile or previous dates indicated this kind of behavior might occur."

Luke rolled back on his heels, folding his arms across his chest. "Seems to me like you picked the first girl who popped up in your database. The press will love this."

Brooke swallowed hard. Had she just ruined any chance Toujour had with one bad date? "I'm sorry. I'll choose better next time."

"Good. Because there definitely isn't going to be a second date with Tamera. I can't help you save Toujour if you don't give me women I can work with." He spun around. "I'll see you tomorrow." He slammed the door, gone as quickly as he arrived.

"What was that about?" Brooke asked Zoey.

Zoey grinned. "Maybe you aren't choosing as carefully as I thought. Did you know that was going to happen?"

Brooke sighed in exasperation, plopping down on the couch. "Of course not. I'm not psychic."

"No. But you do know people. It looks to me like you don't want to pick the perfect woman for Luke."

"Stop it. None of our clients have dated a celebrity before. I should've anticipated that it might bring about different results than previous dates. I'll pick more carefully next time."

"*Right.*"

"If you're going to act like this, I'm going to bed." Brooke left the room and slammed her bedroom door shut. Zoey's laughter floated in from the living room. Brooke sank onto her bed, and couldn't help but wonder—*is Zoey right? Did I pick Tamera, knowing it wouldn't work out?* And if she did, what did that say about her feelings for Luke?

Chapter Seventeen

The media was quick to report on the date. By morning, articles had flooded the Internet. Tamera was painted as a crazy drunk, whereas Luke came off as something of a hero. More than a few articles had questioned Brooke's judgment, Toujour's likelihood of success, and whether or not Brooke had intentionally picked a bad egg for Luke's first date out of jealousy.

Maybe she wasn't as good a matchmaker as she had thought she was.

Brooke walked into Toujour that afternoon, her stomach knotted with dread. She hadn't slept well last night. Charlotte was sure to be furious. Brooke had no doubt a reprimand was coming.

"She can't possibly blame you," Zoey whispered as they booted up their computers at their desks. "How were you supposed to know Tamera is a mean drunk?"

"I should've shown better judgment," Brooke said.

Zoey rolled her eyes. "Yeah, you should become a mind reader too."

Brooke's desk phone rang, and she answered it. A few moments later, she hung up.

"Charlotte?" Zoey asked.

Brooke nodded, then stood. "Well, it was nice working with you."

"Don't be so dramatic." Zoey squeezed Brooke's hand. "You'll be fine."

"I hope so." If she got fired, then it'd make the decision to move easy at least.

Brooke slowly walked to Charlotte's office, taking her sweet time. *No need to hurry to my execution.* Half the parlours were filled with matchmakers and clients, and the rest of the matchmakers appeared to be busy at their desks, scanning the database for matches. At least business was improving, disastrous date or no. She knocked once on the door, and opened the door when Charlotte said, "Come in."

"Sit," Charlotte said without looking up from her computer screen.

Brooke sank into a chair, her back rigid. "Charlotte, I can exp—"

Charlotte turned her computer monitor to face Brooke. "Have you read the articles?"

Brooke nodded. There was nothing more to say.

"This isn't the kind of publicity I want. It makes it look like we let anyone be a client. We're adding sparks to an already blazing fire."

Fuel. The phrase is "adding fuel to the fire." But now wasn't the time to correct Charlotte. "I'm sure Tamera was—"

"I will talk to Kendra about her client later," Charlotte said. She leaned forward, elbows on her desk. "I want you to be honest with me, Brooke. Is it too hard for you to match up your best friend? Do I need to assign him another matchmaker?"

Brooke quickly shook her head. "I don't know what went wrong with Tamera, but I can assure you it won't happen again. My choice had nothing to do with my friendship with Luke."

"I hope not," Charlotte said. "I don't need to remind you what's at stake here. I want him on another date by the weekend. A *better* date."

"Of course," Brooke said.

Charlotte turned the computer screen back around. "Well, what are you waiting for?"

Brooke quickly left Charlotte's office.

Brooke spent the rest of the morning meticulously going over the files of every match the computer had populated for Luke. She had to find him a better date, and fast.

Zoey returned from a meeting with a client and picked up her purse. "Let's go to the café for lunch. You need a break."

"Agreed," Brooke said. She locked her monitor, and they walked next door. The café was reminiscent of a French bakery. The menu was written on a chalkboard in flowery script, and small two-person tables filled the front portion of the room. They took their place in line and waited to order. Brooke inhaled deeply, enjoying the smell of freshly baked bread and chocolate. She peered at the delectable assortment of pastries filling the display case. After this morning, she might order one of each.

"Think Luke is still mad at you?" Zoey asked.

Brooke rolled her shoulders, trying to ease the tension gathering there. "I hope not, or this is going to be a really long meeting." She bit her lip. "Things have been so weird between us lately. I haven't even told him about my dad's upcoming divorce yet."

"Seriously?"

Brooke nodded. "We keep fighting. I didn't think it would be so hard to separate our friendship from a professional relationship."

Zoey snorted. "What professional relationship? He's only doing this for you."

"He's doing it for Toujour."

"Yeah. Because *you* love working there so much."

"He's a good *friend*." Brooke emphasized the word.

They placed their orders, then selected an empty table. "How did it go with Antonio last night?" After Luke had left, Brooke had gone to Antonio's. She'd known he'd read about the date soon enough, and figured it was better to get it all out in the open.

Brooke clenched her receipt in her hand. "Fine."

"Fine?"

"Great," Brooke amended. Antonio had unfortunately brought up some of the same concerns the papers had, and she'd spent most of the night reassuring him she was genuinely trying to find Luke a girlfriend.

"Don't sound so enthusiastic."

"We got in a fight. Nothing major, just a misunderstanding." She wasn't about to give specifics. Zoey didn't need any more ammunition for her Call Off the Wedding campaign.

"Hmmm," Zoey said. Brooke knew she wanted to say a lot more, but appreciated her rare show of restraint.

Their names were called, and they quickly picked up their food, ate, and headed back to Toujour. A reporter jumped in front of them as Brooke reached to open the door. He brought a camera to his eye and quickly snapped a photo. "Miss Pierce, do you take responsibility for Mr. Ryder's failed first date?"

Brooke's cheeks heated. Zoey grabbed Brooke's arm and pushed past the reporter into the building. They quickly made their way to their cubicle.

"This is fantastic," Brooke said. "Just what Toujour needs." She slammed her juice down on the desk, causing a few drops to squirt out the straw.

A deep male voice spoke from behind. "Yeah, the reporters attacked me too. Woo-hoo."

Brooke jumped. "I didn't hear you come in," she said. "I thought Lianna would've told you to meet me in the parlour."

"I'll try to walk louder next time." He looked handsome as sin in a charcoal suit and deep red tie. His dedication to work was obviously sticking. "I'm meeting Mitch at the office in an hour. Will this take longer than that?"

"That depends on how hard it is to get information out of you." Brooke grabbed her laptop and stood. "I think the same parlour we used last time should be open."

He nodded and followed her to the appropriate room. She let him in, then shut the door behind them and set up her laptop. "I'm sorry your date was such a disaster," she said.

"Me too. I'm trying to help you, and that—" He ran a hand through his hair. "Tamera and I were never going to work, but I wanted the date to go well for the press. What if the media coverage hurts business even more?"

Brooke's chest tightened. "They say there's no such thing as bad publicity. I take full responsibility for the date, and I promise to choose more wisely next time."

"Hey." Luke reached forward and grasped her hand. "I didn't mean to make you feel guilty. I was mad, but I'm over it now. It's not your fault. No one could've predicted this. Is something going on that you aren't telling me about? It isn't like you to be so off your game."

Brooke sighed. "Miranda took the girls and left my dad. He has a new girlfriend. But I won't let that distract me from making better matches for you in the future."

Luke squeezed her hand. "Why didn't you tell me he was getting divorced again?"

Brooke shrugged. "I found out at lunch on Saturday. With all this Toujour stuff, there hasn't been time."

"I'm so sorry."

Brooke nodded and cleared her throat. "Thanks."

"Do you want to talk about it?"

"No. I think I got all my ranting out during the car drive home. Antonio helped me talk through it." She motioned to her laptop. "Right now, let's focus on making sure your next date goes better."

Pain flashed across Luke's eyes for a moment, but he nodded. "Okay then. So do I just tell you about the date or what?"

Brooke logged into the database and pulled up Luke's file. "I ask you specific questions about how the date went, if you're interested in continuing the relationship—"

"That's a huge no."

"—and go from there. I'll meet with Tamera's matchmaker later today to compare results."

Luke folded his arms across his chest and crossed his feet at the ankles in front of him. Brooke tried not to stare at his long legs. "What's the first question?"

Brooke glanced at the questionnaire. "On a scale of one to ten, ten being the highest, how would you rate your physical attraction to Tamera?"

"That depends on if we're talking about the beginning of the date or the end."

"There's a difference?"

"She was super hot until she opened her mouth. Some men might think a girl screaming at refs for three hours is attractive, but not me."

"Okay, can you assign a number value to her?"

"If I'm totally wasted and she doesn't open her mouth, I'd dance with her at a club."

This is going well. Brooke typed in a "3" and moved on to the next question. "What do you feel was the best part of your date?"

"This crap is really supposed to help someone find their soul mate?"

Brooke sighed. "Remember what I said about this taking longer if you don't cooperate?"

"Let me make it simple. There isn't going to be a second date. The whole afternoon was a train wreck." His mouth quirked. "It's kind of funny, now that I think about it. But it definitely wasn't at the time."

"Okay, let's try this. Tell me about the date, and I'll fill in the answers as best I can."

So Luke told her, and Brooke's cheeks heated with every word he uttered. "You must think I'm the worst matchmaker in the world."

"I know how you can make it up to me." Luke leaned forward and grinned, making his dimple pop.

Brooke would've called Luke on breaking Rule #15 if she didn't feel so bad. "I never pegged Tamera as a nervous drinker."

"In hindsight, I shouldn't have bought her two beers. But how was I supposed to know she couldn't hold her alcohol?"

"This doesn't make sense. Kendra described Tamera so differently from how you're describing her, and nothing in her file matches up with what you're telling me." Brooke tapped her finger against the space bar on her laptop. "I think the difference is you. Our clients have never dated a celebrity before, and celebrities tend to bring out a different side in people."

Luke rubbed a hand over his face. "That's what I'm afraid of. I don't want someone who treats me like a celebrity. I want someone who treats me like a regular Joe, like you do."

Brooke laughed. "Maybe I'll have to go back in time and find someone who knew you when you were an obnoxious sixteen-year-old, before you were rich and famous. I'll work on it."

Luke moved from his seat to the arm of Brooke's chair. He wrapped an arm around her shoulder, resting his chin on the top of her head. "What a disaster."

Brooke squirmed out of his grip. "At least the papers painted you a hero. Tamera's the one who comes off looking like an idiot. Well, and me."

"Hey now, the papers only said that you were my matchmaker."

"Yeah. The failed date is my fault."

"Don't talk like that."

"I'll find you the perfect girl. Promise."

He held her eyes. "I'm not sure you can find someone who will measure up to you."

Brooke's breath caught in her throat, and she wondered if his lips tasted like the spearmint mouthwash he used. She stood quickly. She was losing her mind. "I think I can fill out the questionnaire based on what you've given me. You can leave now. I would hate to be the reason Luke Ryder takes another sick day."

"I'll take a sick day with you anytime." He wrapped her in a tight hug.

Brooke quickly pulled away and followed Luke out of the office. She needed to get her head on straight.

It wasn't too hard to fill out the rest of the questionnaire before her three p.m. meeting with Kendra, Tamera's matchmaker. Brooke knew Luke so well she could practically hear him saying the words as she typed.

Kendra poked her head around the cubicle. "Ready?"

Brooke grabbed her laptop. "If you are."

They went to the same parlour she'd met with Luke in earlier. Brooke swallowed, taking a seat and opening her laptop as Kendra did the same. "Want me to go first?" Kendra asked.

Brooke nodded. She didn't want to taint Kendra's opinion of the date by what she had to say.

"Tamera thought the date went well right up until the frat boy mishap. She was thrilled with how incredibly 'hot'" —Kendra made air quotes— "Luke was. Even hotter than in the photos, apparently. And she said he was a perfect gentleman. According to her, he bought them enough food to feed a third world country, and she thought that was cool. Something about how he doesn't buy into our society's ridiculous ideas about body image." Kendra rolled her eyes. "Anyway, she's embarrassed about her drinking and the confrontation with the frat boys, but thought it was 'simply adorable' how Luke stepped in the middle of it. She thought he handled the whole thing really well. She was a little disappointed they didn't go out to dinner afterward because she felt they didn't really get to talk, but she still had a great time and would love a second date and the chance to get to know Luke better."

Brooke sighed. "I hate it when this happens."

Kendra's smile turned pained. "He isn't interested, is he?"

"No."

Kendra nodded, positioning her fingers over the laptop keyboard. "I'm not surprised after what I read online. Let me hear it."

"He wasn't fond of Tamera's competitive edge. Apparently she got really involved in the football game and wasn't pleased with how the referees were handling things. And the drinking was a bit of a turnoff." Something Brooke found hypocritical.

"Tamera's never gotten drunk on a date before. I think it was nerves, but I'll mention it. I'm going to set up a relationship counseling session with her later this week. She mentioned that her sister and ex-boyfriend are getting married, and I think it's bringing up old issues. As for competitiveness, some men love that. Sounds like they're just incompatible."

"How's Tamera going to take it?"

Kendra grinned. "Oh, she won't be too disappointed. She didn't think Luke would want a second date after what happened with the frat boys. She had her five minutes in the spotlight and can tell all her friends about the time she dated Luke Ryder, so I think she's happy regardless."

Brooke let out a breath. "Good. The last thing we need is disgruntled women going to the press."

"We all know what you're doing here, Brooke."

Brooke blinked in surprise, and Kendra nodded.

"About the deal with Charlotte? None of us think Luke is really looking for a relationship. We read the papers."

"He says he is, but I'd be lying if I said I wasn't nervous," Brooke said. "That first date didn't help me feel better."

Kendra shut her laptop lid and gave Brooke a reassuring smile. "You're doing a good thing. Hopefully it will work. I think most women will be happy with even one date. No one's expecting to marry the guy."

"Thank you. Setting him up is harder than I thought."

"Better luck next time." Kendra grinned, waving as she walked back to her own desk.

"How'd it go?" Zoey asked as Brooke sat down.

"She wanted a second date, he didn't."

Zoey nodded. "I'm guessing that's how most of Luke's dates will go." She pointed to her computer screen. "We've had one hundred and forty-three people sign up since news of Luke hit the media, so at least we have a bigger pool to pick from. Fingers crossed."

Brooke nodded. Fingers, and toes, and eyes too. This had to work or she could kiss America—and Luke—goodbye.

Chapter Eighteen

Luke wanted to go home after meeting with Brooke, but he went back to Ryder Communications. He walked into his office to find Mitch and Darius standing around the mini-fridge, each holding a glass. They both had stern expressions on their faces.

"What's going on?" Luke asked.

Mitch glanced at Luke. "Good, you're back."

"This is a nightmare," Darius said. "An absolute disaster. Luke, you must fix this."

"Fix what?" Luke looked back and forth between the two men, the dread flowing over him.

"Nathan Kendall." Darius spit out the words as though they were poison.

He's pressing charges. Luke's heart dropped. Not only would that mess things up for Ryder Communications, it would ruin everything for Toujour. "What's going on?"

Darius swore. "It's the home automation system."

Luke barely had time to feel relieved before a new panic took hold. "Fill me in."

Mitch rubbed his eyes. "Kendall Home Systems announced their pre-sale numbers." Mitch held his tablet out to Luke. Luke took it, scanning the article. He nearly choked at the numbers.

"That's a lot of zeros," Luke said.

Darius nodded. "Our stock's already dropped three points."

"We have to issue a press release, letting the public know we're doing our own relaunch of Talia," Mitch said. "No more keeping things quiet. The tech department will have the pre-order button up on the website by tonight." He took the tablet back from Luke and tapped the screen. "We need to give them a firm release date, and work with the stores to do pre-orders through them as well."

Luke didn't want to say it, but had to. "What if Talia isn't ready by January?"

"She has to be," Darius said. "We're all sunk if she's not. We may never recover if we can't one-up Nathan."

"We're not going to let that happen," Luke said.

"Then what are we going to do?" Mitch asked.

Luke's mouth felt dry. What would his father do in this situation? "We'll have to undercut Kendall Home

System's price, at least at first. Even if it means taking a loss. We'll offer existing customers an upgrade to the new system at a significant discount."

Mitch nodded, tapping away on his tablet. "Great ideas. Maybe we could offer them a sneak peak at Talia 2.0. They can get it before the rest of the public or something."

"Good, good," Darius said.

Luke rubbed his eyes. This so wasn't what he wanted to deal with right now. "Whatever it takes. Let's call a meeting with the Talia Team this afternoon. I want every member here and ready to work."

Mitch nodded. "I'll have Krista send out an email immediately." He left the room.

"I appreciate the effort you're putting in," Darius said. "I know you're trying. Let's hope it pays off."

"It will," Luke said.

Darius pursed his lips. "I saw the articles about your first date."

Luke grunted.

"I'm worried your dating life will take away from your focus at the job. I read what happened at the football game. That type of thing is stressful."

Luke tried to play it off. "That was a fluke. I assure you, I'll be able to get the job done—while dating."

"If you're sure."

"We'll launch the first week in January, and it'll be great. Kendall won't know what hit him."

"That's barely two weeks away."

"We'll be ready."

Darius sighed. "You know he's doing the release now because he knows we're struggling."

"Of course he is. Kendall's an oily snake. But we won't be down for long." Luke closed his eyes, willing the pain away. *If Dad was here, this would've never happened.*

The meeting with the Talia Team went as well as could be expected. It turned out the first week in January wasn't doable, but with a tight four week timeline they'd have Talia 2.0 out by the middle of the month. Hopefully without the glitches of the first launch. *But without Dad too.* Their first release without the company founder.

It was nearly nine p.m. before Luke left the office for the day. The gurgling fountain right outside Ryder Communications soothed his frayed nerves once he stepped outside. A guitarist sat near the water, playing Christmas music. Luke's father had never minded musicians earning money by playing on their grounds, as long as they weren't disruptive or offensive. The haunting notes of *What Child Is This?* compelled Luke to stop and listen. That had always been his father's favorite Christmas song. Luke walked over to the man and tossed a hundred dollar bill into the guitar case.

The man's eyes widened, but he didn't stop singing, just inclined his head as a lone tear trickled down his cheek. Luke nodded his understanding and walked away.

"That was very generous."

Luke stopped as a woman stepped onto the path in front of him. Candi. "What are you doing here?" Luke asked.

Candi shrugged, and he worried her bosom would pop out of her shirt with the movement. "I came to see how you're doing."

Luke snorted, brushing past her. She kept pace with him as he headed toward the valet station.

"What do you want?" he asked.

Candi frowned. "You. I know I should've told you about Nathan. But I genuinely care for you, Luke. I was so mad at Nathan that night, and when I saw you, all the old feelings came rushing back." Her red nails skittered along his arm, and he shivered.

"I find it more believable that you and Nathan cooked that night up in a pathetic ploy to try to get company secrets out of me."

Candi laughed. "Kendall Home Systems doesn't need your secrets. They're doing great on their own, thank you very much." She ran her hand down his arm, intertwining her fingers with his. "I might be able to help you out, however."

He shook her hand away. "Not interested."

"Even if it saves the company?"

It would've been a tempting offer, if he'd believed she had anything to offer.

Candi frowned. "What's this matchmaking business about, Luke? You didn't seem interested in 'serious' on Thanksgiving."

"A lot's changed since then."

She snorted. "Like you letting the girl you love match you up?"

Luke clenched his hands into fists. "Stop it. Just stop."

"You always did feel more for Brooke than she felt for you."

Luke whirled on her. "What's your angle? Is there a photographer hiding in the bushes, ready to take an incriminating photo of us? Are you trying to get me to confess something condemning to make Nathan look better in the press?"

Candi raised an eyebrow. "Do you have something condemning to confess?"

He shook his head. "I'm done with this."

"She'll never have you." Candi folded her arms, making her cleavage even more pronounced. "Brooke's a serious relationship girl, and you're a player."

He curled his toes in his shoes. "I'm not a player."

"She's getting married. It's over." She grabbed his hand, pulling him close. "After a night with me, you won't care that you lost. It can be our little secret."

Luke tore his hand from Candi's. "You have a boyfriend, and I'm not interested."

She laughed. "If you haven't convinced Brooke to be more than friends by now, you never will."

Luke wanted to yell at her, but he turned and walked away.

"You'd do well to stay on my good side, Luke Ryder," she called at his retreating back.

He shook his head. *What game is she playing?* But he knew her game. Nathan wasn't stupid enough to share secrets with that viper, and Candi simply wanted what she couldn't have.

The valet must've seen him approaching, because the limousine and driver waited for him at the curb. Luke thanked the valet and got in his car, eagerly leaving work behind.

Had the valet seen him with Candi? Worse yet, had the press? Had anyone heard them fighting about Brooke?

Luke shook his head. Nothing had happened. They'd barely even talked. Even if the press had gotten a picture, it wasn't anything damning. Probably. They did know how to spin lies.

"Why?" Luke asked the ceiling. Why did everything have to happen all at once? Ryder Communications, Toujour, Talia, Candi . . . Brooke. *Which one do you want the most?*

The answer to that question was easy—Brooke. If everything else went away, he'd be fine as long as he had her.

He had to convince her not to marry Antonio. The time for being timid had passed. *I won't lose her. Not without a fight.* He picked up his cell and called her. It was time to stop dancing around the issue. He had a girl to win over.

Chapter Nineteen

Charlotte's reprimand hung heavy on Brooke, and after meeting with Kendra, she scoured the databases for an acceptable second date for Luke. Nothing. None of these women were quite good enough—for Luke or the press.

When seven o'clock rolled around, Brooke was more than happy to shut down her computer and go home. She and Zoey silently gathered their things and walked to the car. They'd both been so busy that afternoon that they hadn't really spoken since lunch.

"Rough afternoon?" Zoey asked once they were in the car.

Brooke sighed. "Yeah."

"Sounds like you need a spa day. Or evening, I guess. What do you say?"

Brooke sighed again. "Sounds divine, but Antonio's coming over to help address save the dates."

"Once you send out save the dates, things start getting real."

Brooke flicked a glare at Zoey before refocusing on the road. "This wedding is happening, maid of honor. Get used to it, and thanks for the support."

"As maid of honor, it's my duty to tell you when you're making a mistake."

"Are you going to help me address invitations or what?"

"Sorry, no can do. I have a date."

"I thought you wanted to do a spa night."

Zoey shrugged. "I would've canceled for a spa night, but I won't for a calligraphy pen and cramped fingers."

"Figures."

They arrived home, and Zoey disappeared into her room to get ready for her date. Brooke pulled the gigantic box of save the dates from her walk-in closet— nearly five hundred announcements. She'd wanted the wedding to be a much smaller affair, but Antonio's family and friends-he-considered-family list was huge. If they moved to Italy, that would be something she'd definitely have a hard time adjusting to.

Next, Brooke pulled out the address list, invitations, envelopes, stamps, and calligraphy pens. She dragged everything out to the living room and assembled it on the beige carpet in a line parallel with the television. Maybe she should've asked the bridal party to help. At least Antonio was an artist, and could help address the envelopes. She wouldn't trust most guys with such a task. But even with the two of them, it would take hours to address all the envelopes. She turned on the television and picked a British comedy that Antonio enjoyed, then sat on the floor with her back against the couch and her careful assembly line in front of her.

Brooke glanced at her cell phone—6:02. He was two minutes late. She took a deep breath, trying to relax. She pulled the address list toward her and began addressing envelopes.

At 6:10, Brooke called him. No answer. At 6:17 she tried again. At 6:32 her phone rang. *Don't be upset. Don't make this into a fight.* "Hello," Brooke said, proud of herself for sounding cheerful.

"*Mia dolcezza.* I'm sorry I didn't call earlier. The muse struck, and I lost track of time."

Brooke closed her eyes and breathed deeply. "No problem. Are you on your way over now?" *You'd better be on your way.*

"No, I'm at the loft, covered in oil paints from head to toe. Brooke, this landscape is a masterpiece. The gallery will adore it. I hate to stop working when the inspiration is so strong. Can we do the invitations a different night?"

Don't get mad, don't throw a fit. "Of course." He was trying to financially support them, after all. And he was nervous about making the gallery in Italy happy.

"You're perfect, *mia bella.* I promise we'll do it soon. Maybe this weekend, after I get back from San Diego."

"No problem. I've already started, but you can help me finish up later." Brooke paused. "Is someone laughing?"

"It's my iPod. I should've turned down the *musica* before calling. It's why I didn't hear my phone ring the first two times."

"Oh. Right."

"Saturday we'll finish up. And I'll stop by to see you before I leave for San Diego tomorrow."

"Sure."

"I love you, Brooke."

"I love you, too." But as she hung up the phone, her feelings were leaning much more toward anger than love. She knew when she started dating an artist that it would be like this sometimes. His job wasn't nine to five. He kept odd hours, and worked whenever the mood struck. And she understood that. Really, she did.

But why did it have to interfere with their wedding?

And if the muse strikes on our wedding day, will he show up late to the ceremony? She pushed the thought away. Of course he wouldn't. Even Antonio wasn't that irresponsible. Besides, he was as excited to get married as she was.

Brooke picked up the calligraphy pen. She really should keep addressing the invitations. She'd taken the time to pull everything out, and besides, the likelihood of Antonio flaking a second time was high. But if she was doing this solo, she was watching something she liked. She flipped through the channels and settled on a modeling competition show she and Luke loved. He always critiqued the models' clothing in a British accent that made her giggle hysterically.

Her phone rang, and she knew without looking at the caller ID that it was Luke. He had an uncanny ability to know when she was thinking about him. Brooke answered the phone with a smile. "I'm watching *Model at the Top*," she said.

His laugh was deep and rich and sent her spine tingling. "Please let me come over and watch it with you. I had a run-in with Candi and I'm in a sucky mood."

"Okay, that needs details."

"Not many to give. She's playing her usual mind games. At first I thought Kendall was behind it, but now I'm pretty sure it's just her."

"Do you think she was hoping the press would get a photo?"

"No. That'd be hard to explain to her boyfriend. Now can I come over or what?"

That little tramp. "Only if you bring donuts and hot chocolate."

"Have you eaten anything real for dinner?"

"Donuts are a real dinner." She shifted, and her knee landed on the corner of the invitation box. She looked down at the save the dates, suddenly remembering what she was doing. "Oh."

"You already have plans."

"Well, Antonio and I were supposed to address save the dates."

Silence. "Maybe another night. I don't want to interrupt."

"Antonio couldn't come. He just bailed." She bit her lip, debating what to do next. She could put the invitations away and do them another night. But she really should send them out in the next week or two. "You could help me."

"I am your man of honor."

Brooke laughed, relieved he wasn't going to be weird about this. "True."

"I'm coming right over. Be there in ten."

Eight minutes later, a knock came at her door. Brooke grinned, pushing herself to her feet and going to answer it. Luke wore an old pair of jeans that were worn in all the right places and a T-shirt she recognized from college. "That was quick," Brooke said. "Where are my donuts and hot chocolate?"

"I sent the driver to get them. He'll be back soon." Luke came inside, shutting the door behind him.

"Sometimes being rich has its benefits," Brooke teased.

Luke smirked. "I guess you could say that. Where's Zoey?"

"Another date with a guy who's totally wrong for her. I think she and Mitch like each other, but neither seems willing to do anything about it."

Luke raised an eyebrow. "High-strung Mitch and chaotic Zoey?"

"I bet if I put them in the database, they'd be a match."

Luke took off his jacket and laid it on the back of the couch. "I don't see it. So it's just you and me tonight then, eh?"

"And an all-night marathon of *Model at the Top*."

"I should've brought the score cards." Luke sat down on the floor, motioning to the piles of invitation materials. "So what am I doing?"

"You're stuffing the envelopes while I address them. I'll show you."

"There's a wrong way to put things in an envelope?"

"There is when it's for a wedding." Brooke grabbed a save the date and showed him which direction to put it in the envelope. "Then you put this envelope into this envelope—"

"Wait, wait, wait. You're sending your save the dates in two envelopes?"

Brooke rolled her eyes. "Well, yeah. That's how it's done."

"Why?"

"So that when the outer envelope gets dirty in the mail, the inner one still looks nice."

"You're kidding me."

"Why would I joke about this?"

Luke sighed. "Good thing *Model at the Top* is on. This is going to be a long night."

"You're not the one addressing five hundred invitations."

The driver delivered the donuts and hot chocolate, and they enjoyed their treat before getting to work. Luke stuffed envelopes and offered unsolicited commentary on the show while Brooke wrote addresses on envelopes. She couldn't help the glow in her heart as she listened to Luke talk. This was the most he had sounded like the old Luke in months.

"So what's the deal with Antonio being AWOL anyway?" Luke asked during a commercial break. He held up a save the date. "Seems like the kind of thing the groom should help with."

Brooke sighed, setting down her calligraphy pen and stretching out her fingers. "His muse hit, so he's home painting."

Luke rolled his eyes. "That's the lamest excuse I've ever heard."

"Painting *is* his job. He's really stressed about this new contract with the gallery in Italy. He wants the first landscape he sends them to be absolutely perfect."

"You'd think he'd want his wedding to be perfect."

"I didn't think men generally cared about that sort of thing."

"Perfect wedding equals happy bride. Happy bride equals happy groom."

"You speak wisdom." Brooke bowed her head dramatically and Luke snorted, stuffing another envelope. She should get back to addressing, but her fingers were seriously cramping and the thought of holding that calligraphy pen had them screaming in protest.

"Are you happy, Brooke?" Luke asked.

She stopped stretching her fingers. "Why would you ask that?"

He dropped the filled envelope, scrubbing a hand over his face. "My feelings about Antonio aren't exactly a secret."

Brooke pushed the filled invitations aside and scooted closer to Luke. "Just give him a chance. You both are so important to me." She swallowed hard. "Can't you at least try to get along?"

"He's such a douche."

"Lu-uke." She drew the word out into two syllables.

He picked up one of the save the dates, holding it out to her. "This is really what you see when you picture your future?"

Brooke took the save the date, really studying it for Luke's sake. He would know if she brushed off the question. The photo was black and white and had been taken in downtown LA. Brooke and Antonio both stood in front of a graffiti-covered wall, holding hands with solemn expressions on their faces. The filter the photographer used made the whole thing look grainy, and it was hard to make out facial features in the photo. They could be any couple. The only pop of color was their names and the date and location of the wedding. The save the date was much more artistic than what Brooke would've chosen, but Antonio had a photographer friend who'd given them a great discount on the photos and design so she hadn't said anything.

Brooke put the photo back. "Antonio loves me. He's always there for me."

Luke drew back, a mask covering his face. "You mean like he was here for you tonight?"

"That's not fair."

"*I'm* here for you, Brooke."

Her heart pounded in her chest, and she jumped to her feet. "Don't."

He stood, grabbing her arm. "*I* love you."

She shrugged his hand off. "Stop it."

"I know I haven't exactly been a model citizen in the past. But I'm changing. I'm trying to deserve you. You don't have to question me."

"You're breaking like every single rule I've ever created." She ran her fingers through her hair. Her hands felt clammy and cold.

"There isn't a rule that forbids me from declaring my love. And if there was, I'd break it anyway."

"You can't do this, Luke. I'm getting married. To Antonio."

Luke stepped close again. She could smell his laundry detergent and cologne, and it made her dizzy. "Give us a chance."

"We'll never work."

"Why?"

"Oh, I don't know. Because you've never had a serious relationship." Brooke paced back and forth, waving her hands as she spoke.

"An eight year friendship is pretty serious."

"Because if we tried, and things didn't work out, our friendship would be ruined. And I can't live with that."

He took a step toward her. "It would work out. And you don't think marrying Antonio will change our friendship?"

"Sometimes you're too much like my dad. Flitting from woman to woman, not really caring if their feelings get hurt."

"That's not fair. I might not have serious relationships, but I haven't abandoned three separate wives and four children either."

"You and I aren't compatible in that way. Not like me and Antonio."

Luke snorted. "I dare you to run our compatibility in Toujour's database. I bet we'd blow your and Antonio's seventy-one percent out of the water."

Brooke held up her hands as though to ward him off, still pacing. "It doesn't matter. I'm marrying Antonio. I love him. That alone is reason enough why we wouldn't work."

Luke shook his head. "No good. You love me too." He stepped in her path, forcing her to stop pacing. He took her face in his hands and gently caressed it. "What are you afraid of?"

Brooke closed her eyes and her breath hitched. She wrenched herself from him. "I'm not afraid of anything. I just know we wouldn't last. Where is all this coming from?" Her hands shook. "You haven't mentioned dating since high school."

"Only because every time I got up the courage, you started dating someone else. You turned me down pretty hard in eleventh grade and made it abundantly clear multiple times that we were just friends. But that's not enough for me anymore."

Brooke's breath quickened. For eight years he'd felt this way. And he'd waited until now to say something?

"He's all wrong for you, Brooklyn, and you know it. But us . . ." He leaned down, his lips hovering above hers.

Her hand struck his cheek before she even knew what she was doing. He drew back, stunned. His hand went to his cheek. Brooke's chest heaved as tears obscured her vision.

"I scared you. Too much too soon." He nodded. "I can understand that."

"We're going to forget this ever happened. Tomorrow things will go back to normal. The wedding has me on edge, and you're struggling with your father's death. We're friends. *Best* friends. And you will always be my best friend. But Antonio's the man I'm going to marry."

"No. It doesn't get to be that easy for you. I'm telling you right here, right now, that I'm throwing my hat in the ring. Because this" —he motioned between them— "is worth fighting for. You might not be willing to risk it. I was too scared to take a chance for a really long time. But now, the only thing I'm scared of is losing the possibility of us. So get ready for the fight of your life, Brooke. I'll see you later." He strode out the door without another word.

Brooke stared after him in shock, then mechanically closed the door. A hand caught and held it. She looked up into Zoey's concerned eyes. "How long have you been standing there?" Brooke asked.

"Long enough. What are you going to do?"

Brooke shook her head and began to cry.

Chapter Twenty

Luke walked away from Brooke's apartment door and down the hallway, toward the elevator. His hands clenched into fists as he tried to stop them from trembling.

There was no going back now. He'd laid it all on the line. He'd either made the best decision of his life, or the worst.

I have to win her. Antonio isn't right for Brooke.

But how was he supposed to "win" Brooke? If eight years hadn't been enough to convince her they were meant to be together, then what could he do?

Luke pushed the chipped button for down on the elevator. He walked on shaky legs to the limousine and climbed in.

The partition lowered. "Where to, Mr. Ryder?" the driver asked, watching Luke through the rearview mirror.

"Mitch's," Luke said. Even his words sounded shaky. "No, my place. Call Mitch and tell him to meet me there. It's urgent."

"Of course, Mr. Ryder." The partition slid back up, and the limo purred to life.

Luke's cheek still stung from the force of Brooke's slap. He ran a shaky hand through his hair. He had no idea what to expect going forward. Breaking rules in the past had resulted in anything from snippy remarks to the silent treatment, and he'd gone way over the line this time.

I told her I'll fight, and I will. But hot chocolate and donuts weren't exactly an amazing start.

"Stop it." He couldn't get the image of Brooke screaming at him, shaking off his hand as though that would shake off his declaration of love.

She loved him. He knew she did.

Didn't she?

Luke scooted across the bench seat to the mini cabinet in one corner of the limo. He fumbled for the bottle of Scotch and unstopped the top, sloshing it into a tumbler. He swallowed it in one drink and quickly poured another.

"We're going to forget this happened. Tomorrow things will go back to normal."

Luke slammed a fist against the window. *She can't do this to me.* His feelings mattered, too.

During the fifteen minute drive, Luke's fingers itched for a basketball or weight bar, desperate for the relief exercise brought. He jumped out of the limo as soon as it came to a stop and hurried into the building, ignoring the camera flash from someone hiding in the bushes. The elevator doors immediately opened. Luke stepped inside and the elevator attendant entered the penthouse key code.

"Welcome home, Luke," Talia said in greeting. "Mitch is in the living room." Luke barely registered that she hadn't glitched on Mitch's name, a positive sign that the overhaul was working. They'd been testing the updates in his penthouse, as well as at Ryder Communications.

"Thanks," Luke muttered. Mitch's apartment was only five minutes away, so he wasn't surprised.

Mitch met him in the foyer. "What happened?" he asked, grabbing Luke's arm. "The driver said you were with Brooke, then came out looking rattled."

Luke shrugged off the hand and headed into the kitchen, grabbing a tumbler and filling it with Scotch.

"How many have you had?" Mitch asked, following him.

"This will be my third," Luke said. He threw back the Scotch and reached to refill the glass.

Mitch's hand landed on top of his. "Okay, calm down. I think you've had enough to drink. Do some yoga breaths."

Luke didn't know what a yoga breath was, but he closed his eyes and breathed deeply. *If Brooke saw you now, she'd be more convinced than ever you aren't the one.*

Mitch took the bottle and put it back. "Let's go sit down. Tell me what's wrong."

Luke followed Mitch into the living room and sank into the arm chair. "I told her."

"Told her what?"

Luke closed his eyes, but all he saw was Brooke's horrified expression. "That I love her."

"What did she say?"

"She slapped me. She told me we were going to forget it ever happened and go back to normal." He ran a shaky hand through his hair. "How can things ever be normal again? I told her I love her. *Love her.*"

Mitch cursed, but his eyes were full of sympathy. He leaned forward, clasping his hands together. "You sure know how to take a bad situation and make it worse. In less than a month, we have to relaunch Talia. If we can't do it successfully, Nathan will steal all our clients and we will be well on our way to working ourselves out of a job. That is what we should focus on. Not Brooke."

"Do you know why I went over there tonight? To help her stuff envelopes with save the dates. For her wedding to Antonio. It's really happening, unless I do something to stop it."

"And we're really going to be out of a job, if we don't do something about that."

Luke swore. "This is Brooke we're talking about."

"I know Antonio's kind of annoying, but I think she really does love him. I'm sorry."

Luke grabbed a candy dish off the coffee table and hurled it at the wall. It shattered, M&M's and shards of glass dropping to the carpeted floor. "She loves *me*. We're meant to be together." He picked up a vase of fresh flowers—pink Gerber daisies, Brooke's favorite—and threw it at the wall too.

Mitch grabbed Luke's arm. "You need to calm down. Breathe."

Luke sucked in a huge, gulping breath. Tremors shook his body as the adrenaline surged through it. "You have to help me. You have to help me convince her."

"You want me to help you break up Brooke's wedding."

"Yes."

Mitch sighed. "This doesn't seem right, man."

"*Please.*"

"Okay, okay. But we've got to balance this with keeping Ryder Communications afloat, and keeping our jobs. Now how are we going to convince Brooke you're the one?"

"I can't believe he said he loves you," Zoey said. She shifted on the couch, causing Brooke to sink toward the middle.

Brooke sniffed, throwing another tissue in the general direction of the trash can. Their normally tidy living room was starting to resemble the disaster zone that was Zoey's bedroom. Tissues overflowed and spilled onto the beige carpet, and a few had even landed perilously close to the save the dates that were still spread across the floor. "How am I supposed to see him tomorrow and keep matching him up with these women and pretend that all of this is normal?"

Zoey rubbed small circles on Brooke's back. "Maybe you don't."

"What?"

"Brooke, this is *Luke*. He's here and he loves you and you love him. It's perfect."

"Zoey, I'm engaged." She motioned to the living room floor. "I'm addressing save the dates. I love Antonio."

"I know. But you love Luke too, and you're lying to yourself if you deny it. The two of you fit. You're different around Luke. Less uptight. More fun. Lighter.

He brings out the happiness in you. With Antonio, you act more moody and stressed."

Brooke shook her head before Zoey finished speaking. "The stress is because of the wedding, not Antonio. I will not be Luke's first real relationship. I won't be the girl he makes all the rookie mistakes with. Our friendship—"

"Don't give me that crap. You tell your clients all the time that a deep friendship is a great foundation for a lasting romantic relationship. And eight years is a pretty solid foundation."

"Luke is a fantastic best friend. But that's all we'll ever be. I have a fiancé that I really do love." Brooke held up a hand. "I know you don't understand it or agree with it, but I do love Antonio. Yeah, he's kind of oblivious at times. And yeah, he has some old fashioned ideas about gender roles. But he's sweet and kind and he loves me. He's a responsible adult who knows how to be in a relationship. We're seventy-one percent compatible." She let her hands drop to her side. "I'm not gambling my happiness on Luke. My chips are solidly on Antonio's number."

Chapter Twenty-One

Antonio held Brooke close, nuzzling her neck. She buried her face in his shoulder and held him closer. Light poured in from the floor to ceiling windows in his studio apartment, illuminating the space where they stood. The sun felt like summer on her skin, and the smell of turpentine and oil paints was familiar and safe. Brooke wanted to stay in that sunlight, basking in the comfort of Antonio's embrace, forever.

"I'm going to miss you," he said.

Brooke tightened her arms around his neck. She needed to leave for work. She'd only stopped by Antonio's for a moment to wish him luck on his business trip to San Diego. But she didn't want to let him go. "I'm going to miss you too."

He captured her lips with his own, pressing a hand against her back to urge her closer. She tried to focus on the kiss, to be present in the moment.

Antonio pulled back. "You've been quiet. Is everything okay?"

Brooke knew she should tell him what had happened last night with Luke. But if she told him, he would never let her see Luke again. *And I probably shouldn't.* She didn't know if their friendship could ever recover from what had happed. But she wanted it to.

"Brooke?"

She blinked. She'd been lost in thought again. "Yeah, sorry. I'm stressed about work."

"Have you had any luck finding another date for Luke?"

"There are plenty of willing candidates and I'm trying to find the right one. I don't want another disaster like the football game."

Antonio kissed Brooke again. "You'll figure something out."

Brooke glanced at her cell and groaned. "If I don't leave now, I'll be late for work."

Antonio let her go. "I should be going too. I'll walk you to your car."

At work, Brooke scoured the list of potential matches the computer had populated, looking for the one that would be just right for Luke. Maybe if she found him a girlfriend, their relationship could go back to normal.

Why, Luke? Why did you have to say you love me?

246

She wished she could rewind time and go back to the days of denial. Life had been so much easier then. So much simpler.

Brooke scanned the list of qualifications for Bachelorette #1. She loved cats . . . definitely not the girl for Luke, despite a seventy percent compatibility rating. Brooke closed out her profile and began reading the next one. She loved the bar scene. So not what Luke needed right now.

Brooke stopped on the profile of Michelle. She looked sweet and wholesome, an elementary school teacher who loved football and had a passion for Star Wars. A white personality, so she probably wasn't competitive. Brooke kept reading, but she already knew that Luke would go on a date with this woman. Hopefully that weekend. Charlotte was annoyed Brooke hadn't already scheduled a date for Friday.

Brooke walked over to Raine's cubical. Raine looked up from her computer. "Hey, Brooke."

"Hey. Do you have a sec?"

"Sure."

Brooke perched on the edge of Raine's desk. "I looked through Michelle's profile, and I think she might be a good match for Luke."

Raine nodded. "Okay. What qualities is Luke looking for?"

"He needs someone who isn't only interested in his celebrity status. Someone who is calm and can balance out his more bold personality."

Raine nodded. She turned to her computer and pulled up Michelle's profile. "Michelle isn't the celebrity gossip type. And she definitely isn't the type to drink when nervous." She flashed Brooke a grin. "I think they'd be a great match, and the computer agrees. Sixty-nine percent compatibility. Let me call her right now and see if she'd be interested in a date. When were you thinking?"

"Friday night hopefully."

"Yeah, we need to give the press something new to talk about." Raine picked up her phone and dialed a number. Brooke's stomach tied in knots as she listened to Raine's side of the conversation.

A few minutes later, Raine hung up the phone. "Michelle's excited to meet Luke and looks forward to the date. I told her I would call her back in a few hours with more details. What did you have in mind for Friday?"

"Something cultural. Maybe the theater?"

"Michelle would love that. Broadway's *The Lion King* is in town right now. I know Charlotte had a few tickets set aside in case a client wanted to go."

"That sounds great. Let me call and confirm with Luke, and I'll get back to you."

Raine nodded, and Brooke walked back to her desk. Now she'd have to call Luke. She wasn't sure what to say or how to act. Usually after he broke a rule, she ignored him for a few days, he apologized by buying her chocolate, then they went to the movies or something and pretended the whole thing had never happened.

Act natural, like everything is normal. That's what you told him you'd do, right?

Brooke swallowed. "I'm calling Luke," she told Zoey.

Zoey gave her a sympathetic smile. "Finally found a good match for his next date?"

Brooke nodded.

"Just hurry and get it over with, quick like a Band-Aid."

"Yeah." Brooke picked up the phone and dialed before she could talk herself out of it.

"Good luck," Zoey whispered.

"Hello?" Luke said.

Brooke closed her eyes, the cadence of his voice washing over her like warm sand. "Hey, Luke." How would he respond? What would he say?

What did she want him to say?

"Hey." His voice was cautious. But it held a warmth, too. One that made her insides squirm.

Brooke grabbed the framed photo of her and Antonio from its place on her desk and slid it closer.

She forced herself to take in his dark curly hair, his stubbled jaw. His kissable lips. "I've got another match for you. Her name's Michelle. I'd like to set up a date for Friday. Will that work for you?"

"Sure," Luke said. "I should be able to get off work by six."

He's still working regularly? Brooke shook her head. She couldn't reconcile this new Luke, who really was the old Luke, with the Luke she'd become familiar with over the past few months. "Great. There's an eight-thirty showing of *The Lion King*. I thought you could go to the play, then take her out for dessert afterward." One of Tamera's complaints had been she didn't feel like she had a chance to talk to Luke, and Brooke was determined not to make that mistake this time.

"Okay."

"Right. I'll get everything arranged and let you know. I'll call you back in a few hours."

"Bye, Brooke." Then, more quietly: "I love you."

Brooke froze. Her hand tightened on the phone receiver. "Don't say that."

"Why not? It's true. And I will keep saying it until I convince you to believe me."

Brooke slammed the receiver down.

Zoey crossed one leg over the other. "Didn't go well, huh?"

Brooke looked around to make sure no one was nearby before answering. "He said he loved me."

"So? He does."

"But he shouldn't say it." Brooke blinked quickly. "I told him I wanted things to go back to normal. Why doesn't he understand that?"

"Why should it get to be all about what you want?" Zoey turned back to her computer. "Luke has feelings too."

Brooke's heart thudded to a stop, then hammered in her ears. She slowly picked up the phone again and dialed the ticket office for the theater. She needed to give them Luke's name so they'd know who was picking up the tickets. Was she being selfish to deny Luke's feelings?

No. He's wrong to try to break up my wedding.

"Box office, how may I help you?"

Brooke sat up straighter in her chair and pushed Luke out of her mind. She had a date to arrange.

Chapter Twenty-Two

It was a long three days without Luke or Antonio. Luke didn't call, didn't text, and their only interactions were Toujour-centered. Brooke tried to forget about Luke, forget about his declaration. She tried to focus on Toujour and planning her wedding and her nightly chats with her fiancé.

It wasn't working.

Brooke wandered into the kitchen Friday morning, feeling her shoulders droop and the bags under her eyes. Zoey sat at the bar, sipping a cup of coffee.

"Morning," Brooke mumbled.

"You look awful. Sit down. I'll get you some coffee."

Brooke slumped into a chair and watched through bleary eyes as Zoey poured a cup and set it in front of her.

"Something new got you losing sleep?" Zoey asked.

Brooke shook her head. "I keep hoping I'll wake up and realize it was all a bad dream, and things are still the same between Luke and me."

"But they aren't. And it isn't what Luke wants."

Brooke laid her head on the table. "Men suck."

Zoey laughed. "Luke's date with Michelle is tonight. Maybe he'll fall madly in love with her and solve all your problems."

Brooke's stomach twisted. She knew Zoey was joking. But Brooke didn't want that, either.

"Are you going to tell Antonio?"

"I can't." The words caught in Brooke's throat as they forced their way out of her mouth. "I know I should, but I love Luke too much to let Antonio know he has feelings for me. Because if Antonio knows, he'll want me to stop hanging out with Luke. And Zoey, I know I should, but I can't. There's got to be a solution to all of this that doesn't involve me losing Luke or Antonio."

Zoey leaned forward, bracing her arms on the counter. "Are you happy?"

"What?"

"It's a simple question—are you happy? When you forget about the stress of Toujour, and Antonio and Luke not getting along, and the wedding, are you happy with your choice?"

Brooke stared into her mug. It scared her to death that she couldn't answer that question. She sipped her coffee and stewed.

Brooke finally had enough clients at Toujour that she stayed busy for most of the day. Her excitement at seeing Antonio again grew as the end of her work day drew closer. By the time Brooke left at seven, she felt a lot better about things. It would be a tense and awkward few months with Luke. But once the wedding was over, everyone would get used to the new status quo and things would calm down.

Brooke practically skipped up the three flights of stairs to Antonio's studio apartment. He opened the door, and she flung herself at him. He laughed, holding her tight and kissing her until she gasped for air. She savored the feel of his stubble against her cheek, his arms around her waist. This was right. This is what she wanted.

"You're right on time," he said, pulling her inside. "I just got back a few minutes ago. I picked up takeout on my way home."

"What did you order this time?" Brooke asked, taking off her coat and tossing it on the worn couch pushed against one wall.

"Mexican—your favorite. It's a peace offering since I didn't cook. I'll come over to your place later this week and make you a real meal, promise."

Brooke grinned. Antonio was a fabulous cook, but he refused to do it in his tiny kitchen. "Sounds like I'm getting the better end of this deal."

"I do what I can. Let me set the table, then we're ready."

Brooke helped get the food on while they discussed how Antonio's business trip had gone, and soon they filled their tortillas with Mexican rice and beans. "So how did things go with matchmaking this week?" Antonio asked once their burritos were made.

Brooke swallowed. She hoped her face didn't show the guilt she felt. "Good. We've had over a hundred new clients sign up this week. Luke's on another date tonight."

"I hope he can save everyone's jobs. I know Zoey enjoys working there."

Brooke bit her lip and looked away. *I love this job too, Antonio—my dream job.* She focused on the glittering city lights visible through the floor-to-ceiling windows. "I selected this date very carefully. I think it'll go well."

"Have you thought any more about Italy?"

Breathe in. Breathe out. "Yes. I'm still not sure."

"We could do Christmas in Paris."

Brooke swallowed hard. "Maybe. This sweet pork is amazing tonight. I wonder if they did something to the recipe."

And just like that, the subject changed. They both avoided bringing up moving, Toujour, or Luke for the rest of the meal. Instead, they talked more about Antonio's business trip and their plans for the week.

"Thanks for dinner," Brooke said when they finished eating.

Antonio nodded, throwing the plates in the trash.

"Can I grab your laundry before I forget?" Brooke asked. Antonio's apartment didn't have a washer or dryer, so Brooke did his laundry at her apartment. "I'm guessing you are in desperate need of clean clothes."

"You're right. Thanks."

"I can't stay too late tonight. Mind if I start sorting it?"

He shrugged. "If you want. I'll finish cleaning up down here, then come up." He swatted her on the butt.

Brooke weaved her way through easels and tiptoed over the drop cloths that covered the main living space, making her way to the ladder leading to the bedroom loft. She'd always loved the twelve foot high ceilings and exposed brick in this apartment. She quickly scaled the ladder and ducked under a wooden beam before straightening. The ceiling was barely a few inches above her head. This apartment definitely wouldn't work once they were married, but still, she'd miss it.

A suitcase sat on the floor next to the unmade bed. Clothes spilled out of it and littered the room. No surprise there. Antonio was messy and unorganized—something Brooke knew would drive her nuts when they moved in together after the wedding. But probably not any crazier than Zoey's messes. With a sigh, Brooke started picking clothes up off the floor. She had no idea what was clean or dirty. She'd have to wash everything.

She quickly gathered the clothes from around the room and moved on to the suitcase. She separated art supplies and toiletries from the clothing. She tossed dental floss onto one pile and a shirt onto another. A flash of silver caught her eye, standing out against the black of Antonio's shirt. She reached for the silver. Her hand stilled, and her heart thudded in her ears.

A single diamond earring. A present for her, maybe?

Brooke set it aside, turning back to the suitcase. She pawed through it, throwing clothes and toiletries aside without thought of sorting. If it was a present, there should be a box. A matching earring to complete the set.

She took a deep breath. *Think, Brooke. There's got to be an explanation for this.* Maybe he'd found it at the hotel and meant to leave it at the front desk. Maybe someone had asked him to hold on to it. Maybe he wanted to get his own ear pierced and was nervous to tell her.

Her hands shook as she again searched the items, looking for something to help this make sense.

Nothing.

Her legs buckled and Brooke sank to the floor, staring at the earring. Her mind exploded with the countless fights she'd overheard between her parents over Shandi. Had Antonio really been on business this weekend? Or had it been a cover?

This couldn't be happening to her.

Her mother's heartbroken voice floated into her head. *"All men are cheaters, Brooklyn. They can't help it. It doesn't matter how good they have it at home, the grass is always greener on the other side."* She remembered so well those late night chats on her mother's bed after her parents split.

Could there really be another woman?

The ladder creaked, and Antonio's head appeared. "The kitchen is clean," he said. Standing straight, his head nearly brushed the loft ceiling.

Brooke didn't move from where she sat on the floor. She held up the earring as though it carried some infectious disease. *Stay calm. Maybe there's a logical explanation.* "Want to explain this to me?"

Antonio looked startled. "What is it?"

"An earring."

"From where?" He looked genuinely confused.

"Never trust a man, Brooklyn." Brooke laughed, but it was hollow. "I found it in the bottom of your suitcase."

Antonio shrugged. "Oh. Maybe it's Jeanette's, from the gallery. She wasn't feeling well one night and I told her I had aspirin in my bag. Maybe it fell in without her noticing."

Brooke rose, her heart pounding. *He's lying to my face!* She threw the earring at Antonio. "You expect me to believe you let some random girl from the gallery go through your luggage?"

He caught the earring. "Yes, because that's what happened. I don't know, maybe the earring got there some other way. But I don't know how. Why are you so upset, *bella*?"

"Let me make sure I understand this. A girl from the gallery in San Diego had a headache. You told her to go up to your room, paw through your luggage, and find pain reliever. In the process she lost an earring." Brooke ticked the items off on her finger as she listed them.

"Five people from the gallery were in my hotel room last night. We had a few drinks and talked business. So yes, when she had a headache, I told her to get the aspirin herself." His voice was so sincere, his face so open and vulnerable. Just like when he told her he loved her for the first time.

Brooke picked apart his argument, looking for a flaw. He could be lying. This could be the forgotten earring of some scarlet woman with whom he'd had a torrid affair.

Or he could be telling the truth. It wouldn't be the first time he'd met with contacts in his room on business, and he wasn't exactly possessive of his personal property. It sounded like something he'd do. She'd blown the whole thing out of proportion.

Of course he's telling the truth. What am I doing? Mom is wrong. Antonio isn't a cheater.

Please let him be telling the truth.

Her voice shook. "You swear on your life that's what happened?"

"Yes." He wrapped his arms tightly around her. "I love you, Brooke. Why would I need anyone else? You are the woman I want to marry."

Brooke sank into Antonio's embrace, burying her face against his strong chest. Her shoulders shook. *Get out of my head, Mom. You're wrong. Not all men are like Dad.* Had she really almost thrown away their future over a simple misunderstanding? She needed to stop self-sabotaging. She knew Antonio. He wasn't a cheater. He loved her, and she loved him.

Brooke took a deep breath and whispered, "I'm sorry. I saw that earring and suddenly my mother was in my head. I could hear all the fights she and my dad had before the divorce and . . ." She shuddered. "And now he's doing it again."

261

"Shhh." Antonio stroked Brooke's head. "If this is going to work, you have to trust me, Brooke."

"I do." *I want to.*

"And I trust you, so let's put it behind us."

"Okay."

Chapter Twenty-Three

Luke waited near the box office where he'd picked up the tickets, hands clasped so he didn't fidget with his tie. People wandered into the theater in everything from jeans to evening wear. Just inside the glass doors, Luke could see a lobby with chandeliers and velvet settees.

He nodded as a group of women passed. He wondered if Michelle would be the type to wear jeans or a dress to a Broadway play. Brooke would definitely have worn a dress, something comfortable but still dressy. How different things would be if he was seeing the musical with her. If they went as a date, and not as friends. If the stupid rules weren't in place.

A woman broke away from the crowd. "Luke?" Her voice was timid, and she was taller than he'd expected—at least five foot ten inches. Her hair was nearly the same chestnut color as Brooke's, but her eyes wider set and hazel instead of blue. Her lips were thinner too, her cheekbones not quite as high.

Stop comparing her. Step one to attaining Brooke was making sure Toujour succeeded and she didn't move to Italy. Which meant paying attention to his date.

Luke reached forward for a brief awkward hug. He saw a camera flash, but this time the paparazzi were being discreet. *Maybe because it's a more formal location. They don't want to get thrown out.* "It's nice to meet you, Michelle."

"It's nice to meet you, too." They both stood there for a moment. Luke hated this part of first dates—the part where he didn't know what to say or how to behave.

"Shall we go inside?" Luke asked, gesturing toward the doors.

Michelle nodded. Luke showed the usher at the door their tickets. He didn't touch Michelle, but unlike his date with Tamera, he didn't feel like she expected him to hold her hand. They made their way past the velvet settees and grand piano that filled the room with music. At the correct door, another usher took their ticket stubs. Michelle looked around in awe as they walked down the aisle to their seats on the mezzanine floor.

"It's beautiful," she said. She pointed to the ornate crown molding painted gold. "I've always loved that style."

"It's great," Luke agreed, although he hadn't really paid attention until she pointed it out. He found the correct row and stepped aside to let Michelle enter first.

"These are fantastic seats," she said. "I can't believe Toujour got such great tickets at such late notice. I wonder how they do that."

"I'm not sure. Brooke always takes care of it."

"Well, this is fabulous. I've been dying to see *The Lion King*. When I told my second graders that I was going tonight, they were so jealous. I promised them I'd memorize the important details and tell them all about it."

That's right—she taught school. "That's really cool," Luke said lamely.

"We're doing a unit on animals right now, and we just finished studying the lion. We've learned all about their habitats and lives. We went on a field trip to the zoo today to celebrate the end of the term."

Michelle prattled on about her job as a teacher, and Luke tried to respond appropriately. But his mind kept wandering to Brooke. If she were here, she'd point out the couple a few rows ahead who were clearly having a fight, or admire the African designs in a brilliant gold on the stage curtain, or laugh at the usher who was trying to help a confused elderly couple find their seats. He was grateful when the lights dimmed and the production began so he could sit back and not have to try and keep up a conversation with Michelle.

An hour and a half later, the lights went up again for intermission. "Wow," Michelle said, fanning herself with the playbill. "This is awesome."

"They're doing a great job," Luke agreed. But the truth was, the production was kind of boring. Broadway wasn't really his thing.

You wouldn't be bored if you were here with Brooke.

He quickly brushed the thought aside. He and Brooke were . . . well, whatever. Right now his priority was making sure Michelle had a good time, and that nothing happened the press would consider headline news. At least, not the bad kind.

"Excuse me," a voice called from the aisle. A camera flash nearly blinded Luke. The woman dropped the camera, held around her neck by a strap. "Samantha Hamilton, *California Globe*. Can I get a statement from you two?"

Luke shifted uncomfortably in his seat. Would fooling the press ever get easier? "Of course," he said. "As long as my date doesn't mind."

Michelle gave a tight smile. "Not a problem."

Samantha nodded, pressing a switch on her hand-held recorder and holding it toward them. "Can I get your name for the article?"

"Michelle."

Samantha frowned. "Last name?"

Michelle's expression didn't change. "Just Michelle."

Samantha grunted. "What do you think of the cast's production of *The Lion King*?"

"It's great," Luke said. "I'm thoroughly enjoying myself."

"Mmm-hmm," Michelle agreed.

Samantha frowned, as though they were patients being difficult during a medical exam. "What can you tell us about yourself? America is dying to know who Luke Ryder is dating now."

"I'm a second grade teacher." Michelle shrugged, as though there was nothing more to tell.

"Uh-huh. And how's the date going?" Samantha asked.

Luke wished a hole would open up in the floor and swallow him. Pretending was exhausting. "I can't speak for my date, but I'm enjoying myself. Michelle is a great girl."

"Yeah, Luke's great," Michelle echoed.

Go away, Luke telepathically told Samantha. But of course it didn't work.

The theater lights flashed on and off, a signal the musical would begin again in five minutes. "One last question, and then I'll let you get back to the show," Samantha said. "This is the one America is dying to have answered. Luke Ryder, will you end this date with a kiss, or will you end it with another drunken brawl?"

Luke's hands curled around the playbill, and he wished he could smack Samantha with it. "We really should get back to the show," he said.

"Are you deliberately avoiding my question?"

Luke glanced over at Michelle. "You're making my date uncomfortable, Ms. Hamilton."

An usher appeared then, his face pulled into a scowl. "Miss, you can't use cameras in here. I'll need to hold on to that until after the show is over."

"I'm not giving you my camera," Samantha said.

"Intermission's over. If you want to argue, you'll have to step into the hallway with me. Otherwise, hand over the camera."

"Where is your manager?" Samantha demanded. "I want to speak with him immediately."

The usher's scowl deepened. "Right this way."

Samantha angrily stomped after him.

Luke laughed uncomfortably. "Sorry about that."

Michelle's nose wrinkled in disgust. "Are they always so invasive?"

"Unfortunately, yeah."

The lights dimmed. "I'm glad I'm not you then," she whispered as the curtains opened.

The rest of the play was just as good as the first half, but all Luke wanted was to go home. To cuddle up next to Brooke and watch a movie. After the final number, the audience gave the cast a standing ovation. Then the lights flicked on and the auditorium started to empty. Michelle and Luke followed the crowd outside. The cool December air was a welcome relief after the stuffy building.

"I have reservations at a dessert café down the street if you're interested," Luke said. *Please say you're tired or too busy or need to wash your hair and get home.*

"That sounds great," Michelle said, buttoning her coat against the chill.

"Do you mind walking? It's only a block away."

"Sure."

They headed in the direction opposite the parking lot. The street was calm and peaceful, but the silence made Luke uncomfortable.

"Did you enjoy the musical?" he asked. There had to be something they could talk about. How long would dessert take? If they ordered right away and he asked for the check with the meal, they could probably be in and out in thirty minutes.

"I did. I wish my class could've seen it. But alas, public schools don't have the budget for that kind of field trip. Getting them to let me take the kids to the zoo was like pulling teeth."

"That bad, huh?"

"Yeah. I love my job, but I don't love the funding issues and parent complaints and politics that come with it. I'll miss the kids, but when the time comes to quit I won't miss anything else."

Luke shoved his hands in his pockets. "You're planning on quitting soon?"

Michelle blushed. "Well, no. Not until I get married and have a baby at least. But when I do have kids, I'd like to stay home with them."

And now they were talking about marriage. *Brooke, the things I do for you.* "That's rare these days. That a woman wants to stay home with her children, I mean."

"I'm old fashioned, I suppose."

"I think it's refreshing. My mom stayed home while raising me." Luke held the door open for Michelle. The restaurant wasn't what he'd expected. The maître d' stood at a rustic podium. Luke squinted. A plaque on the front read *made from recycled barn wood.*

"Just two?" the maître d' asked.

Luke nodded, and they were soon seated at a table, also made from recycled materials. Luke perused the menu and was pleased to see the options weren't too weird. This seemed like the type of place that would serve wheat grass shakes.

"This looks great," Luke said. "Order anything you'd like."

Michelle smiled. "What are you going to have?"

"I think a slice of pecan pie. What about you?"

Michelle scanned the menu. "Wow, they have so many vegan options."

Suddenly the restaurant made sense. "That's right. Brooke mentioned you're vegan."

"Yeah, for three years now. When I found out how the animals we use for nourishment are treated, I couldn't stomach the thought of animal products anymore."

"Uh-huh."

The waiter appeared then, and they both placed their orders. Luke was already out of things to say.

Michelle smiled, and her eyes were warm and understanding. "You can quit trying."

Luke's heart stopped beating, then thrummed loudly in his chest. "Excuse me?"

"I know there isn't going to be a second date. This, us . . ." She motioned between them. "There's no chemistry."

Luke glanced around, but there were no paparazzi in sight. "I'm sorry," he said weakly.

"Don't be. I couldn't handle this anyway." She waved a hand vaguely in his direction.

He winced. "Ouch. Thanks."

She laughed. "I didn't mean it like that. I just couldn't handle being in the spotlight all the time. The fame." She shrugged. "It's not for me. And I know if most girls in America heard me saying that right now, they would freak out and call me crazy."

"I don't think you're crazy. I appreciate your candor, in fact. Now we can enjoy our dessert without the pressure."

As though the waiter had heard them, he appeared with their food right then. Luke dug into the pie. Fantastic.

"There's someone else, isn't there?" Michelle asked.

Luke blinked. "Excuse me?"

"There's another girl."

"How did you know?"

"I can just tell. You don't act like a single man. You're emotionally married to someone already." Michelle paused, her fork creating designs in the whipped cream of her trifle. "Is it Brooke? She shows up in the papers with you a lot."

Luke rubbed his eyes. "Please don't tell anyone."

"I won't breathe a word." They were quiet for a few minutes as they ate. "I hope you get her."

"What?"

"Brooke. I hope you win her over."

"It's complicated."

"How complicated?"

Luke smiled grimly. "You really must not read the papers. She's engaged."

"Oh. That does make things more difficult. But not impossible."

"What do you mean?"

The waiter brought the check then, and Luke paid the bill. He wanted to resume the conversation, but waited until they were walking to the theater parking lot before repeating his question.

"I've waited my whole life to fall in love," Michelle said. "I know I'm not exactly a spinster, but it still feels like I've been waiting forever. If I felt about a man the way I can see you feel about Brooke, I would never let him go."

They paused in front of a car that was obviously Michelle's. An elementary school decal was in the back window, and her steering wheel cover looked like crayons. Michelle toyed with the keys in her hand.

"What would you do to keep him around?" Luke asked.

Michelle grinned. "Whatever it takes."

"All's fair in love and war."

"Exactly."

Luke leaned forward and hugged Michelle, feeling genuinely grateful to be on this date for the first time all night. "Thanks. I had a great time."

"Me too." Michelle unlocked the car, and he held the door open for her. "Fight for her, Luke. Don't let her get away."

Luke stood in the parking lot, watching until Michelle's tail lights disappeared around the corner. Michelle was absolutely right. He needed to fight for Brooke.

He just wasn't sure how.

Chapter Twenty-Four

Brooke leaned back in her office chair, closed her eyes, and breathed deeply. In. Out. In. Out. She focused on the sound of Zoey typing away, trying to time a breath with every third or fourth click.

Ten minutes and Luke would be here to discuss his Friday night date.

Her stomach twisted, and her breaths grew shaky instead of steady.

The weekend had been filled with pointed comments from Antonio about Italy's many virtues. On Saturday, they'd visited the vineyard where the wedding would take place. As they talked over table placement and ceremony space with the wedding planner, Brooke found herself wondering if she even wanted the wedding to happen. It left her feeling confused and guilty, and trying overly hard to be upbeat and enthusiastic.

Antonio was exactly the kind of guy she needed. He had a solid family life. He valued commitment and loyalty. They were compatible in all the ways they needed to be. And she really, truly loved him.

But Luke . . .

"Are you going to be okay?"

Brooke slowly opened her eyes and focused on Zoey. Her brow was scrunched over heavily made up eyes, and her arms were folded across her chest. "I'll be fine," Brooke said.

Zoey raised a skeptical eyebrow. "Brooke, it shouldn't be this hard."

"What are you talking about?"

"If you really wanted to spend the rest of your life with Antonio, it wouldn't matter what Luke did or said."

"It doesn't matter," Brooke said quickly.

Zoey let out a harrumph.

"You shouldn't be talking about this. Luke will be here any moment," Brooke said. She glanced around to make sure he hadn't sneaked up behind her. But all that was behind her was another cubicle wall and the gentle murmur of co-workers chatting.

"I could talk until I was blue in the face, but it's pointless. You're too stubborn." Zoey stood, grabbing her laptop. "I'm here if you need me. You know that, right?"

"I know. Thanks, Zo."

Zoey nodded and left for one of the parlours.

Despite Christmas being only two days away, the phone lines still buzzed on Lianna's desk, and the chatter of matchmakers and clients alike filled all corners of the building. Luke's celebrity status was still helping bring business in. That was something, at least.

Brooke took one last deep breath, then grabbed her own laptop and headed for a parlour. She shut the door behind her, blocking out the noise of Toujour. The sudden silence was welcoming. She wanted to kick off her shoes, sink into one of the arm chairs, and sleep away the disaster that was her life.

If only it were that easy.

She settled into a chair, shoes still firmly on her feet, and brought up Luke's file. What would he say about his date with Michelle? Brooke had selected her carefully. Her gentle personality would complement Luke's. And she definitely wasn't the type to get hung up on his celebrity status.

There was a tap on the door.

Brooke's stomach was suddenly in her throat. She set her laptop on the coffee table and opened the door. Luke looked like an ad for menswear, with his suit hugging him in all the right places and the five o'clock shadow across his strong jaw, and he smelled like spearmint toothpaste. Her breath hitched, and she forced herself to look away.

"Right on time," she said, shutting the door. "I've got your file all pulled up—"

He crushed her to him in a hug, knocking the wind out of her. She didn't mind, though. Not even a little bit. Instead she melted against him, without consciously giving herself permission to do so.

"I love you," he whispered in her ear.

Brooke stiffened, pushing him away. "You can't keep saying that."

"It's true. I'll keep saying it every time I see you, whether you like it or not."

Brooke swallowed, her brain jumping from outrage to jittery happiness quickly enough to make her nauseous. She couldn't even think clearly enough to pick out which rule he was violating. The best course of action was probably to ignore him.

She sat down, pulling her laptop toward her. "On a scale of one to ten, ten being the highest, how would you rate your physical attraction to Michelle?"

"You can't avoid me forever."

Brooke curled her fingers against the keyboard. "Please, I'm working right now. Just answer the question."

"A three."

"A three?" Brooke stared at him in disbelief. She had worked hard to find a good match for Luke, despite her growing misgivings. "Michelle is beautiful. She's cultured and well-educated."

"I agree."

"She's perfect relationship material."

"Absolutely."

"Then why aren't you attracted to her?"

"Because I'm in love with you."

She gritted her teeth. He was impossible. "Stop it. You don't get to do this right now."

"When would be a better time for you?"

Never. She'd just keep ignoring him. Maybe he'd get the hint eventually. "Okay, you were only attracted to her on a three. Next question—what do you feel was the best part of your date?"

"The part where she told me she hoped I could win you over, and if she loved someone as much as I clearly love you, she'd fight for that person."

Brooke slammed the lid closed on her laptop. "You talked to Michelle about me?" Her hands trembled as she set her laptop on the coffee table. She was worried she'd throw it across the parlour if she didn't. "What if the press finds out about that? I could get fired. Toujour could be ruined."

"We were discreet, and the conversation only lasted a minute at most."

"You're undermining my efforts to save the company."

279

"I'm not trying to."

"I can't deal with this right now." Her foot tapped against the floor at a rapid pace.

"I will do anything to convince you we're meant to be together."

"We aren't meant to be together. I'm meant to be with Antonio." The suspicious earring flashed into her mind, but she pushed it aside.

"I believe you love Antonio. But he can't live up to the eight years of history we've had together. He wasn't there for your graduation from high school, or college. He didn't take you to the winter formal or senior prom. You didn't spend spring break in Miami Beach with him. He wasn't the one who comforted you after your parents' divorce and at your grandpa's funeral. A relationship, a life together, is made up of memories. And we have a thousand of those."

Brooke wanted to put a shoe through the pewter gray wall. "Yeah, we have those memories. But I have a lot of other memories, Luke. Memories of the women I found you with when I stopped by with donuts on Saturday mornings in college. Memories of finding you necking in the corner of some club. Memories of you flirting with me, and making me feel like the only girl in the world, only to turn around and do the exact same thing with someone you'd just met." Brooke lowered her voice to a harsh whisper. "If you love me so much, why have you spent most of the last eight years sleeping with other women?"

He blinked, clearly taken aback by that question. "Well . . . I . . ."

"You can't answer that, can you? I love you, Luke. I do. And our friendship means everything to me. But I can't love you like that."

"I haven't been with another woman in months. I'm changing."

"Prove it." She stood and grabbed her laptop. "This meeting is over. With Christmas, it'll be a week or so before I can find you another date. I'll let you know."

Chapter Twenty-Five

She was on a beach with Luke. He looked glorious in his swim trunks. A wave crashed into his legs, and Brooke laughed as he grimaced at the shock of cold. His bronzed skin glistened in the sun, and rivulets of water ran down his well-defined abs.

"Come in," he called, motioning to her.

Brooke shrank against her beach towel, warm from the sun. "No way."

"Don't make me come get you."

"You wouldn't dare."

He sloshed through the water, making his way back to shore. Brooke shrieked and leapt up, running away. Luke caught her around the waist and she laughed. He threw her over his shoulder and headed toward the ocean while she giggled and protested the whole way.

"*Buon natale, mia dolcezza.*" Warm lips caressed her cheek.

Brooke's eyes popped open. Antonio leaned over her, smiling. His curls were messy and matted down on one side, evidence that he'd just woken up himself. The plum colored sheets were soft underneath her skin, the beige walls familiar.

She wasn't on a beach with Luke. She was in her own bedroom with Antonio. Her cheeks heated as she recalled the dream. What was wrong with her?

It's just a stupid dream, she told herself. It meant nothing. She wrapped her arms around his neck, kissing him back. "Merry Christmas."

"I made you breakfast," he said. "An American breakfast, even. Cinnamon rolls."

"Sounds delicious." Her heart pricked with guilt. Antonio was perfect. So why was she pining over Luke?

They spent a leisurely morning together, just the two of them. Zoey had gone home to San Diego for a few days, and so they had the apartment to themselves. After breakfast they sat around the small Christmas tree and opened presents, then they called their families. Brooke's mom had elected to go to Mexico with a recently widowed friend, and Brooke wasn't ready to spend a major holiday with her dad.

After they hung up with Antonio's family in Italy, they settled down to watch Christmas movies. When the third one was over, Brooke rose and stretched. She'd been sitting too long. She grabbed the bowl of popcorn and headed to the kitchen.

Antonio followed with their glasses. "Have you had a good Christmas?" he asked.

"I have." Brooke gave him a quick kiss, then opened the dishwasher and put the bowl and glasses inside. "Have you?"

"*Sì.*"

Brooke smiled and started the dishwasher. She rinsed out a rag and started wiping down the counters.

"The gallery's pushing for an answer. They want me in Rome by March first."

Brooke tossed the rag in the sink and stared at Antonio. "I thought they were willing to wait until after the wedding."

He looked away. "This is my career we're talking about. I've worked my whole life for this type of opportunity."

"And I've worked my whole life for my career. A career that brought you and me together, I might add."

Antonio leaned against the counter and folded his arms. "That's not fair. Charlotte's already offered to transfer you to Rome. If I stay here, I'll never be the gallery's top seller. They'll find another artist, one who's close by and easier to work with, and start promoting him. I won't make it if we stay."

But I won't be happy if we move.

The realization hit like a ton of bricks. *I'm an idiot.* She had thought her hesitation was due to Toujour and the unexpected timing. But the reason she wouldn't be happy in Italy would be because Luke wouldn't be there.

She squeezed her eyes shut tight. Luke, who claimed to be in love with her. Luke, who had put forth his best foot on every Toujour date. Who was working twelve hour days to try to revive Ryder Communications. Who, now that she thought about it, didn't drink anymore.

He's changing.

"Brooke?"

She blinked, bringing Antonio and the black IKEA cabinets he stood in front of back into focus. "Do we have to talk about this today? It's Christmas."

"Time's running out."

She blew out a breath and nodded. "You're right. Let's talk about it." She walked around the counter and to the square dining room table, with its four mismatched chairs. Eclectic, Zoey called them.

Brooke pulled back a chair, and Antonio did the same. She pushed the table centerpiece aside—a square glass vase with artificial lilies—so that it didn't obstruct his face.

"Why don't you want to move?" Antonio asked.

"Toujour is doing great right now. Our clientele is growing like crazy, and Charlotte said we're finally in the black. How can I turn down my dream promotion to move to Italy? I might wait years before I can become head of the office there." She felt like a liar for not admitting her true reservations. But not wanting to move away from Luke didn't mean she wanted a relationship with him beyond what they already had.

"How can I tell the gallery I'm staying in Los Angeles for my wife's job?"

The words were a sucker punch to the gut. "My job isn't as important as yours," Brooke said.

He fiddled with the flower arrangement. "That's not what I meant."

"Then what did you mean?"

"You said if I let you do this thing with Luke, you would consider Italy."

Brooke spread her fingers wide on the table, pressing them into the smooth wood. Trying to keep herself from screaming. "Yeah, *consider* it. And I have. But my life is here. My parents. My half-siblings."

"Luke."

Brooke sucked in a breath and held it. "Yeah. And Luke."

Antonio stood with a curse. "Once again you are putting your friendship with him first."

"It's not just him. It's everything." Brooke ran a hand through her hair. "You sprung this on me without warning. We had plans I was counting on. You can't move up our timeline five years and expect me to grin and say 'let's do it.' This is my home."

"And Italy is mine." He sat back down, this time next to her. "Just like your family is here, my family is there. My *genitori*. My *nonni* and *fratelli*. And now my job is there." He rubbed the back of her neck with one hand.

She leaned forward, resting her head on the table. She closed her eyes as he slowly worked out the knots at the base of her skull. Seventy-one percent compatible. Luke was messing with her head, and she couldn't let him. She and Antonio were meant for each other.

"The only thing not in Italy is you," Antonio said.

His words sank in, and Brooke didn't like what her head told her she must do. Antonio seemed to sense she was at the breaking point, because he kept talking.

"You will love Rome. We can do all the things we talked about . . . visit the sites, eat gelato. The studio will help us find housing and get settled. You can still work for Toujour. You'd probably even like it better there—Italians love a good matchmaker." He wiggled his eyebrows, and Brooke let out an involuntary laugh. "I probably even have cousins who would want to sign on as clients."

"What about the wedding?"

He kissed her temple. "I've already promised we can get married here, in California. Planning will be more difficult from Italy, but not impossible. And we can take our honeymoon in Paris instead of Mexico."

"That's not fair." Brooke gave him a teasing kiss. "You shouldn't get to bribe me with Parisian honeymoons."

"I want us to be happy. And I know we can be happy in Italy."

Brooke played with Antonio's hands, tracing the flecks of paint there. "I thought we were happy here."

He flipped his hands so they were holding hers and squeezed. "We *are* happy, *mia dolcezza*. But we'll be even happier there."

"When do they want an answer by?"

"New Year's."

Brooke's stomach tightened. "That's only a week away."

"I know. I can probably hold them off another week past that."

She closed her eyes, trying to get used to the idea. Italy. She pictured a small apartment over a bakery. Holding hands as they perused a produce stand. Having Antonio's parents over for Christmas Eve dinner. It was a nice picture, one she could get used to. Except Luke wouldn't be there. No more seeing each other almost daily. Lives lived apart.

Antonio or Luke. She was going to have to pick one or the other.

Antonio brushed a curl out of his eyes, a grin touching the corners of his mouth. "C'mon, let's watch another movie."

She hoped she could live with her choice.

Chapter Twenty-Six

Brooke rubbed her eyes, feeling the sting from staring too long at a computer screen.

Four first dates. In the last week, Luke had been on four first dates and no second dates. The press was eating it up, but they had started to speculate the reason Luke hadn't made it to date number two was because of Brooke.

Brooke scrolled through the database again, trying to block out the noise of Lianna's incessantly ringing phone at reception. She had to find someone Luke would like. She prayed she wouldn't. Things were such a jumbled mess. She wanted to rewind time to before Luke confessed his love, before Rick's cancer and death, when things had been easy and simple.

Do you want to rewind before Antonio, too?

No. Despite how hard Luke had tried to convince her otherwise, she was grateful to have Antonio in her life.

Zoey sank into her desk chair, a big grin on her face. "Lianna said she just entered forty new clients into the database."

"Forty more this morning?"

Zoey nodded. "You're a genius, Brooke. Our numbers are up nearly eight hundred percent since November. And it's all thanks to your brilliant idea and Luke's willingness to play along."

Brooke rubbed her temples. "Great," she said, voice flat.

Zoey frowned. "What's wrong?"

"Luke is what's wrong. Again." Brooke motioned to the computer screen. "Over three hundred women, and I can't find one I think Luke will go on a second date with. If he doesn't stick with one for a while soon, the press is going to think Toujour doesn't work."

"Run his profile against yours. I bet you're a perfect match."

Brooke glared. "Not funny."

"Hit refresh." Zoey spun around to face her own computer. "Maybe one of the new girls will be his fake match."

"Haha." But Brooke did as Zoey suggested and started going through the list of new women.

And that's when she saw her. Andi, a socialite with wealthy parents and a law degree. She was beautiful, with dark blonde hair and tanned skin. Brooke clicked, opening up her hobbies. Tennis, spin classes, and old movies. There wasn't a lot to go on yet, since Andi hadn't completed the intake appointment and therefore hadn't filled out her complete profile. But she looked promising.

"Looks like she's been assigned to me," Zoey said. Her face practically rested on Brooke's shoulder.

Brooke jumped, putting a hand to her chest. "Don't do that."

"Sorry." Zoey looked unrepentant. Her arms were folded across her chest and she still peered over Brooke's shoulder at the computer screen.

"Yeah, she is your client," Brooke said. "Looks like you have your first appointment scheduled with her today."

"Want me to see if she's interested in a date with Luke?"

No. "Feel her out to see if she'd be a good match first, since we don't have much to go on yet. But yeah." Brooke's gut told her Andi and Luke would get along very well.

"I'll make sure to let her know it's strictly for show and Luke is off limits."

"Zoey!"

"What? He is. At least until you figure out what you're going to do."

"I've already figured out what I'm going to do," Brooke said. "Talk to Andi."

"I don't know if I can do it, Mitch." Luke ran the miniature rake through his tabletop Zen garden, creating abstract designs in the sand.

Mitch clapped Luke on the back in sympathy. "Another blind date?"

"Yeah." Luke dropped the rake and ran a hand through his hair. "These dates are killing me." Christmas had been bad enough, with uncharacteristically impersonal gifts exchanged between him and Brooke. And it had been a hard day without his father. He'd been on four first dates since the holidays, bringing his total up to six. Four dates in a week. It had been exhausting. The women had been nice enough, but none of them were Brooke.

"Who's up this time?" Mitch asked. He grabbed two sodas from the mini fridge and slid one across the desk to Luke. The sunlight streaming in from the window glinted off the aluminum can, momentarily blinding him.

Luke popped the top and took a swig, blinking to clear his vision. "Her name's Andi. She's a lawyer from a socialite family. Brooke seems confident." His shoulders hunched. He didn't want Brooke to be confident. He wanted her to set him up with horrible women she knew he would hate and never want a relationship with.

But it hadn't happened. There was nothing really wrong with any of the girls. They just weren't the girl for him.

"Where's the date this time?" Mitch asked.

Luke made a face. "Ice skating. It's supposed to be romantic or some crap like that." He motioned to the stack of blueprints in front of him. "Tell the Talia Team I've signed off on these and they can get to work running the final test cycles tomorrow. We're already a week behind schedule, and we can't delay the relaunch any longer."

Mitch nodded, making a note on his tablet. "I'll do that before I leave tonight."

"Thanks." Luke rose, slipping into his coat. "I still need to go home and change. If I don't leave now I'll be late, and Brooke will hate that."

Ice skating. Honestly, what was Brooke thinking? The whole thing was a little too romantic.

"See if you can beat your last date record of two hours," Mitch said with a smirk. "I've got ice cold sodas at my place and the game if you can."

"You got it."

295

An hour later, Luke parked his car and walked into the skating rink. The temperature dropped ten degrees as soon as he walked inside, and he buttoned his coat to ward off the chill. He should've brought gloves. The smell of nachos wafted over from the snack stand, and he inhaled sharply. They'd definitely need to get some of those tonight.

The floor squeaked as his soles rubbed across it with each step. It was a strange plastic material with raised dots, probably so you could safely walk on it in ice skates.

His eyes swept past the skate rental counter and snack bar, searching for Andi. He found her leaning against the white ticket counter in the center of the room. The nicely tanned skin and honey blonde hair unmistakably matched the picture Brooke had shown him. A red scarf was wrapped tightly around her neck. The man behind the desk was grinning as Andi laughed.

So she was a natural flirt. Then why wasn't she already in a relationship? Luke pulled out his phone and checked the picture again, just to make sure. Yup, it was her.

Andi looked up as though sensing his presence. She grinned, said something to the man, and walked toward Luke.

"Hi," she said, her voice still bubbling with laughter. She stuck out a hand in an oddly formal gesture. "I'm Andi."

Luke took the hand uncertainly. "Luke." He motioned to the counter. "Shall we get our tickets and skates?"

"Sure." Andi fell into step beside him. "I really hate first dates, don't you?"

Luke's eyebrow hitched. This was new.

The man behind the counter glared at Luke, seeming to realize Andi was there for him.

"Two tickets," Luke said. The jilted employee quickly completed the transaction, stamping their hands so they'd be admitted to the rink.

"First dates are so awkward and uncomfortable," Andi continued as soon as they moved away from the ticket counter. "Agonizingly painful experiences, and you've had some real doozies lately. At least according to the press. I was thinking, let's pretend we're not on a date. Let's pretend we're friends. Sound good?"

"Sounds great, actually," Luke said. But he couldn't stop the suspicion from crowding in on him.

They picked up their ice skates and found an unoccupied bench. They sat down and unlaced their shoes.

"So what brings you to Toujour?" Luke asked. It had become his standard question when the conversation lagged.

Andi flipped her hair over her shoulder and stood on wobbly legs. "My best friend," she said. Luke rose, and they baby-stepped their way across the floor. Andi grabbed onto the plexiglass wall surrounding the rink and carefully stepped onto the ice. Luke was right behind her.

"Your best friend," Luke said. "There's gotta be a story there." Hopefully not one similar to his. He wouldn't wish that on his worst enemy.

Andi laughed. They tentatively started skating, sticking close to the wall. "Oh, there is. It's kind of Rachel's fault my high school sweetheart dumped me six months ago. She's a newlywed and seems to think I will only be able to heal from the indignity of being dumped once married. Whoa." An ice skater flew past them and she stumbled. Luke stuck out an arm to catch her. *Click.* Some lucky cameraman had caught the moment.

"Thanks," Andi said. "Anyway, Rachel can be relentless, and she pre-paid for three months at Toujour and gave it to me as a Christmas present. I figured it would be easier to go along with it than to try to convince her I'm over Mark. That's why I was excited when Zoey told me they'd matched us up. I knew you weren't looking for serious either."

Luke grabbed her hand, pulling her to a stop. "What makes you say that?"

Andi rolled her eyes, pulling him forward. "Oh, c'mon. You're totally gone on Brooke. It's obvious even from photos. Aren't you two best friends or something?"

"Or something," Luke agreed.

"Yeah, I'm 'or something' too." Andi sighed. "I think I might have a crush on Rachel's brother."

"Then why don't you go out with him?"

"It's complicated. I don't think any of our friends or family would exactly be thrilled. But you . . . ha!" She shook her head, sending locks bouncing around her shoulders. "My parents and Rachel will die when they see the papers tomorrow. Definitely no 'you need to find a nice guy to date and get over Mark' conversations this week. Take that, Rache."

Luke had no idea what to make of this woman. None of his dates had gone like this. "I, uh . . ."

Andi spun around, grabbing his hands and skating backward so they faced each other. Her hands were warm and soft, a sharp contrast to his chilled one. "Don't tell me Luke Ryder is without words." She grinned.

"I don't know what to make of you."

"There's nothing to make of me." Andi shrugged. "I'm just me. So, tell me about Brooke."

Luke glanced around, wondering if a reporter was on the rink. But since it was a Monday, there weren't too many skaters out, and none of them were close by. "I'd rather not."

"Oh, psh. No one's listening here. And if they are and somehow print our conversation, I'll sue them for unlawful invasion of privacy."

Luke laughed. He let Andi pulled him forward. "Is that even a real thing?"

"I'll make it a real thing, then I'll sue them. I'm very good at my job." Andi let go of one of his hands and moved so they were skating side by side again. But she didn't let go of his other hand. "So what's the deal with you and Brooke?"

A skater flew past, and Andi and Luke both wobbled on their skates. Andi laughed as they slowed to a snail's pace.

"I love her, but she's getting married to someone else," Luke said.

"Yeah, that sucks. What are you going to do about it?"

"I told her I loved her."

Andi shook her head. "Not good enough. Women respond to actions, not words."

"What, like I'm supposed to overwhelm her apartment with flowers and chocolates?"

Again she shook her head. "You're rich—buying things takes no effort or sacrifice. You have to do something to really show her you're committed. That she means more to you than anything. You know—the big gesture."

"A big gesture, huh?"

Andi nodded.

"If I save Toujour, that'll go a long way toward convincing her. If I don't, she's moving to Italy."

"Well, that fits in with my plans perfectly then."

Luke chuckled. "Ah, you do have ulterior motives."

"Obviously. I need Rache off my back for a few months. But my plans benefit you too. I think we can help each other. You need a fake relationship for the papers. I need a fake relationship so Rachel can stop feeling guilty." She grinned. "Well, what do you say?"

It was crazy. There were so many ways this could blow up in his face.

But it also could be just what he needed. What Toujour wanted.

Luke pulled her closer, tightening his grip on her hand. He hoped the photographers got a picture. "You make a persuasive argument. Deal."

Chapter Twenty-Seven

*B*rooke chewed on her nail, her foot tapping impatiently as she waited for Luke to arrive. She half-listened to the phone conversation Zoey was having with a client. Zoey shot her a questioning look, and Brooke shook her head.

She hated this part of it—hearing how his dates went. She was equal parts elated and disappointed when things never seemed to pan out. On the one hand, it had her questioning her matchmaking abilities. On the other hand, there was still a chance.

A chance for what? she silently demanded. She grabbed the framed photo of her and Antonio off her desk and forced herself to stare at it.

She'd mailed the save the dates yesterday. Antonio never had gotten around to helping her address them. She should've mailed them before Christmas, but things kept getting in the way.

But what about Luke? her brain screamed.

Miss Match

What about him? Yeah, he's in love with me right now. But in six months? His relationships never last. If we dated, our friendship would be doomed.

A hand landed on her shoulder. "Hey," Luke said.

"Hey," Brooke said. A month ago, she would've leaned in for a hug. But now . . .

The poster on the wall of a happy couple laughed at her.

Brooke unplugged her laptop and headed toward one of the parlours, Luke following behind her. These days, Toujour was a constant hive of activity. Matchmakers tapped away on their laptops, and the parlours were almost always full. Brooke shut the door behind them in the parlour she'd scheduled and sat down. She opened her laptop and focused on Luke. No, focusing on Luke was a bad idea. Then she had to look into the depths of his cerulean blue eyes and see the emotion there.

"You know the drill," Brooke said.

"Hotness factor—a solid eight."

Brooke's hand stilled over the keyboard. He hadn't rated any of the other girls higher than a six.

"I want a second date."

Brooke's heart thudded in her chest until the only sound was the blood pumping through her veins. *Not happening, not happening, not happening.*

No, this is a good thing. For him and Toujour.

"Okay . . ." *Act professional. Be the matchmaker, not the best friend who is desperately in love with him.*

Wait. What?

"Andi's a great girl," Luke continued. "It won't be difficult to spend more time with her."

And just like that, Brooke's worry faded. *Same old Luke.* What was she thinking? In *love* with him? That was a relationship that would go nowhere fast.

Brooke finished the rest of the questionnaire. Her heart sank lower and lower with each word he uttered. Luke liked this girl. She could tell.

"I'll talk to Zoey and see what Andi says," Brooke said as they finished up. "If she's interested in a second date, we'll get that set up."

"Thanks." Luke rose, and Brooke followed suit. "Brooke?"

"Yeah?"

"I'm only doing this for Toujour. I'm not going to fall in love with her."

Brooke hugged her laptop closer to her chest. *Love is friendship set to music.* She tore her eyes away from the quote on the wall. "Andi's a nice girl."

"Yeah, she is." Luke brushed a strand of hair behind Brooke's ear, and she flinched. "But I love you, Brooke. Always have. Always will."

Brooke's breath stalled, then rushed out in a gasp. "Why do you keep saying that?"

"Because it's true. And I'll keep reminding you of that every day until you believe it."

"Antonio's gallery is pushing for a March first move date. He was supposed to give them an answer almost a week ago." Brooke didn't know why she said it—it just came out.

Luke drew back. "You told him no, right? Toujour's doing great now. I'm sure Charlotte will make you head of the office in no time."

"Maybe it's better if I leave."

Luke's hand grasped hers. "You don't mean that."

"Luke." Brooke glanced at the door, making sure it was still solidly closed. It was, but she lowered her voice all the same. "I do. We can't . . ."

His fingers tightened around hers and he pulled her closer. "We can't what?"

"We can't do this."

"This?"

"This." She pulled her hand from his and motioned back and forth between them. "Us."

He swore. "Why not?"

She turned around and paced the small room, focusing on the dark wood floor. "Because I'm engaged. Because you aren't ready for a relationship. Because it wouldn't work."

"I think the reason you aren't willing to try is because you're scared. You're scared because you know once you let yourself admit you don't want Antonio—that you want me—you'll be consumed by the feeling. You're worried because as soon as you let yourself care that much, you are no longer in control. You no longer get to decide whether or not your heart breaks. And you can't stand the idea of giving another human being that much power over you. Even me."

"I love Antonio." Brooke wanted to yell, scream, throw something. "Why doesn't anyone believe me when I say that?"

"Because it's not true." He pounded a fist against his chest. "It doesn't feel true."

"I need to go with him. I can't have you constantly trying to rip our marriage apart. You need to move on, get over me, find someone else. Maybe Andi can help." The words burned her tongue like acid.

Luke cursed. "I don't love Andi. I barely even know her. Don't leave. Don't do this to me."

She lowered her eyes, blinking back the tears that threatened to fall. Toujour was going to be okay. She'd accomplished her task of saving the office. But she needed to go with Antonio. "I think I have to."

Luke reached forward and grasped her arm. "Give me until the wedding. If you really go through with it and marry the guy, I'll back off. We will just pretend this" —he motioned between them— "never happened and things will go back to normal, whatever that means. But until you say 'I do,' there's still a chance. And I will fight with my last breath until that chance is gone. Think about that, Brooklyn." He opened the door and stormed out of the room.

Brooke stared at his retreating figure, her heart heavy in her chest. Zoey slipped into the room, shutting the door behind her.

"Please tell me the whole office didn't hear that," Brooke said.

"I think you're okay. I had to press my ear against the door in a decidedly unladylike fashion to make out the words. Everyone will just think you got in a heated argument."

Brooke put a hand to her face. "I can't believe this is happening. With Luke, of all people. It's so wrong."

"Or so right. You're not really going to go through with the wedding now, are you? The poor man is desperate. If you don't at least give him a chance, you'll always wonder about what might have been."

"I can't lose him as a friend."

"Honey, I think you already have. If you marry Antonio, things won't go back to normal between you and Luke. And what would Antonio say if he knew his wife was still hanging out with the man who tried to steal her away? That's not fair to anyone involved."

Brooke closed her eyes, willing her heart to stop constricting, her chest muscles to relax, her breathing to slow. *In, out. In, out. Just breathe.* "I don't know what to do. I've mailed the save the dates. Ordered the cake. Picked out a wedding dress. Antonio doesn't deserve this." Her voice broke. "I don't deserve him."

"No, you don't. You are way too good for him, and I really hope you figure that out before making the biggest mistake of your life. Because that's exactly what Antonio is—a big, fat mistake. He's an okay guy for someone else. But he's not for you." Zoey sat down in the chair Luke had occupied minutes before and opened the laptop. "Now, it gives me no pleasure to do this, but it's time to do our jobs. Andi had a great time with Luke and would love a second date. What did he say?"

Brooke swallowed. "He wants to see her again too."

It was agony to go over the date with Zoey. Andi appeared to have enjoyed herself as much as Luke had.

"It's all for show," Zoey assured Brooke as they finished up. "At least on Luke's end. I can't get a read on Andi quite yet. But she seems to feel more friend feelings for Luke than love feelings. I've gotta go meet another client, but try to not obsess, okay? I'm going to help you figure this thing out."

Brooke nodded mutely and walked back to her desk. But she couldn't help obsessing.

"Don't do this to me."

Brooke plugged her laptop in, trying to shake the conversation with Luke out of her head.

"I think the reason you aren't willing to try is because you're scared."

Eight years ago, Luke had told her he wanted them to date. And she had told him no, that their friendship was worth more than a high school fling. Then he had moved on to other women, rather quickly in fact, and she'd been convinced she'd made the right decision. But they weren't in high school anymore, and Luke was changing.

Brooke booted up her laptop and brought up Luke's profile.

"You're worried because as soon as you let yourself care that much, you are no longer in control. And you can't stand the idea of giving another human being that much power over you."

Brooke looked around to make sure she was alone. The cubicles next to hers and Zoey's were all either empty, or the matchmakers were distracted by work.

Brooke stared at Luke's profile picture, chewing on her lip. She hovered the pointer over *run compatibility match* and clicked. A screen popped up. *Run match against database or specific client?* it asked.

Brooke lightly tapped her index finger against the mouse. She was crazy to do this.

She had to know.

She clicked *specific client*. A new box popped up and the cursor blinked. Brooke glanced over her shoulder, then quickly typed *Brooklyn Pierce*.

Anther screen popped up. *This file is frozen. Do you still wish to run compatibility match?*

Brooke hit *yes*.

A progress bar appeared on the screen. Brooke watched as it slowly filled with green. One of the matchmaker's laughed, and Brooke jumped. Her cheeks burned. How would she explain this if she was caught?

She was only doing it for her own peace of mind. Just because she and Luke were compatible as friends didn't mean they were compatible as a couple. When the database proved that, she'd be able to put the whole thing out of her head forever and focus on Antonio.

Her heart twisted as she thought of him. She needed to come clean and tell him everything, and then they needed to go far away from Luke and focus on their new lives together. She closed her eyes against the pain.

The computer let out a chime. Brooke took a deep breath and opened her eyes.

Luke's profile picture was on one side of the screen, and Brooke's was on the other. Blinking between their photos was a giant, green number.

Eighty-three percent.

Chapter Twenty-Eight

She needed to tell Antonio about what was happening between her and Luke. She wanted to tell him.

She couldn't tell him.

Brooke sat on his worn couch, pretending to read but really watching Antonio paint. Light streamed in from the floor to ceiling windows, and she was tempted to snap a picture with her cell phone. The stark white of the canvas and the splattered paint on his jeans against the backdrop of exposed brick held a kind of beauty that almost made her want to take up painting herself. *Why can't I tell him? I should be able to tell him.*

The compatibility test meant nothing. She never should've run it. She'd had numerous couples ultimately end up with one of their less compatible matches. A computer generated number was only part of what made a match successful.

I have to tell him.

Antonio dropped his paintbrush onto the pallet and turned to face her. "What are you thinking about, my love?"

"You," Brooke said, forcing a smile.

He grinned, removing his painter's smock. He sank onto the couch and pulled her into his arms. "Mmm," he said, squeezing her tight. "You seem troubled, *mia dolcezza*. Tell me what's on your mind." He leaned down and slowly kissed her. "I want to help if I can."

Brooke turned her face into his chest so he wouldn't see the tears that threatened. She was as bad as her dad, thinking about Luke while promising her life to Antonio. It stopped here. She had made her decision, and she trusted that choice.

"I think we should move to Italy," Brooke said.

"Really?"

"Yeah. You were right. It's the best decision for us."

Antonio let out a whoop and jumped up, pulling her up with him. He kissed her soundly on the lips. "You won't regret this. We will have such a *fantastico* time in Rome. I already know what area of the city I want to look in for an *appartamento*. Oh, Brooke. We're doing the right thing."

"Yeah," Brooke agreed, forcing a smile. "Please, though, I don't want to tell anyone yet."

His brow furrowed. "They'll find out soon enough."

"I know. But I want the focus to be on Toujour right now." She looked down. "I need to find a way to tell Luke. He's going to be crushed."

Antonio's gaze darkened. "Is there something you need to tell me?"

Brooke frowned. "I think he loves me." *I know he does.*

Antonio cursed, stepping away. "I knew it."

Brooke grabbed his arm. "Nothing has happened between us, I swear. I've never so much as kissed him. But we need to get away. Please, don't tell anyone yet."

Antonio frowned, then nodded. "I can feel us pulling away from each other, Brooke."

"We won't let it happen."

He leaned forward and kissed her again. "I love you. Italy will be our fresh start."

Brooke smiled too. She wanted to feel elated. Any other girl would be thrilled to move to Italy with her new husband. But all Brooke could think about was Luke, and the ache in her heart that would never quite heal.

Why had he gone and ruined everything?

Brooke took a deep breath and knocked on her dad's door. Antonio's shoulder brushed against hers, a show of support that she appreciated. She wasn't comfortable coming here now that Lexi had moved in, but when she'd asked her dad what he wanted for his birthday, he insisted all he wanted was for her to visit.

The door opened, and Lexi let out a shrill laugh. "They're here, Daniel," she called over her shoulder.

Brooke tried not to let her annoyance at Lexi's presence show. Of course she would be here for the birthday dinner. "Hi, Lexi."

"I'm so glad you could come." Lexi shut the door behind them. "Let me take your coats."

Antonio and Brooke both handed over the coats and followed Lexi into the spacious kitchen. Dad stood behind the stainless steel stove. Brooke blinked and set the present she'd brought on the counter.

"Happy birthday," Brooke said. "If I'd known you were cooking, I would've insisted we go to a restaurant. I thought you were ordering in."

"Hey, Sugar Bee." Dad stepped away from the stove and gave Brooke a one-armed hug. "It's good to have you here."

"I'm not sure I'm in the right place," Brooke said. "I haven't seen you in a kitchen in at least twenty years."

"Lexi taught me how to caramelize almonds for the salad. I wanted to give it a try."

Miranda had been a professional chef, but Brooke had never seen Dad make the effort for her.

"Have you had a good birthday?" Antonio asked.

"A fantastic one. Lexi and I took the twins to a movie this morning, and tomorrow Shandi's bringing Jason by. I got to see all my kids for my birthday, which means it's perfect."

Brooke looked away, studying the flecks in the granite counter top. She wasn't sure how her dad's improved efforts to be a good father made her feel.

Soon they were all eating around the kitchen table. Brooke begrudgingly admitted that Lexi actually seemed like a very nice girl, cheating with a married man aside.

After dinner, they played a few games in the sun room, and then Antonio and Lexi got into a spirited debate about impressionist painters. "Let's leave them to it," Dad said, nudging Brooke with his shoulder.

Brooke looked at Antonio, who was still deep in conversation with Lexi. Brooke reluctantly nodded and followed her dad into the living room, sinking next to him on the leather couch.

"How's wedding planning going?" Dad asked, flinging an arm over the back of the couch.

"Okay." Brooke swallowed hard, gazing at the print of a Monet painting on one wall. She'd never seen it before. It must be one of Lexi's. Brooke had told her mom about Italy a few days ago. It was time to tell her dad, even if they were keeping it on the down low for everyone else. "Antonio accepted the position with the gallery. We're moving to Italy at the end of February. It's going to make wedding planning a bit more complicated."

Dad patted Brooke on the knee. "Well now." He cleared his throat and looked away. "I can't say I won't miss you. But if you're happy, I'm happy."

Brooke eyes brimmed with tears. She quickly blinked, pushing a few down her cheeks.

"You are happy, aren't you?"

"Of course."

Dad frowned. "Antonio isn't here right now, Brooklyn. I can hear him and Lexi still arguing in the sun room. What's going on?"

Brooke shook her head. She didn't want to have this conversation with her father. "Nothing."

"You can't lie to me. I know you too well."

Brooke laughed. "We've barely had a relationship since you left Mom."

"That hasn't been my choice." He frowned. "I haven't always been the best dad or role model. But you're still my little girl. And I know something's going on."

Brooke fiddled with a throw pillow. "Luke isn't too pleased about the move, that's all." Not that she'd worked up the courage yet to tell him they were definitely going.

Dad snorted. "Of course he isn't. Boy's been in love with you since high school."

"Dad."

"What? It's true. He loves you the way sugar loves to cause tooth decay."

Brooke rolled her eyes. "Wow, romantic."

Dad took her hand in his. "Why haven't you given that boy a chance?"

She pulled her hand away. "He's not relationship material."

"That's Nadeen talking, not you." He sighed. "I blame myself for that. I gave your mother plenty of reasons to hate men."

"You gave Shandi and Miranda plenty of reasons too."

"I know I'm not great at relationships, and I know I've given you a lot of baggage because of that. I'm sorry."

Brooke glanced at her father, surprised to see tears in his eyes. "Then go back to Miranda, Dad. Try to work it out for the twins' sake. Don't do to them what you've done to me and Jason."

"That ship has unfortunately sailed. But we aren't talking about me—we're talking about you and Luke. And Luke's been putting up a front so you don't see how much you're hurting him."

Brooke clutched her mug in her hands. *Eighty-three percent.* "Don't say that."

"Brooklyn, I'm only going to say this once—Antonio will never make you happy. Not really. He's a great guy. But not for you. Luke's the guy you love. Even the tabloids see it."

Tears dripped onto Brooke's pajama pants. "I don't love Luke like that."

"Yes, you do. And Brooke—he's not me."

Brooke gasped, her eyes flying to her father's.

Dad nodded, his own eyes sparkling with tears. "I know I've hurt you badly. And I know your mother and I turned you sour on relationships. And then me and Shandi. And now me and Miranda. But don't let my past rob you of your future. Talk to Luke. Give him a shot."

The talking in the sun room stopped, and Brooke quickly wiped at her eyes. "Sounds like they're done arguing," she mumbled. "I'd better go check on Antonio."

Dad grabbed her hand as she rose. "Don't write Luke off. And don't make your choice out of fear."

Antonio and Lexi appeared in the living room, both laughing. Brooke quickly went to his side. "Have a good conversation?" she asked.

He nodded, leaning down to kiss her. "I think I've finally convinced Lexi I'm in the right."

"Hardly. I agreed to disagree on the subject."

"Ready for dessert?" Lexi asked. "I made Daniel's favorite."

Brooke nodded. But all she could think about was the conversation with her father.

Chapter Twenty-Nine

Luke sat on the floor outside Brooke's apartment door, nervously tapping the box against his leg. *This is a stupid idea. I should leave before she sees me.*

If he wanted to give her a meaningful gift, Christmas would've been the appropriate time. But he hadn't thought of this idea until after the holiday.

He heard the ding of the elevator, saw the number for Brooke's floor light up above the elevator door, and tensed. It could be someone else on this floor. But it could be her. If he took the stairs, he could still leave before she saw him. Then a horrifying thought occurred to him—what if Antonio was with her?

He was about to stand and disappear into the stairwell when the elevator doors pinged open. Brooke stood there in her white peacoat, her pink Birkin bag slung over one shoulder. Alone. Luke blew out a breath and rose. "Hey," he said awkwardly.

"Hey. What are you doing here?"

He held up the package. "I brought you a present. Sorry I didn't call before dropping by." He'd been afraid she wouldn't answer, or would tell him to stay home.

Brooke's brow furrowed. "Oh." She shuffled her feet awkwardly. "You already gave me my Christmas present."

"This is different."

"Okay." She stared into his eyes, and he could feel her studying him, trying to figure out his angle. She unlocked her door. "Want to come in?"

"Sure." He followed her inside, looking around. The small living room was tidy, the throw pillows neatly arranged and coffee table clear. "Where's Zoey?"

"On a date, of course. Relishing her day off."

"Right. So . . . how was dinner at your dad's yesterday?"

"Great."

He took her hand in his. "I hate how things are between us."

She pulled away. "You made them this way, Luke."

"I don't regret my choice."

She closed her eyes, digging her palms into them. "And I don't regret mine." The words were soft, but sliced like a dagger.

Luke shook his head. *I'm not giving up.* He held out the package. "Here. Open it."

She took it cautiously, sliding a finger under the tape and unwrapping it. She set the box on the kitchen counter and lifted the lid. Her brow scrunched together. "Um . . . thanks."

Luke chuckled, stepping up behind her and lifting an item out of the box. "This is a ticket stub from the first movie we saw together." He dropped it on the counter and removed another item. "This is the first draft of the 'rules.' And this is the wrapper from the candy bar I bought Chris when you fake-laughed so he could win a bet."

Brooke laughed, her fingers eagerly combing through the contents of the box. "I didn't laugh so he would win the bet, I laughed so you would lose it. I can't believe you kept all this." She picked up a brittle, dried rose. "Is this the boutonniere from winter formal junior year?"

He nodded. "Our first date."

Brooke dropped the boutonniere back into the box like it had spontaneously ignited. "I seem to recall we went with other people."

"But we ended up leaving together." Luke motioned to the box. "I've kept everything from the very beginning. What I feel for you—it's not going away. It's been building and growing for eight years. And in eight years, I'll have an even bigger box, full of more moments from our life together."

Brooke set the lid on the box. "Whatever you're doing, it won't work."

"Why are you so afraid to try?"

"Because I don't trust you!"

The words sliced through Luke like a knife. Brooke covered her mouth, as though horrified to have let her true feelings escape.

"I wish I could take back the past. But I'm trying to show you I've changed. I've got Ryder Communications back on track. I'm helping you save Toujour. I've quit drinking. How else can I prove to you I love you?"

Brooke shook her head. "I'm moving to Italy."

The words stole the breath from Luke's lungs. The door opened, and Zoey stood there, her eyes wide in surprise. "Oh. I didn't expect anyone to be home."

Brooke quickly wiped at her eyes. "I thought you were on a date."

"I left early. He was a serious jerk." She motioned back and forth between them. "Want me to leave you two alone?"

"No," Brooke said.

Luke brought a hand to his eyes. Italy. That was it then. She'd made her choice. "I'll see you Monday." He had a date tonight with Andi, and Monday he'd have to return and report.

"See you," Brooke said, her voice empty.

Luke turned and left.

"I'm losing," Luke told Andi as they sat in their box, waiting for the basketball game to start. The chairs were cushioned and comfortable, and a counter behind them held an array of tasty snacks. A television set in one corner, in case they wanted to watch the game on television while at the stadium. He felt confident the paparazzi could only see and not hear them behind the glass partition. "She's moving to Italy. She's made up her mind."

Andi gave Luke a sympathetic smile. She looked gorgeous, with her hair spilling over her shoulders and a half-eaten pretzel in one hand. But Luke hardly noticed.

"She really said she's moving?" Andi asked.

"Yeah." He sat back in his chair, running a hand through his hair. "I pushed too hard, and she wasn't ready."

Andi ripped off a chunk of the pretzel and plopped it in her mouth, chewing thoughtfully. "Why is she with Antonio? What does she get out of that relationship?"

"I have no idea."

Andi gave him a pointed look. "If you want me to help, you've gotta answer my questions."

"Okay, fine. I think she views him as safe. A security blanket. She likes that he sought out a matchmaker, and she's always talking about how compatible the computer system says they are. She loves how his parents and grandparents and sisters have all been married for forever."

"Your parents were married for a long time, weren't they?"

A roar came from the crowd as the team mascot shot T-shirts out of a gun. "Almost thirty years."

"So why doesn't she see you as stable?"

Luke grabbed his Dr. Pepper and took a swig. He'd given up alcohol completely the last few weeks. "When we first met, I was kind of a player. I was all about the chase, and once I caught the girl, I quickly lost interest. When Brooke didn't return my feelings, I kept pretending to be the player so she wouldn't see how much it stung."

"But you're not a player." Andi smiled. "Not anymore."

"How do I show her that I've changed? How do I convince her I'm worth taking a risk? I don't think she loves me enough to leave him."

"There has to be something you can do to convince her. A grand gesture or something, like I told you on our first date." The buzzer rang, and the crowd let out a collective sigh.

Luke held out his hands, palms up. "Do you have any ideas? Because I'm fresh out of them."

Andi shoved the rest of the pretzel in her mouth, chewing. She tapped a foot in thought while she finished eating, and it reminded him so much of Brooke that his heart physically ached. "Is there something from your past that's especially meaningful? Maybe the moment you first realized you were falling for her?"

And that's when it hit Luke. "I know exactly what to do," he said.

"Tell me about that."

As Luke spoke, ideas started to come together. Andi asked questions and offered suggestions, and soon they had a fully formed plan.

Andi smiled. "Not too shabby, Mr. Ryder. Let's get to work."

"Don't you want to watch the game?"

Andi made a *psh* sound with her mouth. "This is way more important. She's moving to Italy next month, right? We've got to act fast."

Chapter Thirty

Luke took a deep breath, staring at himself in his bedroom mirror. Today was the official relaunch of Talia. His team had worked beyond hard over the last month and a half, and they were finally ready to celebrate.

A knock came at the door, and Mitch opened it. "Ready?" he asked.

"Ready," Luke said.

"Good. Andi's already in the limo."

As they drove to the same hotel the gala had been held at, Luke couldn't help but think how much things had changed in six weeks. He hoped tonight wouldn't end in as big of a disaster as the last gala had.

Andi patted his knee and smiled encouragingly, but didn't say anything. Luke took her hand and squeezed it. He appreciated her silence.

Luke saw the camera flashes from a block away. "Let's do this thing," Mitch said, and they stepped out of the limo. Luke pasted on his best media smile and posed for photos, arm wrapped around Andi, before entering the grand ballroom. The holiday decor had been replaced with marketing materials and booths where attendees could test out Talia 2.0's various features. Red banners hung from the ceiling with Talia's logo, and Ryder Communications employees in easily distinguishable polo shirts were present everywhere to answer questions.

Luke scanned the room for Brooke. He found her near the dance floor. Right next to Antonio.

Luke breathed deeply through the pain. He still had six weeks before she moved. Six weeks to change her mind.

Andi took his hand and squeezed. "You okay?"

Luke opened his mouth to respond, but a hand clapped on his shoulder. Darius.

"I must say, Luke, I never thought we'd get here," Darius said. "But the numbers we're seeing from the pre-orders are very encouraging. I think we're nearly out of the woods."

"Couldn't agree more," Luke said, making his voice light and airy.

"This must be the lovely young woman you're dating."

"Yes. Reginald, this is my girlfriend, Andi. Andi, Reginald is chairman of the board of directors."

Andi took Darius' hand in hers. "Such a pleasure."

Darius chuckled. "I assure you, the pleasure is mine. We'd begun to wonder if a woman would ever snag Luke on a permanent basis."

Andi laughed. She was good at playing her part, Luke would give her that. "I consider myself lucky he remained unattached for so long."

All too soon, it was time for Luke to give a presentation on Talia 2.0. He did a demonstration of the new and improved program, and the response from the audience was thunderous applause. Luke knew this time they were delivering a solid product. But a part of him still missed the old Talia, bugs and all. He knew his father would be proud he'd made the changes though.

"Well done," Andi said when he had managed to escape the hand shaking and congratulations after his presentation. She leaned forward and gave him a quick kiss on the cheek.

And that's when Luke saw Brooke. Her arm was looped through Antonio's, but her eyes were hurt. He wished he could talk to her—assure her the kiss was all for the press. But he couldn't.

Luke took Andi's hand and quickly led her to Brooke.

"Great job," Brooke said. Her smile seemed forced, her eyes sparkling with tears. "This product's going to go nuts."

"Let's hope so. The pre-sale numbers are encouraging."

"That was a great speech," Antonio said. His eyes gleamed wickedly. "I barely even noticed you stumbling over your words at the beginning. The product is fabulous."

"Antonio," Brooke said. She had a tight smile on her lips, the one that said I'll-reprimand-you-for-this-later. "The presentation was perfect."

"Luke."

They all turned. Mitch hurried through the crowd, muttering "excuse me" as he accidentally bumped into someone.

Luke raised an eyebrow. "Something wrong?" *Please say no.* Flashbacks of the last gala had his stomach twisting.

"You aren't going to believe this." Mitch handed his phone to Luke. A web page was pulled up. "Kendall issued a recall of all their home automation systems. They didn't put it through proper testing, and three fires have been started from the control panel. A house burned completely down."

"Oh my gosh," Brooke said.

"It's fine, no one was hurt and Kendall will pick up the tab for whatever insurance doesn't cover," Mitch said. "Do you know what this means?"

Luke stared at Mitch, and then they burst out laughing.

"We're in the clear," Mitch said. "You did it, man."

Luke nodded, his eyes locked on Brooke's. One crisis averted. Now to avoid another one.

"Are you sure you won't run the office here?" Charlotte asked Brooke.

Brooke shook her head. "I'm happy to transfer to Rome."

Charlotte sighed, pushing away from her desk and placing a book on a shelf. "I can't say I'm not disappointed. I'm happy to have you in Rome, but there's no one else I trust as much to run things here when I go back to France."

"So we're in the clear?" Brooke asked.

Charlotte nodded, her eyes sparkling. "I think it's safe to say the company is stable here, at least for a while."

"Andi and Luke seem very happy." Brooke twisted her engagement ring around and around on her finger. Luke kept saying he loved her, that Andi was all for the press. But every time Andi kissed him, every time Brooke saw a photo of them holding hands, it stung.

She wished she was moving to Italy tomorrow. It was hard to put Luke behind her when he was constantly around. She could feel the distance growing between her and Antonio, and she was desperate to reclaim what they'd once had. He was her choice, who she wanted to be with. Compatibility ratings weren't everything.

Charlotte sank back into her chair, her eyes soft. "Surely you know Andi and Luke won't last. I've trained you well enough that you should recognize the signs. They're attracted to each other, but not in love."

Brooke looked down. "And if they aren't the real thing, what will happen when they break up? For Toujour, I mean."

"Nothing. Couples get together. They break up." She leaned forward. "And this is strictly between the two of us, but I have another celebrity who has approached me all on his own about signing with Toujour. This guy really wants to find someone." Charlotte straightened her pencils on her desk. "If you were to date Luke, Brooke, I wouldn't be overly worried about the effect it would have on Toujour."

Brooke's head whipped up. "Excuse me?"

"I've been a matchmaker for twenty-one years. I know what love looks like."

Brooke opened her mouth to protest, but Charlotte waved a hand. "I've got work I can't put off any longer.

And if you change your mind, the promotion here is still on the table."

Chapter Thirty-One

Brooke glanced around the conference room at Toujour. It teemed with employees, all laughing and talking as they drank wine and enjoyed finger foods. A banner reading "congratulations" hung on one wall with balloons underneath it. But the focal point of the room was the cover of *Allure* magazine. A picture of Charlotte graced the front, with the headline, "Matchmaker Revolutionizes Love with Toujour."

A national magazine. And Toujour was in it. This on the heels of a popular movie star signing with the company, all of his own accord. Andi and Luke's relationship was still going strong in the press, but the actor's signing had started to draw the spotlight away from them. Brooke had a feeling that if Luke and Andi did break up, things would be okay.

But would they break up?

She glanced over at Luke, standing in the corner of the room with Andi. Their heads were close together, both of them laughing. They seemed to be getting along really well.

Charlotte came over to Brooke, a satisfied smile on her face. "The party is great. Thanks for taking care of it. What's that saying? This party is the best thing since sliced cake."

Brooke hid a smile. "I was happy to do it. I'm so relieved Toujour won't have to close."

"You and me both." Charlotte let out a sigh. "I wish I could persuade you to stay."

Brooke swallowed hard. The Rome office would be so different from here—nearly fifty matchmakers instead of ten, not to mention the culture shock she'd experience. "I need to go," she said.

"Where's your fiancé? I would think Antonio would want to celebrate this with you."

"He was falling behind on a deadline, so he's painting." And they'd had a huge argument last night about some stupid wedding detail. She frowned. Ever since he returned from Italy, they'd never seemed to get back in sync with each other.

Charlotte gave Brooke a sideways glance. "That's too bad. Well, I'd better get this party started." She walked to the head of the conference table and tapped on her wine glass.

Zoey sidled up next to Brooke. "Looks like we'll make rent next month after all," she whispered.

"Thank you all for being here today," Charlotte said in her heavily accented French. "Two months ago,

I thought something like this would be impossible. We owe it all to Brooke and Luke." She lifted her glass, her gaze meaningful. "To Brooke and Luke."

Brooke and Luke. Brooke forced a smile and raised her own glass, taking a small sip along with everyone else. Their names had always been linked together. It was never Brooke and Antonio. It was Brooke and Luke.

"Speech," Zoey called. Brooke swatted her.

"Yes, we should have a speech." Charlotte turned to Luke. "The ceiling is yours."

"The floor," Lianna corrected, and everyone laughed.

Luke stepped away from Andi and took Charlotte's spot. He cleared his throat. "What can I say? If not for Toujour, I wouldn't be standing in this room right now, with the love of my life." His eyes locked onto Brooke's, drawing her in. "Toujour gave me my life back. It gave me a reason to fight, a reason to become a better man. For that I will always be grateful." He raised his glass. "To love."

"To love," everyone echoed. Luke walked back to Andi, who offered him a smile. And that's when Brooke saw it—friendship. She saw what she would've seen a long time ago, if she hadn't been so close to the situation.

There was no love for Luke in Andi's eyes, or in his for her. Only friendship and a mutual respect. Luke really wasn't into Andi.

And I really love Luke.

Zoey playfully shoved Brooke. "Your turn," she said.

Brooke nodded, walking to the front of the room. She glanced out over the crowd. "I want to thank Charlotte for going along with my crazy idea, and Luke for agreeing to it." Through the glass of the conference room wall, she could just make out the corner of the cork board in the front lobby, covered in wedding invitations. *I don't want to go to Italy,* she realized. *I want to stay right here, forever.* Luke smiled at Brooke, and her heart melted. *I want to give Luke a chance. I believe in our eighty-three percent.*

The realization took her breath away.

Zoey nodded her head encouragingly. Brooke cleared her throat. "I believe in matchmaking, and I believe it works. I'm glad we're finally proving that to everyone. Ten couples have put their files on hold this week after finding love. If not for Luke, those couples never would've met each other." She lifted her glass. "To many happy years, and many happy couples."

"Hear, hear!" one of the other matchmakers cheered. The room broke up into pleasant chatter, and Brooke made her way back to Luke.

He reached forward and gave her a hug. She savored the feel of his arms around her, melting into him. "I'm glad it worked," he said.

"Me too." Brooke pulled away, focusing on Andi. "And thank you, Andi. You're a big part of this too."

Andi smiled. She glanced around, then leaned forward so only Luke and Brooke could hear. "I'm ready for the charade to be over." She gave Luke a teasing wink. "Think we can break up soon?"

Brooke blinked. Was Andi joking or serious?

"Sure," Luke said. He nudged Andi with his shoulder. "I was kind of getting sick of you anyway."

Brooke had refused to see it for weeks. She could move to Italy with Antonio. They could get married. And they would be happy, mostly. But it wasn't what she wanted. She wanted to stay here with Luke, in California. She wanted to be head of the Los Angeles office.

She wanted him.

"Are you okay?" Luke asked, his brow furrowed.

"Yes," Brooke gasped. She shook her head as though to clear it. She'd been such an idiot all these years. Luke wasn't her father. He was worth the risk.

She had to break up with Antonio. She couldn't believe she was even considering it. But it wasn't fair to either of them. She loved Antonio. But she loved Luke more.

"I have to go," Brooke murmured.

Luke raised an eyebrow. "Looks like the party might continue for a while still."

"I know. Can I come over later tonight?" She swallowed. "We can talk."

"Sure," Luke said, his eyes softening with hope. "Can I . . . help you with anything?"

"No, thanks. There's something I need to do, and I've gotta do it on my own."

She gave Zoey a reassuring wave and left the room, her footsteps determined. She wasn't being fair to anyone by continuing to force something that wasn't right. It was time to give Antonio back his ring, and take a risk with Luke.

Chapter Thirty-Two

Brooke trudged up the stairs to Antonio's top floor apartment for the last time. She paused at his door, staring at it for a long moment. Their entire relationship flashed through her mind—meeting him in the club on their first official date, where they'd danced the night away and he'd made her feel like an Italian princess. Shyly admitting to him she was ready to put her file with Toujour on hold and be exclusive. The proposal. All the million little moments, both good and bad, that together added up to a life. A relationship. A future that would never be. There would be so much to do after she walked out of that apartment—a venue to cancel, gifts to return, a wedding dress to sell. Was it worth it? Was Luke worth it?

She remembered his teasing grin the first day they'd met. The easy way he'd accepted her ridiculous rules for their friendship. Lying on the hood of his truck, looking at stars on warm summer nights. The way her skin burst into flame when he casually brushed his fingers over her arm. The sting of her hand as she slapped his cheek, realizing he'd loved her for years. The blinding fear that something would happen, and she'd lose him for good. The heat in his gaze when he locked eyes with her, trying to reassure her he was in it for the long haul.

Was Luke worth this risk? *Yes.*

She took a deep breath. "Just get it over with," she whispered, and knocked. She waited for the patter of Antonio's feet, but heard nothing but silence inside. Brooke knocked again.

Nothing.

Maybe he's out on a walk. Or in the restroom. She stood there for a moment, debating what to do. She should leave and come back later.

But then she might lose her nerve. Breaking Antonio's heart wouldn't be easy.

Brooke raised her hand and knocked again. She heard a few footsteps, then the door opened. "Brooke." Antonio was dressed in paint-splattered jeans and a white T-shirt, lifted to expose a strip of his belly.

"Hey," Brooke said. She shifted from foot to foot. He looked adorable, with his mussed hair and sleepy eyes. "Did I wake you?"

"Just taking a quick nap." He didn't open the door to invite her in. "What's wrong? I thought you were at the party."

Brooke took a deep breath. Maybe it would be easier to do it here, do it now. "There's something I need to tell you." Her eyes stung with tears, and she looked down, blinking quickly.

You can still back out. You don't have to do this.

But she did.

"Antonio, I can't marry you."

He let out a strangled growl. "What?"

"Antonio?" The voice came from inside the apartment, and was definitely feminine.

Antonio's eyes grew wide with panic. He glanced inside the apartment.

Something clicked in Brooke's head. The midday sleepy eyes. The door he'd kept half-closed since opening it.

"Do you have a woman in there?" Brooke whispered.

Antonio's eyes flew back to hers. "Just a model. For a painting."

Brooke pushed Antonio aside, entering the apartment. Sunlight streamed through the windows, setting the place aglow. There, in the middle of the room surrounded by drop cloths, stood an easel. And on the easel set a painting. But not a landscape.

A portrait of a nude woman. Lying on his couch. Antonio's favorite gray scarf draped over her legs but covering nothing.

Brooke whirled on Antonio. "Who is she? *Where* is she?" *When did he start doing nudes?* She felt sick. Violated.

"Antonio?" the sleepy voice asked again. It came from above. The loft. A blonde head appeared at the top of the ladder. She was completely naked. The woman let out a shriek and stepped back.

Brooke stood there, taking it all in. The woman had been in his bed.

He's cheating on me. She couldn't absorb it. *He's cheating on me!* And she had worried about feeling things for Luke. Meanwhile, Antonio was sleeping with someone else.

Brooke picked up the red stiletto near her foot and threw it at Antonio.

"It's not what you think," he said.

"You're cheating on me," Brooke said. She let out a disbelieving gasp. "I can't believe this is happening."

The woman appeared at the top of the ladder, this time dressed. "I thought she was at a party," the woman spat.

"Jeanette, I think you should go." Antonio reached for Brooke, his eyes desperate.

She slapped his hand away. "Don't touch me."

Jeanette scampered past, sending both of them a heated glare. The door shut with a bang.

"It isn't what you think—" Antonio began again.

Brooke folded her arms, the sting of betrayal slicing across her heart. "And what do you think I think?"

He sighed. "Jeanette's a model. I've been painting her."

"Yeah, I saw."

"For the gallery, Brooke. She came over for a session early this morning. I was still upset about our fight. I didn't mean for it to happen." He reached for her again, but Brooke swatted his hand away.

"No. You can't talk your way out of this one." She held a hand to her forehead, cheeks heating in humiliation. "I'm such an idiot. The earring was hers, wasn't it? You were with her in San Diego." She leaned over, heaving. She was going to be sick.

"I met her in San Diego. But I swear, nothing happened until today. I felt you pulling away and panicked."

Brooke looked deep into his eyes—the eyes she had planned on spending the rest of her life with. Bile rose in her throat, and she struggled to keep it down. "I came here to call off the wedding. To tell you that Luke wants . . ." She swallowed. "I haven't been completely upfront with you. He wants to see if we can make it work. But I've been putting him off. Because of you. Because of my commitment to us. And then today, I realized that I do love him, and I'm not being fair to you. And I came here, before I allowed anything to happen with Luke. How could you do this to me?"

"You're leaving me for Luke?"

"You just slept with another woman. I think the wedding's off, regardless of why I came over."

"It was a mistake," Antonio said quickly. "Jeanette was a mistake, and leaving me for Luke is a mistake. Can't you see that he's the one destroying our relationship? I felt insecure because of him, and Jeanette was . . ." He shook his head. "That's not important. All that's happened is we both got cold feet and made mistakes. But we can salvage this. Italy will be a fresh start."

Brooke let out a strangled cry. "I love you, Antonio. Deciding to call off the wedding has been agonizing."

"And I love you. So don't call it off. Let's fix this."

"No." Brooke looked down at her left hand. Her engagement ring sparkled in the sunlight streaming in from the loft's windows. She still remembered shopping with Antonio for this ring and picking it out. The butterflies in her stomach that had erupted when she tried it on at the store. The tears that had streamed down her cheeks when Antonio slipped it onto her finger after she said yes. She'd worn it every day since— woken up each morning and gladly slipped it on. The past few weeks, she'd been overwhelmed with her guilt for even thinking of Luke that way. For betraying Antonio with her thoughts.

But he'd cheated on her for real.

"Jeanette means nothing to me, Brooke." He swiped quickly at his eyes. "If I could go back in time and change it, I would."

Brooke slipped the ring off her finger. "But you can't. And seeing you with her confirms the decision I'd already made." She dropped the ring onto the floor and picked her way through the drop cloths.

Antonio jumped in front of the door, the ring clutched in his fingers. "We can work this out."

Brooke unclasped the painter's palette necklace he'd given her and threw that on the floor too. "You know about my hang-ups with my father. How much I hate cheaters."

"I didn't plan for it to happen. She was only here for a modeling session."

Brooke snorted. "Looks like the message somehow got misinterpreted."

"I love you. Please."

"We're over, Antonio. I never want to see you again." She shoved him aside and left without a backward glance.

Chapter Thirty-Three

"Did you hear that?" Andi whispered to Luke as the glass conference room door swung shut behind Brooke. Luke watched Brooke walk up the row of cubicles and round the corner to the lobby before disappearing from sight.

"I know." Luke leaned closer to Andi as someone bumped into him from behind. "She said she wants to see me tonight. What do you think she wants to talk about?"

Andi nudged him with her shoulder. "I think she's going to give you a chance."

His stomach flipped. A loud laugh came from two matchmakers at the refreshment table, and he jumped at the sudden noise. "Maybe we're misinterpreting."

Andi shook her head. "I saw her face. And that's the face of a woman in love."

Luke's heart fluttered. "I don't know if I dare hope."

"Well, start hoping, mister. Do you think you can get everything set up for tonight?"

"But what if we're wrong?"

Andi slapped him on the shoulder. "I think this is your moment, either way." She tugged on his hand. "C'mon, let's go."

Andi and Luke said their goodbyes to the small party and escaped the boardroom. Luke pushed open the front door of Toujour, holding it as Andi passed. He took a deep breath of the cool air, full of car exhaust and pollution. Anything was better than the Dragon's Blood that saturated every inch of Toujour. "There's no way we can pull this off in just a few hours," he said.

"Oh, stop being such a pessimist." Andi raised her voice to be heard over the honking horns of rush hour traffic. "Sure we can. We already know what you're going to do. We just have to pull it together."

The warm January sun spilled over Luke, making him believe anything was possible. He thought about Brooke and the shy way she'd looked at him when asking if they could talk. She was either going to tell him she never wanted to see him again, or that she was leaving Antonio. Luke had a feeling it was the latter. He hoped he was right.

"There's a party shop a few blocks away," Andi said, pointing down the street. "It'll be quicker to walk. We can get everything there."

"Okay," Luke agreed, following Andi down the sidewalk. Luke's mind swirled. Eight years of hoping and longing. And it all came down to this.

They paused at the corner, waiting for the crosswalk to change to the white walking symbol. It flipped from red to white and let out a beep, indicating it was time to cross. Andi stepped into the street. And that's when Luke saw the bicycle barreling around the corner, heading straight toward her. The bicyclist was looking over his shoulder, and hadn't seen Andi enter the crosswalk.

"Look out!" Luke yelled, grabbing Andi and pushing her behind him. The bicyclist glanced up, but it was too late. Luke felt the front wheel hit him and he went down. His shoulder hit the blacktop hard and it dug into his forearm. Breaks screeched and a few horns honked. He saw the bicyclist fly over his head before the searing pain registered. Luke let out a curse. His ankle and shoulder throbbed. He lifted his arm and saw blood. The beep of the crosswalk reverberated in his head, loud and distracting.

Andi dropped down next to Luke. "Are you okay?" she asked.

He let out a hiss. "I think so."

"Crap, you're bleeding. And your ankle's swelling. I'm calling an ambulance." She whipped her phone out of her pocket. Then she yanked off her jacket and pressed it against his arm.

"You'll ruin it," he said.

"Shut up and let me help."

"Go check on the bicyclist."

Andi swore. "You're right. Keep pressure on that arm." She rose and ran to where Luke had seen the bicyclist land. Sirens sounded in the distance. Luke hunched over, pressing Andi's jacket tight against his arm. His whole body throbbed.

Andi sank back onto the ground beside Luke. "The bicyclist is all right. He has some road rash, but he was wearing a helmet. Someone stopped and is with him. Ooo, that's bleeding a lot. And I think you broke your ankle or something."

The sirens pounded in Luke's head, drawing close. The ambulance screeched to stop a few feet from Luke, the lights swirling in a sickening pattern. The back door opened and two paramedics jumped out.

The next hour was a blur. The paramedics wrapped his arm in gauze and stabilized his shoulder and ankle before loading him into the cramped ambulance. Andi and two paramedics hopped inside.

"Is there anyone we should call?" one of the paramedics asked.

Brooke. Her name was on the tip of his tongue. But no. He would give her her space. She said she wanted to see him tonight, which meant she'd call soon enough.

At the hospital, Luke was taken to a bed with only a curtain separating him from other patients. Doctors and nurses filed in and out of the room, attaching monitors and writing things down on charts. Someone came in with a tray and stitched Luke's arm up. X-rays showed his shoulder was only bruised and his ankle merely sprained.

"I've gotta get home," Luke told the doctor. A voice came over the intercom, announcing something Luke didn't care about or catch. What if Brooke didn't call, but just showed up at his apartment and he wasn't there?

"We'll get you out of here soon," the doctor said. He clicked off the pen light he'd been using to check Luke's pupils yet again and started scribbling on the chart. "I'll have the nurse start processing your discharge papers."

Luke's phone rang. He grabbed it, and his heart started thudding when he saw it was Brooke. "I've gotta take this," he said. The doctor nodded absently, still making notes in the chart. "Hello?"

Is it Brooke? Andi mouthed. Luke nodded. Andi gave him a thumbs up.

"Hi, Luke." Brooke sounded exhausted, and Luke clutched the phone in concern, his own pain vanishing. "Can I come over? We need to talk."

Luke cleared his throat. "I'm actually not home right now." The doctor clicked his pen closed and left the room. Luke hoped it was to get the discharge papers.

"Oh." Her voice became even more subdued.

"Don't freak out, but I'm at the hospital." She let out a gasp, and Luke spent the next few minutes explaining what had happened, without going into the details of why he had been crossing the street.

"I'll be right there," Brooke said.

"I should be home soon."

"I don't care. I'm coming to the hospital."

He put a fist to his mouth, unable to hide the smile at her concern. "I love you, Brooke."

The phone went silent. And then, so faint he almost didn't hear it, she whispered, "I love you, too." And then the line went dead.

Luke stared at the phone. "She said she loves me."

Andi squeezed his good arm. "That's fantastic." The she laughed. "I'm breaking up with you."

"What?" Luke blinked, staring at Andi.

She laughed again. "Go get your happy ending, Luke. I'm ready to go get mine too, whatever that is." She kissed him on the cheek. "I expect an invitation to the wedding."

Chapter Thirty-Four

Brooke left Antonio's apartment. She walked down the stairs. She got into her car and drove away. And she never once looked back. She wanted to cry—felt like she should be crying—but all she felt inside was empty and hollow.

The wedding was off. Her fiancé had cheated. And she was in love with her best friend.

Deciding to call off the wedding hadn't been an easy choice. Making the decision, only to find out she'd been cheated on, had destroyed her fragile trust in men. She shook her head, and a sob rose up in her throat. She pulled to the side of the road and laid her head on the steering wheel, trying to calm her shaking shoulders.

She wasn't sure how long she sat there and cried. Eventually she started the car again and drove back to her apartment. She hoped Zoey was there. She knew Zoey had a date, but not until later tonight, and the party at Toujour should be over by now.

Brooke trudged up the stairs to her apartment and unlocked the door. "Zoey?" she called.

"Here." Zoey walked into the living room. Her eyes widened, and she rushed to Brooke's side. "What happened?"

"The wedding's off." Brooke dropped her purse and sank onto the couch.

"What?"

"I gave Antonio back his ring."

"But . . . what happened?"

Brooke let it all spill out. About how she went to tell Antonio the wedding was off and she was going to give Luke a chance. How she found him with the woman. How her heart ached with the power of his betrayal.

Zoey wrapped her arms tightly around Brooke. "I'm so sorry."

Brooke put a hand to her forehead. "There's so much to do. People to contact. Vendors to call and orders to cancel—if they can even be canceled."

"As maid of honor, I will gladly help you with anything you need."

Brooke smiled wanly. "Thanks."

"So what are you going to do about Luke?"

Brooke shook her head. "I was going to tell him I wanted to start dating. But now . . ." A tear fell into her lap. "I need time to process this. I don't know if I'm strong enough to take that kind of a risk right now."

"Hey." Zoey took Brooke's hands in hers. "That's crazy talk. Luke is not a risk. He's perfect for you."

"Eighty-three," Brooke whispered.

"What?"

"I ran our numbers in the database. We're eighty-three percent compatible."

Zoey grinned. "Of course you are. Don't let Antonio ruin that." She squeezed Brooke's hands. "The two of you are ready to be together. Take time to process if you must. But tell Luke how you feel. Start working on building a future with him."

"I should go see him?" Brooke asked.

"You should go see him."

"I want to see him." Brooke felt her heart lighten at the realization. Antonio's betrayal hurt—probably would for a while. "Seeing Antonio with that woman only confirmed my decision—it didn't make it."

"Then go see Luke," Zoey said. "Tell him you love him. He's waited a really long time to hear that."

Brooke gave Zoey a quick hug. "Thank you." She grabbed her purse and headed to her car, calling Luke as she walked.

"Hello?" Luke's voice sounded strange. Was he drunk? But no, his words weren't slurring.

"Hi, Luke." Brooke said the words cautiously. She needed him to be strong right now. Her Luke. The

Luke who wasn't grieving. Maybe she should wait and do this tomorrow.

No. If I don't do it now, I might chicken out. And he hasn't had a drink in weeks. He's different now.

She cleared her throat. "Can I come over? We need to talk."

"I'm actually not home right now."

"Oh." Maybe he was out with Andi. She slumped against the car door, not sure if she should get in.

"Don't freak out, but I'm at the hospital."

Brooke let out a gasp. She fumbled with her keys, dropping them once before getting in her car. She started the engine and whipped out of the parking lot as she listened to him explain that he'd been hit by a bicyclist. Pain killers, she realized. He was drugged, not drunk.

"I'll be right there," Brooke said. She was maybe ten minutes from the hospital.

"I should be home soon."

"I don't care. I'm coming to the hospital." No one could keep her from him now.

"I love you, Brooke."

Brooke stopped, her heart pounding. Here it was— the moment. She could take a chance on Luke, or she could lick her wounds in solitude. "I love you, too." She heard an intake of breath on the other end of the line, but she ended the call before he could reply and focused on her driving.

Brooke quickly parked and raced into the hospital lobby. "I need to see Luke Ryder," she breathlessly told the receptionist.

"Brooke?"

Brooke turned around. Andi stood there, smiling uncertainly.

"Hey," Brooke said. She reached for her engagement ring to twist around and around, but froze when she touched nothing but bare skin.

Andi's eyes followed the gesture, and she broke into a smile. "You broke up with him."

Brooke nodded.

"You're going after Luke."

Again, Brooke nodded. *This is soooo awkward.*

Andi threw her arms around Brooke's neck in a tight hug. "You two will be so happy together," she said.

Brooke blinked, then returned the hug. "What about you two?"

Andi laughed. "I already broke up with him."

"You were serious about that?"

Andi laughed again. "The press has been getting pretty bored with our relationship. A breakup is just the thing to spice it up." She grinned. "I've got my own secret romance. Oh, don't look so surprised. Luke can tell you all about it."

Brooke laughed. "I've really been off my game to not notice that."

"You've been preoccupied." Andi gave Brooke another hug. "He's a good guy, and he loves you very much. You two will be so happy together." She pointed down a hallway. "He's right down there. I think they're about ready to let him go home."

"Thanks," Brooke said. She walked down the hallway toward the ER. She told the receptionist who she was, then followed the woman back to a triage room. She stopped outside the partition separating his bed from others, taking a deep breath to calm her nerves. Then she walked in.

Luke's eyes lit up when she entered and his mouth quirked into a grin. "Hey."

Brooke leaned down, giving him a hug. His arms wrapped around her, and she closed her eyes. "Look at you," she whispered. She pulled a chair close to his bed and sat down. "You've done it this time. How are you feeling?"

Luke reached out for her hand, and she let him take it. "Fine. My arm's still numb, and they gave me some pain meds for my shoulder and ankle." He peered closely at her. "How are you? You look . . ."

Brooke laughed, hiding her head against his chest. "I know, I'm a mess. It's been quite a day."

Luke ran his finger over her knuckles. His hand froze. "Brooke, where's your ring?"

She lifted her head and locked her eyes with his. "There's not going to be a wedding anymore. At least not to Antonio."

His hand tightened around hers, his eyes alighting with concern . . . hope. "What happened?"

"I went to his apartment to tell him we needed to call it off." She took a deep breath. *Here it goes.* There would be no turning back now. "I didn't think it was right to marry him when I'm so desperately, head-over-heels in love with you."

Luke sucked in a sharp breath. "You love me?"

Brooke nodded, tears glistening at the corners of her eyes. "Yeah. I love you, Lucas Ryder. I always have, and I always will."

His good arm wrapped around her and lifted her out of the chair until their lips touched. Their first kiss. Fire exploded in Brooke's veins, and she leaned into him. Her mouth parted, and his arms tightened around her. She had never felt a kiss so deeply. Her toes tingled. Her face burned. She let him kiss away all the hurt and pain of the last few hours, relishing the experience. It felt so . . . *right*. Like they'd been together all along.

"I can't believe it," Luke whispered against her lips as he kissed her over and over again. "I can't believe this is happening."

Brooke put her hands on his face, giving him one last kiss before she sat back down.

"How did Antonio take it?" Luke asked.

"Not too well. But considering I found him with a naked woman, I think he'll rebound quickly."

"What?"

So Brooke told him the rest of the story. Luke's mouth clenched tighter and tighter as she spoke. "That animal," he spit out. Then he called Antonio something even worse.

Brooke put her fingers lightly over his mouth. "Shhh. It's done."

"So . . . what about us?"

Brooke traced a pattern on the thin hospital blanket. "I feel so betrayed. So scared to try again. You were right, Luke—I was scared to admit I need you. I'm scared to give someone else all the power."

"I won't abuse it. I will spend the rest of my days making you happy."

"I know. But I'll need you to be patient with me."

"I can do that."

"We're really going to try to make this work?" She motioned between them.

He captured both her hands in his. "We *will* make this work." And then he kissed her again.

366

Chapter Thirty-Five

Luke eyed himself critically in his bedroom mirror. He reached up and straightened his tie, then flicked an invisible piece of lint off his suit jacket. Tonight, he wanted everything to be perfect. They'd only celebrate their two month anniversary once, after all.

The press went wild over Brooke and Antonio's breakup, and then her almost immediate status as Luke Ryder's girlfriend. Brooke had mentioned multiple times that she was worried there would be fallout where Toujour was concerned, but it had only pushed sales higher. The company was now solidly in the black, and Charlotte would announce Brooke's promotion next month.

As for him and Brooke, the last two months hadn't been all smooth sailing. But they were working through it together.

Luke stuck his hand in his pocket, tracing the outline of the leather box hidden there. He took a deep breath and prayed this night would go well.

An hour later, the limo pulled up outside Brooke's apartment. Luke got out of the car on shaky legs. He rode up the elevator and knocked on her door.

Brooke opened it almost immediately. Her hair was piled elegantly on top of her head in cascading curls. Her makeup was more dramatic than usual, and it made her cheekbones and eyes pop. The deep purple dress hugged her body before flaring out at the knees.

She touched her hair self-consciously. "You said formal. How do I look?"

"Absolutely gorgeous." He pulled her into his arms and kissed her deeply, all his nerves vanishing. When he was with her, nothing scared him.

"You don't look so bad yourself," Brooke said.

He held out his arm, and she took it with a grin. "Your limo awaits, m'lady."

"Oooo, the limo. This is fancy."

"Well, it is our two month anniversary."

"Where are we going?" Brooke asked.

"To Ryder Communications."

She raised an eyebrow, her lips curved up in a teasing grin. "That's our fancy date?"

"No. But the helipad is there, and we need to take the helicopter to our fancy date."

"Wow. You really are going all out."

He kissed her. "Absolutely. You're kind of a big deal."

Brooke blushed, and it made her that much more adorable.

"How were the numbers at your meeting this morning?" Brooke asked. "Is Talia's relaunch still going strong?"

"Yeah." He grinned in satisfaction. "Kendall Home Systems' might have to file bankruptcy after recalling their home automation system, but Talia 2.0 is doing fabulous. The board is solidly on my side now. I think dating you has helped."

Brooke laughed. "Glad to be of service."

They flirted and talked the entire limo ride. At Ryder Communications the building was dark, most of the employees gone for the day. But the security guard let them in, and they rode to the roof where the helicopter waited. Luke helped Brooke into the helicopter, and they admired the city lights as they flew to San Diego, where they boarded another limo.

"Our old stomping grounds," Brooke said as they drove through their old neighborhood. The glittering city lights reflecting off the sea. She turned to him with a grin. "We haven't been here together in years. Think we can stop by the high school?"

"I think that can be arranged."

Luke watched as Brooke's smile grew wider and wider the closer they got to the high school. They passed by the Denny's where they'd built a tentative friendship. The street where they'd attended a Halloween party together. The apartment complex Brooke had lived at. Then they pulled into the empty school parking lot and sat there looking at the dark buildings.

"I would love to go inside again sometime," Brooke said. "High school feels like a million years ago."

Luke opened his door and got out. "Let's go inside," he said, motioning for Brooke to follow him.

She laughed. "It's not going to be open."

"Humor me."

Brooke did, climbing out of the limo and walking hand in hand toward the front entrance of the school. He smiled as they passed the tree they'd eaten so many lunches under. Then he reached out and pulled the door open.

Brooke stared in amazement. "You didn't."

Luke grinned. "Welcome to winter formal."

"Oh my gosh." Brooke tugged his hand and with a laugh he followed her inside. They passed the front office and lunch room, heading down a hallway toward the gymnasium. Brooke pushed open the door and let out a gasp. "It's beautiful."

Luke looked around the gym and had to admit that Andi had done well. It looked like a more elegant version of a typical prom. Tiny white Christmas lights sparkled all around the room. Crepe paper hung from the ceiling, but Andi had somehow managed to make it look nice and not tacky.

"Oh, Luke. It's perfect." Brooke wrapped her arms around his neck and gave him a long kiss. "Thank you."

He motioned to the balloon archway that created the backdrop for a typical high school dance photo. A photographer stood nearby, waiting patiently. "Shall we get our photo?" Luke asked. "I believe I was denied one at our first winter formal, since you decided to go with Chris instead of me."

"He asked me first," Brooke defended. She laughed. "I wanted to go with you though."

She eagerly grabbed his hand and pulled him toward the photographer. They did a few cheesy poses, and then Luke took her hand. "Let's get a real one," he said.

Brooke nodded, wrapping her arms tightly around him so they stood cheek to cheek. The photographer snapped the photo, and then Luke pulled away and dropped to his knee.

Brooke's hand covered her mouth. "Luke?"

"Brooklyn Pierce," he said, taking her hand in his. "Eight years ago we stood in this room at winter formal and I told you I was falling in love with you. You said it was a passing thing, and my feelings would fade. But every day I fall deeper and deeper in love. I cannot imagine life without you." He reached into his pocket and withdrew the ring box with a trembling hand. "I know we've only been dating two months. Most people will say we're moving way too fast. But I've been waiting eight years to do this, and I don't want to wait another day. Brooklyn Pierce, will you marry me?"

A single tear fell down Brooke's cheek. Her mouth stretched into a brilliant grin. "Yes. Oh please, yes."

Luke slipped the ring onto her finger, then stood. He pulled her into his arms and kissed her deeply.

"I can't believe this is happening," Brooke whispered.

Luke pulled away. "I have some new rules for our relationship," he said gruffly. "Eight years ago you implemented more rules after I told you I loved you, so it seems only right I get to pick them now."

Brooke laughed. "Let's hear them."

He took her hands in his, his tone turning serious. "Rule #1: I promise to never let a day pass without kissing you. Rule #2: I promise to always hug you, especially for longer than three seconds. Rule #3: I promise to cuddle just for cuddling's sake every day. Rule #4: I promise to take you on a real date at least once a week. Rule #5: I promise to never let a day pass without showing you how deeply I love and care about you. We'll always work through our problems together. Because with you, Brooke, nothing is impossible."

Brooke wiped away a tear. "I have a rule to add, too," she said.

"Yeah?"

"Yeah. Rule #6: I promise to never doubt your love for me again." And then she kissed him.

Brooke and Luke's Rules for Their Marriage

1. Under no circumstances can we let a day pass without kissing.
2. Hugging is ALWAYS okay, especially if it's longer than 3 seconds.
3. We'll cuddle just for cuddling's sake every day.
4. We'll go on a real date at least once a week.
5. We promise never to let a day pass without showing how deeply we love and care about each other.
6. We promise never to doubt each other's love.
7. We can't cancel dates just because we're busy.
8. We promise never to go to bed angry.
9. We promise to always be there for each other.
10. Extravagant and expensive gifts are encouraged, but not necessary.
11. If one of us needs help, the other will drop everything and come running—no questions asked.
12. We'll never let a day pass without saying "I love you."
13. We won't let our lives be ruled by a set of ridiculous rules. In love, there are no rules.

FREE DOWNLOAD

NOTHING SLOWS DOWN LOVE LIKE THE FRIEND ZONE.

"This was the book I've been looking for!"
—Angela, reader

Get your free copy of *Meet Your Match* when you opt in to the author's VIP reader's club. **Get started here:**

http://lindzeearmstrong.com/claim-your-free-book

ENJOY THE REST OF THE SERIES!

Sometimes love needs a helping hand...

Acknowledgments

As always, this book wouldn't have been possible without a lot of encouragement and help. First and foremost, thank you to my husband, who tells me things like, "Don't worry about cleaning the bathrooms. I'll do that while you write." (Seriously, are there sexier words than those? I think not.)

Thank you to my kids, who frequently allow me to edit uninterrupted for at least three minutes at a time while they play.

Thank you to my accountability partners, Candice and Liz. They are always honest and encouraging, which is exactly what I need.

To my critique group, the Authorities—LaChelle, Darren, Jacob, and David. They keep me constantly striving to improve my writing and are always spot-on with their feedback.

To all my iWrite friends. They always make me feel welcome and awesome.

To my beta readers. You rock! My books would be awful without you.

And most of all, to my readers. Knowing people are reading and enjoying my stories keeps me going!

About the Author

LINDZEE ARMSTRONG is the #1 best-selling author of the No Match for Love series and Sunset Plains Romance series. She's always had a soft spot for love stories. In third grade, she started secretly reading romance novels, hiding the covers so no one would know (because hello, embarrassing!), and dreaming of her own Prince Charming.

She finally met her match while at college, where she studied history education. They are now happily married and raising twin boys in the Rocky Mountains.

Like any true romantic, Lindzee loves chick flicks, ice cream, and chocolate. She believes in sigh-worthy kisses and happily ever afters.

To find out about future releases, you can opt in to Lindzee's VIP reader's club on her website, at www.lindzeearmstrong.com.

If you enjoyed this book, please take a few minutes and leave a review. It really helps other readers discover books they might enjoy. Thank you!

10834221R00217

Made in the USA
San Bernardino, CA
01 December 2018